THE BOOKS OF NORENE I

WOLVES AND WEREWOLVES

JANE SEFC

authorHOUSE®

AuthorHouse™ UK
1663 Liberty Drive
Bloomington, IN 47403 USA
www.authorhouse.co.uk
Phone: 0800.197.4150

Published by AuthorHouse   02/06/2018

ISBN: 978-1-5462-8836-7 (sc)
ISBN: 978-1-5462-8837-4 (hc)
ISBN: 978-1-5462-8835-0 (e)

To my best friend, Jana,
for her support and her patience.

PROLOGUE

John Mathewson squinted into the sun. He was high on a horse, moving slowly towards the south. His silvery hair blended with his iron helmet, which covered most of his face, and his white beard had grown long enough to cover the coat of arms on his chest. The heat of the day caused him to feel quite hot under his armour. He felt sweat trickle down his back and arms.

He raised a water bag to his mouth and took a long sip. He swallowed and glanced to his right. His five loyal knights, each on a magnificent stallion, were beside him. John looked over his shoulder at an impressive army behind him. Thousands of soldiers marched in silence. The army was a mixture of all types of soldiers carrying all sorts of weapons. They couldn't be picky and had to work with whatever they could get. Those who had horses rode in the front as cavalry; those without horses carried bows and arrows and walked behind the cavalry with determined looks on their faces; and foot soldiers, armed with swords, axes, and spears, marched in the rear.

John faced front again and looked at the far horizon. Ahead, just over a high ridge, was the country of Wolfast, a land long ruled under the iron fist of a cadre of twenty werewolves, all of whom were members of the aristocracy. John's homeland, called Norene, spread to the north from the hills. For millennia it had been Wolfast's province. John hoped that all of that would change on that sunny and hot afternoon.

Slowly they approached the ridge. The hill was blocking their view of Wolfast, hiding any possible army marching from the south. Norene's borders were all outlined with hilltops. This was the only place where an army could easily get to the other side of the ridge.

Forest spread for miles and miles to his left, but in this spot, it was replaced by fields and pastures. John could see animals fleeing the grasslands as soon as they felt the vibrations and saw the soldiers approaching, but the vultures flew to the trees near the hill and watched the army, expecting a great feast afterwards.

A man on a horse appeared on the hill. A murmur spread through the ranks. The man on the hill stopped and watched the army below.

"I think it's their spy," one of the knights said.

"I think it's their army," John whispered as he stopped. His horse neighed and, with a quick movement of its head, threw its forelock out of its eyes.

John signalled to the others to stop, not taking his eyes off the hill. The army behind him stopped and anxiously awaited orders. Some soldiers prepared to attack; some just waited.

The man on the hill didn't vanish back behind the horizon; rather, he was joined by two other men on horses. They stopped next to the first man and watched the army below. Next, a few more men appeared and joined the three men. And more figures appeared after them. More and more came, and soon thousands of enemy soldiers came into view.

John hadn't been expecting this many soldiers, and he hesitated for a very brief moment. Then the images of his wife and children flashed in front of his eyes, and he knew that he could not step back. This wasn't about him, his pride, or his ego; this was about the children of Norene. And he would see that history remembered them as fighters for freedom, not as cowards.

Behind him someone bashed a shield with a sword causing a loud thudding sound to spread through the ranks. Another thud came, then two or three more, and then more and more soldiers joined in, bashing their weapons against their shields in slow rhythm. The sound reminded John of battle drums. It was intoxicating. His heart started to follow the rhythm, and the rhythm beat faster and faster and louder and louder. He raised the sword above his head, turned to face his army, and shouted with his strong and deep voice, "For freedom!"

"For freedom!" the soldiers shouted back.

"For freedom!" he shouted even louder, and the soldiers yelled in agreement, raising their weapons high in the air.

John turned around and spurred his horse. Out of the corner of his eye, he saw the knights at his side. The cavalry followed them. The horses sped up with each step and soon were advancing at a gallop. The enemy's army moved forward, and John tightened his grip on the reins. He shouted at the top of his lungs and leaned closer to the horse's back. Arrows flew over his head and landed in the enemy's ranks. John quickly looked over his shoulder and then back at the enemy again. They were approaching. And John knew that his soldiers were going to win this battle or die trying.

The armies clashed when each was halfway from its starting point. The cavalry pushed their way through the enemy ranks, and the soldiers followed, fighting bravely. John rode his horse amongst the fighting soldiers, feeling proud. His army immediately pushed its way deep into the enemy ranks. It seemed that the werewolves stood no chance; yet he knew that to win the battle, they had to finish the enemy. The enemy was like a dragon, and he needed to kill it. And the best way to kill a dragon was to decapitate it.

He rode through the battlefield until he found the werewolves' leader, Wolls, among the fighting men. *There! Right there!* That was the head of the dragon. He pulled on his horse's reins to turn him, and then he spurred his horse forward. With his sword in his right hand, he smote an enemy soldier who got in his way. He continued to the werewolf.

Suddenly, and for no apparent reason, his horse fell to the ground, taking him with it. John saw the ground approaching and quickly covered his head with his shield. He made a somersault and landed on the ground heavily, rolling until he stopped in a puddle face down. His left hand had been trapped somewhere above him by the shield attached to it, his sword having flown out of his grip. He lifted himself off the ground, feeling confused. Cries of the battlefield came to his ears, and his senses caught up. He was still alive. Gingerly, he got up, picked up his sword, and looked around. He was surrounded by his own cavalry as they moved through the enemy ranks. He found Wolls in the crowd and staggered towards the werewolf.

John caught a glimpse of his horse running towards the forest. On the one hand, John was glad that his horse was all right, but on the other, he would definitely have been safer in the battlefield from the back of a horse.

He reached the werewolf, lifted his sword to attack, and then froze. Wolls had just lifted a man twice his size with one hand high above his head. The werewolf turned away from the lifeless body in his grip and locked his eyes on John. With a nasty smile on his face, Wolls threw the man to the ground. John watched the body and realized in horror that the werewolf had broken the soldier's neck. He tore his eyes off the body and focused on Wolls. He felt his courage leaving him. He readied his shield and tightened his grip on the handle of his sword.

"Well, well, well," Wolls said as he turned to face John. He didn't have any shield or armour. He wore only a long tunic and carried a short sword. John hated everything about him: his slick, black hair falling on his shoulders; his fake, maniacal smile; his brown-reddish eyes, and his silky voice. "The great John Mathewson," the werewolf said as he switched the sword from his left to his right hand. "I always thought you were younger."

John didn't say anything. He knew it was hard to kill a werewolf and was doing quick calculations in his head. He knew that werewolves were allergic to silver, but the trick of killing a werewolf didn't lie in a weapon but in the damage created to the brain. Cutting off the head was the safest way to kill a werewolf. Breaking his skull open would also do the trick, and both options were very inviting at the moment. Going for the heart was trickier. Only a direct hit would kill a werewolf, and this would be guaranteed only with a silver weapon.

John realized that the werewolf was grinning. A little shiver ran down his spine, and he remembered that werewolves—very much like wolves—could smell fear.

"So," Wolls said as he stepped forward. John took a step back. "How do you wish to die?"

"In my bed twenty years from now!" John screamed as he charged. He didn't know why he'd said it, but the words gave him courage, as if saying them out loud confirmed the possibility that he would survive this fight.

Wolls's grin froze, and a brief look of shock appeared on his face. Obviously, he hadn't expected John to find enough courage to attack. He lifted his sword and stopped John's blow to his head with little difficulty. A maniacal smile appeared on his face.

Although John didn't expect Wolls's return blow to be as strong as it was, he managed to heave his shield at the werewolf's head as he flew back a few steps. He straightened up. The werewolf staggered backwards and stopped, surprise visible in his eyes. John's heart was beating painfully in his chest as he tried to absorb the shock.

Wolls lifted his hand slowly and touched the blood running down from his nose.

He can bleed, John thought with a huge relief. The werewolf *could* bleed. This meant that he could be injured, and he could be injured quite easily.

Anger twisted Wolls' otherwise handsome, rugged face. He threw the sword to the ground with such strength that the sword rebounded and landed far behind him. And then he leapt.

John hadn't expected that at all. He hadn't expected that Wolls could reach him in one leap. And he definitely hadn't expected that Wolls would change to a wolf in broad daylight.

Wolls landed on John with his front paws, and they both fell to the ground: one man, one wolf tangled together in Wolls' tunic. Even though John had been stunned by the leap, he got his shield ready and his sword in front of him. He could feel the body landing on top of him as they fell down. Years of training had taught him to be always ready, and now it paid off.

He kicked Wolls's dead body off him, and with the shield threw him to the side. Even in wolf form, the werewolf was heavy. John slowly stood up with his shield in front of him, his right hand hanging by his side, numb from the blow. His sword was sticking out of the beast's throat. John watched the werewolf intently, unable to comprehend what had just happened.

It took another few seconds for his brain to catch up with the latest events, but eventually it did. And he realized another thing. They had won. They were free at last!

Andrew and his three colleagues worked in a cave in Minerst Mines, located in the heart of Wolfast. They were mining in silence, hardly talking to each other. In the same rhythm, they lifted their pickaxes and hit the wall. With each hit, stones fell to the ground. The only sound was the pickaxes against the stone and the clunk … clunk … clunk …

They moved slowly and silently forward, chipping at the wall. Hours and hours of monotonous movement made Andrew's arms ache. Yet his arms were big and strong. The stone stood no chance. Clunk … clunk … clunk …

Occasionally, a man with a shovel and buckets came and took away the fallen rocks. The miners hardly paid him any attention. He was just a part of the background. Clunk … clunk … clunk …

Something shiny fell to the ground with a soft clink. The miners stopped and looked at a small light-blue gemstone that lay at their feet. The weirdest thing about it was that it was spherical—completely spherical without any dirt on it. It looked as if someone had cut the gem, polished it, and then placed it back into the mine.

The miners stood still for a long while watching the gem in disbelief. Andrew could feel the goose bumps erupt all over his body. No one moved for nearly a minute. Finally, Andrew walked over to the gem, leaned forward, and reached for it. The miner closest to him grabbed his shoulder and pulled him back. "Andrew, don't!" he shouted.

Andrew looked at the miner and then at the gem. He hesitated and then freed his arm. He picked up the gem gingerly and put it on his palm. It was as big as an acorn. The rest of the miners stepped back. "I think we've found it," Andrew said in a hushed voice as he studied the gem on his palm. "I think this is it."

The others kept looking at the stone in awe. It was beautiful. It took Andrew a few seconds to realize that he actually didn't find it odd that the stone was polished. He felt as if he was holding a natural gemstone. He shook his head and closed his palm. The other miners straightened up and looked around, puzzled. Andrew himself felt as if he was waking up from a dream.

"I should take this up," Andrew said as he looked at the others, who nodded meekly. He stepped forward hesitantly as if still not sure what to do. As he looked at his closed palm, he looked back at his colleagues, who nodded encouragingly. "Right," he said reassuringly, and he moved up the tunnel. His first steps were quite slow, but then he picked up his pace. A few more steps, and he started to jog. And then he broke into a run. The tunnel was long, and it led only to a junction of five tunnels. He hurried up one of the tunnels with his fist pressed against his chest wondering why he was the one taking it to the surface. He ran into the broad daylight and stopped.

After the darkness of the tunnels, the sun blinded him, and it took his eyes several seconds to adjust. He looked around until he saw his employer up on a horse next to a young man, also on horseback. The employer, Mr. Tim Robertson, was a short man who could have stood to lose a lot of weight. He was quite round and didn't really have any neck. He was about fifty years old. His blond hair was cut very short, and his face was freshly shaved. He looked like a huge egg in clothes. The young man next to him was a stranger. Andrew had never seen him before, or heard of him.

As he approached both men, Andrew realized that there was something mesmerizing about the stranger. It was difficult to figure out his age because he looked both twenty and fifty years old. His posture and figure suggested a royal origin, and his manners reminded Andrew of the manners of a general. Andrew knew that all the miners had been trying to avoid the stranger. They weren't scared of him; they just had a huge respect for him. Though the young man had always been very nice to the miners who had seen him, Andrew had a feeling it would be a very bad idea to provoke him.

Now, Andrew became frightened. He couldn't quite put his finger on the reason for his fear; he just knew he was terrified of the stranger. He looked at his hand, still clenching the gem, and chills ran down his spine. He looked around, hoping he would find someone else who could take it to Mr. Tim for him.

A strange feeling came over him as he looked up at the men on the horses. The young man was looking straight at him. Andrew gulped and moved towards them. It felt like ages before he finally reached them. The young man followed him with his gaze all the way, and Andrew asked himself over and over again: *Why the hell did I pick up the gem?*

Andrew stopped in front of Mr. Tim and, though he carefully avoided the young man's stare, he could still feel it fixed upon him. Mr. Tim looked down at him with one eyebrow slightly raised and waited. Andrew opened his mouth, but when no sound came, he closed it.

"What is it?" Mr. Tim asked in a very kind manner.

Andrew took in a sharp breath, stretched out his arm, and opened his palm. And there it was—a small, light-blue, spherical gemstone. The stranger reached out and picked it up. Andrew's eyes flashed to his face. Although he never really paid any attention to men in this way, he had to admit that the young man was very handsome. He had a sort of a smile on his young face and a gentle look in his almost-black eyes. He caught Andrew's gaze and smiled at him encouragingly. Andrew couldn't help but smile back.

"I think this deserves a reward," the young man said, and he handed Andrew a golden coin.

Andrew took the coin, not believing his eyes, and brought it close to his face to inspect it. "A whole crown?" he asked unbelievingly as he looked at the stranger.

"Yes," the stranger said, nodding with a hint of amusement on his face. "A whole crown."

Andrew bowed to him and froze. He wasn't sure if it was his imagination, but he thought that the man's eyes turned bright blue for a brief moment. Andrew stepped back, his eyes wide with fear. He turned around abruptly and ran down the hill as fast as he could without falling. He ran around his colleagues, who had been waiting for him, and into the forest. He didn't stop until he was out of sight.

"What was that about?" Tim asked with furrows on his forehead. He looked at the young man, who couldn't help but chuckle. The stranger looked at the gem in his hand and then checked it against the light. "Do you think this is it?" Tim asked as he leaned closer to have a better look.

"How many gems come from mines in perfect round shapes?" the young man asked, still looking at the gem intently.

Tim thought about this for a few seconds and then shrugged. And then the gem caught his eye. It was a strange shade of light blue; something between spring's sky and a mountain lake, or something like a hydrangea. The more he tried to figure the colour of the gem, the more difficult it became. The gem seemed to change in colour. It took him a while to realize that the gem was getting darker and darker. It turned bright blue then dark blue. And then it was so dark, it was almost black.

When the gem became completely black, a small white dot appeared in the centre. Then the dot got bigger and bigger. The dot wasn't only white, but it was emitting light as well. And as it got bigger, it got brighter. When it was half the size of the gem, Tim had to close his eyes. He couldn't see the young man properly, but he had a feeling that the light was blinding only him. The light was so bright that he could still perceive it through his eyelids. He covered his eyes with his hand, but that didn't really help. He turned away and pressed his hand against his eyes.

He waited for the light to go away, and it took him a while to realize that the light was finally gone. The white light in front of his eyes was dimming down until he saw only the white dot burnt to his retina. He put his hand down and peeked through small slots between his nearly closed eyelids. When he saw trees in front of him, he opened his eyes. He still could see a small white dot, and he knew that he would see that dot for a long time before it would finally fade away from his vision. He turned around and met the young man's gaze.

"Is everything okay?" the young man asked in a worried tone.

Tim nodded and looked at the gem in the man's hand. It was light blue once again. "What was that?" he asked as he blinked, trying to get rid of the dot on his retina.

"Just some light," the young man said nonchalantly. Tim reached for the gem and hesitated. The stranger nodded encouragingly and put the gem on Tim's palm. Tim watched it intently, waiting for the gem to change its colour. No matter how he looked at the gem, it was still the same. He tried to move it, so that it would catch the light from the sun, but it still remained light blue. He tried different positions of his hand, but it didn't change the colour at all. A short cough to his left reminded him that he was not alone. He looked at the young man who watched him curiously.

"Why doesn't it shine for me?" Tim asked, perplexed, as he looked at the light-blue gem. "Where is the white dot?"

He looked at the young man again, expecting some explanation. The young man smiled and looked him in the eye. Tim felt like a little boy at that moment, as if he had a toy that he couldn't operate and an adult was trying to find the correct words to explain how to do it. Tim closed his palm, pressing the gem against his flesh.

"The gem chooses to whom it will reveal itself," the young man said at last. "But don't worry. It isn't dangerous per se."

Tim looked at his fist and back at the young man again. Suddenly, he felt a strong urge to run—to throw the gem away and just turn around and run. For a brief crazy moment, he imagined opening his hand and letting the gem fall to the ground. And then another feeling came—a strong desire to keep the gem forever. What would happen if he never opened his palm?

A strange sensation ran through him. At first it was pleasurable, but then it changed rapidly. A lot of emotions ran through him. Many thoughts and memories emerged, and a great many emotions and thoughts vanished. The sensation was very brief, yet very powerful. Tim felt lightheaded and a bit dizzy. He swayed and closed his eyes.

A memory from two weeks ago resurfaced. It was a memory of the young man approaching. Tim remembered the stranger riding towards him on a horse and then a rush of feelings that overcame Tim the first time he laid his eyes on the stranger. From that moment, it felt completely natural that the man would be there, even though he had never explained his presence. He had not even told anyone his name.

With dread, Tim looked at the young man, who was watching him silently. Then the realization hit Tim heavily. This was no man. This was something much more powerful and very likely something very dangerous. Tim's heart beat painfully in his chest, and beads of sweat appeared on his forehead. "Who are you?" he asked in a whisper. "Why are you here?"

The stranger didn't answer. He just watched Tim, his ever-present shadow of a smile finally vanishing from his face. They eyed each other for a while. A few seconds later, Tim felt a relief. The stranger was not dangerous; at least not to Tim. Those eyes were friendly and kind. Tim looked at his palm again and realized that there was one question he wanted to ask even more. "What is this thing?"

The stranger watched Tim's face intently for a very long time. Then his eyes wandered towards Tim's hand. He sighed and tore his eyes off Tim. "That gem is ancient. No one knew it was here until an earthquake happened three weeks ago."

"I remember that quake," Tim said as he nodded. "Four of my mines were caved in."

"That's why I came here," the man continued, looking at the entrance of the mine. "I was sent here to get the stone and then hide it somewhere where it would be safe."

"You can hide it with me," Tim said without even realizing what he was saying. His brain caught up with him a few seconds later with a simple question: *Why even suggest something like that?*

The young man looked at Tim in surprise. He opened his mouth to say something, but closed it again.

Once more, Tim felt like a little boy who had just said something cute, but stupid.

"You don't want to keep an eye on that stone," the young man said in a matter-of-fact tone of voice. "That gem is maybe pretty—"

"It's beautiful," Tim said breathlessly.

The young man looked a little amused, but nodded and continued: "Though it is beautiful, you wouldn't be able to show it to anyone. You could only lock it up someplace and never talk about it."

"Consider it done!"

"You don't understand," the young man said as he leaned closer to Tim. "Being a guardian of that stone is a curse, not a privilege. There are some … creatures, who would love to get that stone, and they mustn't even know where it is. You, being a mere human, cannot use that stone for your protection, and there is no way you can hide it sufficiently."

"Have you ever heard of Strongfort?"

The young man shook his head.

"It's a vault that very few people know of, and even fewer know that it has a lot of secret rooms. I can hide it there. No one would ever find it."

The young man straightened up on his horse and looked at Tim pensively. "I have to admit that it isn't the worst idea," he said hesitantly. "All right, I give you a week to hide that stone. If I like the way it's guarded, I will leave the stone with you."

Tim smiled happily. He looked at the gem in his hand and convinced himself that the colour was changing slightly, and it was darker than it had been before.

"I want you to take this," the young man said. He pulled a little pendant with a small red jewel in the centre from one of his saddle bags. "If you or your successors decide that the stone can no longer stay here, press that jewel, and someone will come for it."

Tim nodded and took the pendant. While he held the stone in one hand and the pendant in the other, he had an idea. The gem was beautiful, but it was very small and round. If a jeweller turned the gem into a pendant, it wouldn't roll away. If any trouble came, Tim could even guard it by wearing it around his neck beneath his clothes.

He looked up, but the young man was gone. He turned to the mine, but no one stood there. All the miners were gone too. He was all alone in front of an empty mine. The place not only looked deserted, it looked as if no one had been there for months. The wind blew from the mine and howled when it reached the hill. Leaves on the trees behind him rustled.

He spun around and watched the forest nervously. A strong fear overcame him, and his imagination started to play nasty tricks on him. Another howling sound came from the mine. He turned back towards the mine and watched the entrance, his entire body shaking. A shadow moved inside. He screamed and spurred his horse at once.

He galloped around the mine without even stopping and checking what was going on. He rushed through the forest to the city. All he wanted to do was to get away. Suddenly the idea of wearing the gem around his neck seemed stupid, and he wanted to place the gem in the vault as quickly as he could.

A CENTURY
LATER ...

CHAPTER 1

Ethan Philipson was sitting in an armchair in a huge library, reading a book. The torches on the walls were lit, bathing the library in bright light. It was nearly midnight, but Ethan didn't mind. He was leaning against one armrest with his leg hanging over the other one. His blond hair was falling into his blue eyes, but he barely noticed. Breathlessly, he continued reading, his eyes running from one side of the page to the other rapidly.

The library door banged loudly, and he jumped to his feet, sending the book to the floor. He spun around and looked at the door, his heart beating fast. A servant stood in the library, taken aback. "I'm sorry, Your Majesty," the servant said quickly. "I didn't mean to startle you."

"That's all right," Ethan said as he picked up the book from the floor. "I was just reading a very scary passage and didn't hear you come … Carry on."

"Actually, sire, I came for you," the servant said and stepped closer. "It's your father, the king. He is not feeling very well. He asked—"

Ethan sprinted towards the door and smashed it open, bumping accidentally into the servant on the way. Out of the corner of the eye, he saw the man lose his balance, but Ethan didn't stop. He ran through the corridors until he came to a halt by his father's chambers. A maid stood by the door, looking terrified. When she noticed Ethan, she bowed and stepped aside to let him pass.

Ethan entered the bedroom. Few candles were lit, but the baldachin was lowered, and his father lay on the pillows in shadow, breathing very heavily. Two guards and a steward stood by the door. Ethan walked slowly to his father's bed.

King Philip, Ethan's father, was very much loved in Norene. Under his rule, the kingdom had prospered, and people's lives had greatly improved. Unfortunately, for the last two years, his old age had begun to catch up with him. Ethan had inherited his father's looks, which made him very popular in Norene, but the handsome and charismatic face of his father was long gone. The illness had changed the king beyond recognition.

"Get the doctor!" Ethan screamed at the servants. The maid turned on the spot and ran out of the room, but the steward calmly turned to Ethan and said in whisper: "We already sent for him, Your Majesty, before we sent for you."

The king opened his eyes and looked up at his son. He reached his hand towards Ethan, who quickly sat on the bed to be closer.

"It's all right," Ethan said quietly. He reached for the glass of water that stood on the bedside table. "The doctor's on his way."

He lifted his father from the pillows and held the cup to his mouth while the king drank. Hurried footsteps echoed in the corridor, and Ethan looked over his shoulder. A man ran into the room. He was not much older than the prince, but he was much chubbier.

"I came as soon as I heard," the man said quietly as he stepped closer. "Did anyone send for the doctor?"

"Yes, Lord Adrian," the steward said immediately with a little bow. "The doctor should be here very soon."

The king pushed the cup away and lay calmly back on the pillows. He seized Ethan's wrists and pulled closer. Ethan leaned in, spilling a little water on the sheets.

"I'm glad you are of age," the king whispered. He coughed violently. "I was afraid I would not be here long enough for you to be able to take over," he added when he caught his breath again.

Ethan shook his head. He couldn't bear the idea of losing his father so soon. Though Ethan was only twenty-one, his father was past seventy. It had seemed for a long time that the king wouldn't have an heir, but finally, when the queen was over forty years old, Ethan was born. Unfortunately, she died giving the birth, and the king was left alone, but he had stepped up and raised Ethan on his own. And he had done a great job.

"No, Father," Ethan said in a whisper. His voice refused to work for him suddenly. "You will get better, and you will continue your rule."

"I don't think so," the king said hoarsely. "But I feel much better knowing that you can take over. I hope I have taught you well."

Footsteps echoed in the corridor once more, and a tall and rather skinny man rushed into the room carrying a little black bag in his hands. He hurried towards the bed and leaned over the king as he put the bag on the floor. He was so tall that his head was nearly touching the baldachin.

Ethan stepped back to give the doctor more space. He paced the room while the doctor examined the king, occasionally exchanging worried looks with Lord Adrian. Once or twice Ethan wanted to ask the doctor what his opinion was, but couldn't bring himself to do so.

Half an hour later, when the king finally fell asleep, the doctor motioned towards the corridor. Ethan and Lord Adrian followed him outside.

"Can you help him?" Ethan asked breathlessly.

"I gave him something to help him sleep, but I'm afraid there isn't much we can do. The medicine is no longer helping. It seems he's giving up. I would like to remain in the castle to be close. Would you be able to accommodate me here?"

"Sure." Ethan nodded and looked around. The steward hurried towards him and motioned for the doctor to follow him. Ethan wanted to thank the doctor, but he and the steward were gone before he could find his voice. Ethan watched after the doctor and the steward and then looked at Lord Adrian. "I really hoped he would get better," he said in a whisper. "Why would he give up?"

"Because you are of age," Lord Adrian answered calmly. "He didn't want to leave his people without a proper king. It's almost a month now since you turned twenty-one."

"I don't want him—" Ethan stopped abruptly and turned away from Lord Adrian.

"Maybe he's just tired and tomorrow will be better," Lord Adrian said quietly, looking at the bed. "Don't lose hope."

When Ethan didn't say anything, Lord Adrian turned to the guards. "Inform the doctor and the prince immediately if anything—"

"I'm not leaving," Ethan interrupted Lord Adrian and turned around. "I'm sleeping here. I'm not leaving until he gets better."

Lord Adrian looked at the prince and opened his mouth to say something, but then only smiled wearily and nodded. Ethan spun around and walked back to his father's bedroom. His father was now sleeping peacefully, his breathing back to normal. His wrinkled face seemed even older, and Ethan got really scared. He hadn't wanted to hear for the last two years that his father would die. He believed that his father would get better, but tonight was proving him wrong.

A maid entered the chambers and carried bedding to the sofa in the corner. Ethan ignored her. He didn't feel like sleeping. He walked over to the table near the wall and picked up the chair that stood next to it. As he carried it to his father's bed, the maid bowed and left. On the sofa, there were pillows and blankets she had left for Ethan. He didn't even glance at them. He put the chair down next to the bed and sat down.

Julian, the guard in Strongfort, walked his usual route. Working in the vault was boring because nothing ever happened there, and working a nightshift was extremely dull. The building was a little fortress in the mountains hidden above a river that flowed between two small hills. The guards lived there all year long, leaving occasionally to visit their families. Though the job was boring, it was incredibly well paid, so the guards didn't really mind this monotonous work.

The talk amongst the guards was that the place hid a lot of treasures that even they never saw. Some of the treasures were ancient and some had been brought there recently in the dead of night to ensure that no one knew where they were. The word was that the fortress had hundreds of secret rooms that held treasures beyond anyone's imagination. However, all they were actually guarding was art, so Julian suspected that the legends were circling amongst the guards to spice up the boring assignment.

Julian walked up the corridor, which was lit by torches. The only sounds were his boots hitting the stone floor. He sighed and looked through the window. The corridors were built around the fortress's square-shaped yard, so all he had to do was walk in circles. Occasionally, he saw other guards through the windows, and this was usually the most eventful moment of the nightshift; but not today. Suddenly, a shadow caught his eye, and he stopped. He looked down the corridor and put his hand on the hilt of his sword. He never liked doing the nightshifts because the place was draughty and cold, but he had to admit that the fortress was never spooky. Torches were lit all the time, the windows were shut tight, and there were always other guards in the corridors as well. He hadn't seen a shadow like this before. There weren't many shadows in these corridors.

He pulled out his sword and carefully walked towards the shadow. As he got closer, he realized that it was a hole in the wall. He didn't know that the walls could open and deduced that this was one of those secret rooms that the legends described.

He reached the entrance and looked at the room from the corridor. The room was pitch-dark, and he wasn't crazy enough to just enter it. He looked over his shoulder at the yard, but didn't see another guard there. He looked up and down the corridor, wondering if he should raise the alarm, but decided against this. To raise the alarm, he had to get to one of the two ends of the corridor where the alarm bells were placed. This would give enough time to anyone hiding in the room to sneak out.

With his free hand, he took the nearest torch from the wall and threw it into the room. The torch landed on the stone floor with a soft thud, and the light illuminated a very small room. The only thing in the room was a little table in the middle. The table was empty, but a clear spot in the centre of the thick layer of dust showed that a small round object was missing.

As he hurried into the room, out of the corner of his eye, he caught another shadow. He turned around, but before he could protect himself with his sword, or even have a better look, he was thrown to the side. He hit the table as he swung his sword at the shadow, missing completely. The table landed on the ground heavily, and Julian fell on top of it, smashing it to pieces.

He looked up, but the shadow was gone. He quickly rose back to his feet and hurried after the shadow, not even noticing a gash on his left calf. He stopped in the corridor and looked left and right. He sprinted after the thief, ignoring the pain in his leg. Based on the thief's movements, he assumed that the thief was a woman. She was dressed in tight black clothes with a black mask on her face. It seemed she didn't have any weapons with her.

They turned left to another wider corridor, and Julian managed to grab the alarm bell that was hanging on the wall. He rang the bell as hard as he could as he continued to run after the thief. He wasn't sure if other guards could hear it—this was the first time he himself heard the alarm bell—but he didn't have time to check. He rang it four more times, throwing it to the ground with the fourth ring. The thief sped up, slowly but surely escaping Julian. He prolonged his own step, but he was getting weak and tired.

The thief drew away with each step, but suddenly four guards appeared on the other end of the corridor, and the thief stopped abruptly. The guards stopped dead and watched the woman and Julian in surprise. It took them only a second or two to see what was going on, and they pulled out their swords and hurried into the corridor. The thief looked over her shoulder, jumped to the door next to her, and pressed the handle. The door was locked. She swirled and then looked at the window.

Julian was almost upon her when the woman suddenly jumped to the window. In one fast movement, she kicked the shutters open and nearly flew through the window to the outside. Julian followed her immediately without even thinking.

He climbed onto the ledge and looked around. He was on the fourth floor—four storeys between him and yard's stone tiles. He saw that the alarm had awakened almost every guard in the fortress. They were running through the yard to the entrance to the east wing, which meant that the path through the yard was blocked.

Julian looked up and saw the thief disappearing over the edge of the roof. He didn't want the thief to get away, so he hurried after her. The adrenalin, the adventure that shook up the tedious routine, and his light-headed youthfulness were the reasons that he didn't hesitate for a second. He jumped, grabbed the ledge of the fifth floor, and pulled himself up onto it. Then he took a deep breath and jumped towards a gargoyle that was hanging from the roof. Only when he was reaching for the gargoyle, which was too far away, did his brain come up with the possibility that it might not have been the best idea. Luckily, and against all odds, he grabbed the mouth of the gargoyle as his body smashed against the wall.

He steadied himself and looked at the strange stone beast above him. His heart was painfully beating in his chest as he hung there, catching his breath. The adrenalin was slowly fading away, and he started to play with the idea that he would remain hanging on the gargoyle until someone came and rescued him, but his hands and arms screamed in protest. He mustered all his strength and pulled himself up onto the roof. He rolled over the edge and landed, panting, on ceramic tiles. He looked up and, to his surprise, saw the thief nearby.

She was standing several feet away, looking at something in her hands. The wind was blowing, and the moonlight illuminated her slim figure. Julian clearly heard the screams of his fellow guards as they ran to the east wing, but the thief didn't look up. She either didn't hear them or didn't care.

He lifted himself a little, kicked himself off the tiles, and jumped towards her. He grabbed her ankles and pulled her towards him. The woman fell on the tiles with a high-pitched shriek of surprise, and a necklace flew from her grip. They both watched the little light-blue pendant on a golden chain fall onto the tiles, slide, and fall over the rim on the other side of the roof. Quickly, they crawled to the edge of the roof and looked down at the river below.

Julian was so absorbed in watching the river that he didn't even notice the woman move. She spun around quickly and kicked his head. The world around him dimmed, and he barely felt the tiles passing beneath his body as he rolled off the roof. He landed on something cold and hard, reflexively grabbed it, and felt his legs dangling in the air. He tightened his grip and managed to get the roof in focus. He was holding onto the gargoyle. The same gargoyle he had already used for climbing onto the roof. He tilted his head to have a better look and watched the woman disappear over the other edge.

The adrenalin almost completely left his body, and he felt weaker and weaker. He tried to pull himself up onto the roof, but he was so tired that he slid down until he was hanging from the gargoyle's neck. He wasn't sure how long he could hold on.

A drop of sweat was slowly moving down the side of his face, and then it fell onto his shoulder. He wiped his forehead against his stretched arm and immediately noticed something liquid and dark. It was blood, most likely his own. He felt his grip weakening when a window somewhere below him opened and he was somehow pulled inside the fortress. The last thing he saw before fainting were concerned looks on the faces of the other guards.

Amy climbed down the side of the fortress from one window to the next like a cat and landed on the rock on which the fortress was built. She walked carefully over the rim of the cliff until she reached the rope that she had left there before. She climbed it all the way down to the forest and landed on the dry leaves. She let go of the rope and sunk to her knees. She had to gather her thoughts and catch her breath.

She knew she had screwed up. She hadn't expected the guard to follow her. Though the lord of the fortress always chose the best men as guards, the job was so uneventful and tedious that the guards lost their touch. This one had to be new and still full of energy. She should have hurried and only later checked to make sure she had got the correct necklace, but she hadn't wanted to risk leaving with an incorrect item.

She took a deep breath, looked at the fortress above her, and then turned around and hurried towards the river. She reached the bank and stopped on the spot. She quickly pulled the mask off, leaned over, and tried to catch her breath. Suddenly, she sensed the presence of another person. She looked up and saw a familiar figure—tall, slender, with broad shoulders. Even in the moonlight she could clearly see how his brown hair draped down over his forehead. His eyes were watching her intently— those deep green eyes that were glowing in the dark.

"Where is it?" the man asked with excitement in his voice as he stepped closer and scanned her up and down.

"I don't have it," she replied. The man stopped and looked her in the eye. She tried to keep the eye contact, but had to turn away.

"Well, you will have to go back," he said in a matter-of-fact tone of voice. "We have to come up with a plan as soon as possible. It took me almost a hundred years to track it down. I really don't want to risk that they will take it someplace else and hide it there."

"I don't think that will be an issue," she said, still looking down. The man stepped closer, watching her profile intently. Her throat tightened as she tried to continue. She opened her mouth, but no sound came out. She gulped and remained silent.

"What do you mean?" he asked in a quiet voice.

She would actually prefer if he were screaming. This calmness in his voice was a hundred times worse. She sighed, closed her eyes, and whispered, "I lost it in the river." No answer came. She didn't dare to look up or open her eyes. She took a deep breath and told him what had happened. All of it. When she finished, she lifted her gaze and looked the man in the eye. "I didn't want to risk taking the wrong one," she said quietly. She wanted to explain why she had made the mistake, why she had let it slip through her fingers.

The man put his head into his hands and turned away from her. She looked at the ground and hugged her shoulders. She didn't know what he was thinking, but she realized that the necklace was lost forever. "I'm sorry," she whispered. He didn't move or say anything. "I've failed you," she continued meekly. "I am really sorry. I wish I had a dog that could smell the trail and find the necklace, though—"

"What did you say?" the man asked and spun around. She looked at him in surprise and tried to remember what she had been saying.

"I said I was sorry," she said at last.

"No, after that."

"That I wish I had a dog?" she asked hesitantly.

"We need a dog," the man said and grabbed her by shoulders.

She didn't budge. "But a dog won't understand what we need," she said. "Besides, we have nothing that smells like the necklace."

"Exactly," the man nodded happily. "But the magic the necklace emits has some special odour. All we need is a dog that can understand what we are looking for and will follow any strange trail along the river—before the necklace reaches the sea."

The woman watched the man for a while; concentration furrowed her brow. Then a realization appeared on her face, and her eyes became round. She looked at the river and then back at the man. "We're not talking about dogs, are we?" she asked. The man let go of her and turned to watch the river. "You want to go and ask the werewolves?"

"Yes." He nodded with his back to her. "It's their country, and they can be helpful."

"Why should they help us? And even if they did, how do you plan on getting the necklace? They might want it for themselves."

"Let *me* worry about that," the man said as he turned to the woman. A smile appeared on his face. "You just find me a window of time during which I can talk to their new leader alone and unnoticed."

9

CHAPTER 2

B ess stepped out of the palace and took a deep, refreshing breath. He was very tall and strong, but his features were gentle. His nearly black hair was always combed back into a small ponytail, and his chin was shaved clean. He always followed the newest fashion, and even today was wearing a black suit.

It was nearly midnight, and the full moon was rising up in the sky. Guards, pacing in front of the palace, stopped and looked at him. There was a question in their eyes, but he didn't feel like sharing any information. He stepped away from the palace and looked over his shoulder at the building. It was really beautiful, but he would never be able to look at it in the same way. The chills ran down his spine. He shook them off and hurried down the road.

Bess had worked in the capital of Wolfast for nearly twenty years, and he had worked for the werewolves for the last ten. He was not a werewolf—it was not necessary to be one to work for them—and he really didn't like his employers. He was responsible for research on political situations in Lanland. Sometimes it was unbelievably difficult to explain to the werewolves why some situations happened and why other countries of Lanland behaved the way they did, but he liked his job. Well, he had liked his job. Finding one's employer beheaded behind his office desk had not been a picnic for him.

The werewolves couldn't die from disease or old age, but they could be killed. They sometimes died during fights and war battles, during various accidents with water, fire, or weapons, or just because another werewolf wanted to be the leader. Today's death of the current leader happened because Mors wanted to rule, and the current ruler didn't want to leave the post.

After Bess raised the alarm, he had been interrogated on the subject. For a moment, he had wondered if they would blame him for the leader's death, but he managed to persuade them that he wasn't responsible. There was no way he could have bitten off the leader's head. As soon as the situation calmed down a little, Bess handed Mors—the new leader—his resignation and hurried out of the palace before Mors could say anything.

Though it was late at night, there were still a few people in the streets. When they saw him, they stopped and watched him until he walked out of their sight. He felt like a marked man. Everyone knew that he had worked in the palace, and based on their reactions, he surmised that they already knew that something had happened. It seemed that the news had got out of the palace and was spreading like a wildfire. He avoided their stares, but could still feel them. He stopped in front of an inn he sometimes visited and looked up at the sign. He stood there for a while and then came to a conclusion: he needed a drink.

He opened the door, and the murmurs of the people in the inn filled his ears. He entered and closed the door behind him. The murmuring died away, and everyone looked at him. A few men stretched their necks to have a better view, and one man even moved his chair to the side to see him better. Bess scanned the hungry faces around him. No one said a word. He hesitated and then walked to the bar. He sat with his back to the rest of the people and looked up at the innkeeper, who watched him with his mouth hanging open.

"Pour me the strongest spirit you have," Bess said hoarsely as he put two golden coins on the table. The innkeeper picked up a clean metal cup and poured him a drink. He put it in front of Bess and eyed the money on the counter. The amount was huge. It would pay for all the drinks in the inn for a whole day.

Bess picked up the cup and froze when it was halfway to his mouth. He looked at the liquid as if trying to see something in there. Then he sighed and gulped it down. He coughed violently as he put the cup down. Since he usually drank only a beer or two, he wasn't used to strong alcohol. Still coughing, he motioned to the cup, and the innkeeper poured him another drink.

When Bess managed to get the coughing under control, he picked up the cup. Suddenly, he realized that the inn was dead silent. He looked over his shoulder and scanned the room. Everyone was looking at him. The expectation was electrifying the air in the room. He turned back and slowly drank the contents of the cup.

"So, what's new at the palace?" the innkeeper asked when Bess finally finished the second drink. Bess just shook his head and pushed the cup closer to the innkeeper. He was aware of all the stares fixed upon him, but he didn't feel like talking. The innkeeper poured Bess another cup and pushed it back towards him. "This one is on the house," he said with a smile.

Bess nodded gloomily, picking up the cup. His head was starting to swirl, and he was losing focus. The vision of his boss came to his mind, and he shrugged violently. He gulped the third drink and put the empty cup on the counter. Out of the corner of his eye, he saw some people gesturing, and the innkeeper poured him another cup. "This one is from Johaness," he said. Bess waved his hand above his head as a thank you and did a down-in-one. The innkeeper took the cup away with a concerned look and leaned against the counter so that his face was only a few inches from Bess's.

"What's the matter, Bess?" he asked. "You look like a piece of shit. I am really starting to worry about you. Last time you had a drink, you nearly puked after the first cup."

Bess focused on the face in front of him and motioned for more. The innkeeper shook his head and straitened up. "No, you've had enough," he said sternly. He looked around at the others in the inn and frowned. "No!" he shouted. "He really has had enough. I'm responsible for all of you. I am not pouring him another drink no matter who pays for it."

He looked at Bess again and his expression softened. Bess was slowly swaying on the stool, looking completely at a loss. The innkeeper leaned over the counter again, and Bess focused on him. "Talk to me," the innkeeper said quietly. "Let out whatever is bothering you. You will feel better. Spirits are not an answer."

Bess swayed some more and then steadied himself against the counter. He hiccupped. Even after the alcohol hit his brain, he felt no better. There were so many things that worried him, and even the strongest spirit couldn't silence them.

"I just saw what a body looks like after a werewolf attack," he said at last. He could feel how everyone in the whole inn froze. "It's not only a dead body, but a dead body with no head and … and with—" He closed his eyes and pressed his lips together. He sat still for a while, swaying slightly, and then looked at the innkeeper. He leaned closer and loudly whispered: "The werewolves are maniacs. Pure maniacs."

He looked at the counter and hiccoughed. He looked the counter up and down with a frown on his forehead and then checked the floor behind him. He tried to look beneath the stool he was sitting on, but he lost his balance. Someone grabbed him and steadied him on the stool. He looked at the innkeeper, but the man was too far away. He kept his stare at the innkeeper until his brain caught up, and he looked to his left. There stood a young skinny redheaded man with a lot of freckles, holding him by the shoulder.

"Hi, Finn," Bess said happily as he patted Finn's forearm, which was still steadying him. "How are you going? I had just the worst day of my life … I …" Bess hiccupped and looked over his shoulder. Then he looked at Finn and put his index finger on Finn's mouth. "Hush! No one's supposed to know yet, but Mors is the new leader. He killed off the last one and won't stop until he gets to sit in the fucking chair behind that damn table. All covered in blood … blood *everywhere*." He threw his arms in the air and fell backwards. Finn pulled him back onto the stool and leaned him against the counter. A few men in the inn half stood from their chairs, but when they saw that Finn had the situation under control, they sat back down.

"They said they needed me," Bess continued, addressing his words to Finn. He leaned closer and grabbed his shirt. "They said I was irreplaceable." He pulled Finn closer towards him and looked him in the eye. Finn looked worried, but didn't pull back. Bess hiccoughed and continued in a hoarse voice: "I think they be nuts! I … I—" He jumped up, dragging Finn with him. Finn supported him while Bess looked over his shoulder with his eyes wide and full of fear. He looked at the far window, not really seeing anyone or anything else. A few men turned around and looked at the window expecting to see a ghost or a werewolf, but the window was empty.

"I have to go," Bess said suddenly. He turned to face Finn. He let go off his shirt and patted him on the shoulder. Finn kept his hands in front of him, ready to grab Bess. "Don't worry," Bess added in a calm voice, "I won't tell anyone … *anyone* what you just told me." He hiccoughed and walked around Finn towards the door, using the counter for support. The fact that Finn didn't say a single word didn't bother Bess at all.

Finn opened his mouth to say something but looked at the innkeeper with a frown instead. The innkeeper just shrugged and watched Bess with a worried look on his face. Bess staggered to the door and crashed into it. He sniggered, opened the door, and stepped to the street, which was illuminated by the moonlight. He stopped and wondered which way to go, while the rest of the people in the inn slowly stood up and walked after him. He staggered down the street and turned into the darker alley behind the inn oblivious to the curious stares behind him.

The moon was shining brightly, and the howling in the distance made an interesting background. Bess walked from one side of the alley to the other, using the walls occasionally for support. He stopped in the middle of the alley and looked over his shoulder. He stood there for almost a minute, listening to the howling in the background with a nagging feeling that something was wrong. After a while, he shrugged. Staggering forward, he started to sing, using the howling as a musical accompaniment.

He turned around the corner, stopped, and listened to the night again. He had a feeling he'd heard some shouts between the howls. He turned around slowly and waited. Some very strong suspicion built up in his gut. He looked up at the sky and hiccupped, rocking back and forth on his heels. The full moon was high above his head. A full moon in the country with werewolves. And he was out there all alone.

There are only several things that can make a man sober up in an instant. One of them is a growling behind the man's back on a night like this. Bess spun around and looked at a werewolf who was stepping out of a shadow. He screamed. The werewolf leapt.

Amy, wearing tight black shirt and trousers, sneaked up to the palace in Wolfast and leaned against the wall. The full moon was shining on the silent palace, creating a lot of strange shadows. She peeked around the corner and then leaned against the wall once more. She put on a black mask and readied herself. She broke into run and sprinted around the palace until she reached an inside corner near the entrance from the garden. Still sprinting, she ran towards the entrance and then jumped up. With one leg on each wall, she half climbed, half ran to the top window, which was open. She stopped below it and looked over her shoulder to make sure that no one had seen her.

The garden was dark and quiet. A small animal hurried through the grass, and an owl hooted, hidden somewhere in the tall trees. There were no people in the garden. The guards were mostly in front of the palace, not behind it. No one expected an intruder from a garden surrounded by tall walls. That sort of arrangement always helped her.

She stretched her neck and looked inside the window. The room was dark and empty. She grabbed the ledge and prepared to jump into the room. As her feet hit the stone ledge, a male scream penetrated the silence of the night. Her leg slid, and she fell down, still grabbing the ledge. She hit the wall painfully, but quickly pulled herself up and fell into the room.

She landed on the floor, her heart beating like hell. She looked around and then peeked out through the window. The garden was still very quiet. Even the crickets had stopped chirping. Panting, she hurried away from the window. She had made quite a lot of noise when she landed in the room, and she wanted to get away as quickly and quietly as possible. She reached the door and opened it slowly. The light from the torches fell into the room. She heard quick footsteps approaching and silently closed the door. Someone was coming. She looked around nervously and then noticed a wardrobe in the corner. She ran to it and climbed on top of it in two quick moves just as the door handle rattled.

The door hit the wall, and light fell into the room. Amy slid towards the wall silently and watched two guards enter the room. The second one carried a torch above his head. The light illuminated a table in the middle, which was covered with documents, and shelves filled with books and parchments along the opposite wall. The guards looked around the room in silence. The first one walked to the window and looked out, while the second one peeked underneath the table.

"See?" the first one said as he closed the window. "There's no one here."

"I'm sure I heard something," the second one replied stubbornly as he lifted the torch even higher. Amy pressed herself against the wardrobe, hiding in the shadow. The first guard rolled his eyes and walked out of the room without a word, but the second one remained by the table. Amy held her breath.

The guard turned around and watched the wardrobe for a while. Then he walked towards it and opened the door. He lifted the torch and looked inside. The wardrobe was filled with papers and books, but it was so full it could not be used as a hiding place. He scanned the contents and looked at the top of the wardrobe. Amy lay still pressed against the top of the wardrobe, hardly breathing. The guard closed the wardrobe and walked to the door. He turned at the threshold and, with his hand on the handle, looked at the room once more. He listened to the silence of the night for a while and then stepped outside.

Amy waited for him to close the door and then listened to the fading footsteps. She stayed on the wardrobe for another ten minutes, and when it was clear that the corridors were silent again, she carefully and as silently as possible climbed down. She walked to the table and stopped with her hands placed against her hips. Her eyes darted around the room, taking in every detail. She looked at the table and wrinkled her nose. Most of the documents were covered in blood, and the table smelt weird.

She picked up one document and, by the moonlight from the window, scanned through the passages that were still legible. She put the document down and turned towards the documents in the shelves. Without proper light, she couldn't read anything and was in no mood to take the books and parchments out of the shelves.

She walked to the door, opened it carefully, and peered outside. The corridor was empty. She listened for a while, and when no sound came, she sneaked out.

Bess woke up and sat up abruptly. At first, he thought that it had all been just a nightmare, but he was not at home. He had never seen this room before, but the similarity of the interior to his former office told him that he was in the palace. He was lying on a bed. Slowly, he turned his head, taking in the room. And then he saw Mors sitting next to the bed, reading a book.

Mors looked up and smiled at Bess. Anger overcame Bess, and he jumped at Mors immediately. Something tugged painfully at his throat, and he fell backwards, slamming against the bed's frame. He looked over his shoulder and saw a chain fastened to the wall. He raised his hands to his neck and felt an iron collar.

"You're not the first man turned into a werewolf against his will, you know," Mors said in a matter-of-fact tone of voice. He was still sitting comfortably on the chair with the book resting on his knees. "Your reaction is not unexpected."

"Why me?" Bess asked quietly. He let go of the collar. Mors shrugged and looked at the closed door. Bess followed his stare, but didn't see anything. Neither did he smell anyone, which was a completely new experience for him.

"Well," Mors said as he tore his eyes off the door. "You're smart."

"And this is my punishment for that?"

"No, but most of the werewolves are …" Mors paused and waved his hand in circles while looking for the right adjective.

"Halfwits?"

"Yeah, but that's not the word I was looking for."

"Blockheads?"

"That too," Mors nodded. "But I meant to say that they are savage."

"Coming from the man who bit off another man's head," Bess said calmly. Mors looked at him with a smile. Bess really didn't like that smile. When he thought about it, he realized that he didn't like Mors at all. Up until the previous day, he had hated Mors the least compared to the way he felt about the rest of the werewolves, but that had changed in the light of the most recent events.

Mors stood up and started to pace the room. "You are by far the smartest werewolf now. You know diplomaty—"

"Diplomacy."

"Yeah, that," Mors said impatiently, waving his hand dismissively. "You know about other countries, and you know etiquette. That is a rare thing amongst the werewolves."

"You don't say," Bess said with sarcasm in his voice. He had worked with the werewolves for ten years. Half of them didn't even bother to pick up a spoon while eating.

"I just couldn't let you go," Mors said, and he stopped in front of Bess. "You're more than a researcher to me, you're an advisor."

"You didn't have to turn me into a werewolf if you needed an advisor," Bess said as he stood up, stretching the chain. "I wanted to leave. I handed you my resignation. I left the palace right away. Which part of that sounded like 'I wish to stay. Please turn me into a bloody werewolf'?"

Mors smiled and looked at the floor. Bess tried to step forward, but the chain pulled him back. He really wanted to attack Mors. Even the idea of biting Mors's head off was very inviting.

Mors looked up and slowly nodded.

"We will revisit this conversation another time," Mors said, and he turned around. Bess watched him as he walked towards the door and then opened it. He stopped at the threshold and looked at Bess. "I will understand if you wish to leave," he said. "But please, just consider other options."

They looked at each other for a moment, and Bess realized that he couldn't even imagine going away. He wouldn't be really welcomed anywhere. Besides, the only person capable of teaching him anything he needed to know was standing at the door. Well, there were also other werewolves, but truth be told, only Mors was any good. True, he was a maniac, but he was no idiot—unlike the rest of the group.

Mors smiled as he closed the door behind him. All new werewolves were unhappy when they found out what had happened, but all of them came around eventually. Once they realized they had nowhere to go, they decided to stay. And Bess was smart. Mors was positive that Bess would stay.

He walked into his new office and closed the door behind him. The desk was clean and had been tidied up, but it still reeked of blood. That was to be expected, since it had been covered in blood only a day ago, but it bothered him. He was wondering if he should have it changed when another smell came to his nose. He spun around and saw a man standing by the wardrobe in the corner. The man had the greenest eyes Mors had ever seen. He even wondered if they didn't glow a little.

"Who are you?" Mors asked while, behind his back, he fingered a tiny dagger, which he usually used as a letter opener. "What are you doing here?"

"I came to offer you a deal," the man said in a deep and somehow comforting voice. He stepped away from the wall. His eyes were so mesmerizing that Mors couldn't focus on anything else. "As a new leader of the most vicious group of aristocrats in Lanland, you probably need money. And I need a little favour."

Mors nodded absentmindedly and let go of the dagger. He really needed money. The country itself didn't need money; Wolfast had excellent natural recourses. However, with his own money he would be able to keep the power. Power and money were two things the werewolves listened to, and he had neither. He had just become the leader, and he had to show that he deserved that power, yet he didn't have money to buy that power. He *definitely* needed money. "What little favour?" he asked suspiciously.

The man smiled and walked closer. Mors tore his eyes off the man and looked at the table. He felt as if those green eyes were everywhere.

"I need you to find me something," the man said. Mors looked up with furrows on his forehead. "It's a necklace that belongs to me, but I lost it. It fell to Frain River and could now be anywhere between Wolfast and Norene. Unfortunately, it could possibly travel all the way up to the North Sea, and then it would be lost forever. I believe that even a werewolf wouldn't survive a visit to the bottom of the sea."

"We aren't dogs," Mors said in a raised voice as he straightened up. He felt insulted. Werewolves were no one's pet. They didn't sniff stuff! "It's out of the question!" he shouted, and he stepped towards the door.

The man placed his palm on Mors's chest and calmly and gently pushed Mors back towards the table. Normally, Mors would grab the dagger and attack, but something about this man made it clear that any attack would be his last. And Mors wasn't suicidal. Suddenly, he smelled something else over the bloody table: a woman's scent. He looked over the man's shoulder and saw a thick shadow in the corner behind the wardrobe.

"I understand that the request may seem a little degrading worded like that," the man said calmly, and Mors tore his eyes off the shadow, "but I will pay you for that necklace. And if there's anyone in the world who can find it, it's a werewolf."

Mors stepped away from the man and walked around the table. He stopped on the other side and turned to face him. He definitely felt safer with the heavy wooden furniture between him and the stranger. Then he remembered that the last time he was in that room, the table had been very useful to him during his attack. He stepped further back until he hit the wall. "Who are you?" he asked just to break the silence.

"You can call me whatever you like," the man said. "You can call me Rex."

Mors looked the man up and down. It was clear to him that the man's name wasn't Rex at all. The pressing question, which Mors didn't dare to ask, was why the man would hide his true identity. Was it because he didn't trust the werewolves, or was he hiding from someone else?

"Why do you want that necklace ... Rex?"

Rex smiled and stepped closer. Mors pressed his back against the wall and immediately wished he could step through it. He wouldn't even mind the drop. He glanced at the corner and noticed that the shadow didn't move at all. Rex leaned over the table and looked Mors in the eye. Mors couldn't help but stare into those green glowing eyes.

"As I said before," Rex said calmly, "it belongs to me. I inherited it from my mother, and it got lost. It leaves behind it a strange trail that you or your men could trace. As a reward, you will get your weight in gold. If you don't want to help me, just say so, and you will never see me again."

Mors tore is eyes off the man's stare and looked away. His gaze fell upon the shelves on the wall, and his brain started to work really fast. He needed money. And he had a perfect man for the job. All he had to do was to call Axel and send him along to the river, all the way to North Sea, to find some unknown necklace in a river that was flowing to the sea.

"What if we cannot find it?" he asked, not taking his eyes off the shelves.

"Then I will pay you for your troubles and walk away," Rex said. "Do we have a deal?" Rex straightened up and offered his hand to Mors. Mors looked at it terrified but stepped closer and shook it above the table. He looked up at Rex and gulped.

"Great." Rex smiled happily.

CHAPTER 3

A two-year-old wolf stopped between the trees and pulled back its ears. It was almost white with the exception of a bit of light-grey hair on its ears, chest, and belly. It was rather skinny and very cautious, which was a result of the happenings of the last month. It was a lone wolf that had been forced to leave its pack behind when they were attacked by another pack of wolves. It had travelled for over a month until it found a nice forest near a little village called Samforest. It liked it there. The forest seemed to have everything it needed. Since it was getting thirsty, and since it heard and smelled the river nearby, the young wolf walked through the forest with a sole purpose in its mind.

It reached the bank of the river and cautiously stopped in the shadow to have a better look. Some trees had fallen into the wide river and had been washed ashore in this area, creating a barrier on the right bank. The river was calm and very inviting. The wolf approached the river, still watching the area. It was very cautious, but since nothing happened, it relaxed, stopped by the water, and took a long drink. Then it caught some light out of the corner of its eye. It looked up and quickly scanned the trees nearby. It noticed that something shiny was dangling from a branch.

The wolf stepped away from the river and hesitated. It looked at the river and then at the forest on the other side. There were no animals or people visible. The wind was blowing from the river bringing a lot of interesting smells, but nothing dangerous. The wolf looked at the shiny thing and tilted its head. It stepped carefully and very slowly closer. It stopped a few steps away and crouched a little. It hesitated and then took another step. A high-pitched noise came from the thing, and the wolf tilted its head to the right. It didn't know what a necklace was, but it definitely liked this one. The wolf straightened up, stepped a little closer, and quickly tilted its head to the left. The sound obviously came from the little bright round gemstone on the chain that was hanging from the branch.

The wolf took another step forward and leaned in with its legs far behind. It reached the necklace, quickly sniffed it, and jumped back until it was a safe distance away. Nothing happened; even the sound didn't stop. The necklace was not only pretty, it also smelled nice. The wolf walked around the branch from which the necklace was hanging and tried a different approach. It stretched its neck as far as it could and nudged the necklace.

The high-pitched noise stopped immediately. The wolf tilted its head in surprise. Then everything went quiet. The river calmed down, the wind stopped blowing, and the birds quietened down. It felt as if the whole forest had taken a deep breath. The wolf brought its hind paws closer and kept watching the necklace, which was getting darker and darker in colour.

A little dot appeared in the middle of the stone. The wolf stepped closer and sat down in front of the necklace, watching it intently. The dot kept getting bigger and bigger until it was half as big as the stone. But the dot was not only getting bigger, it was also emitting light. The wolf leaned closer to have a better look, and he watched the dot change to a small ball of fire. It seemed as if the fire was inside the pendant—in its heart. The fireball was getting bigger and brighter. Soon it matched the size of the pendant, and it exploded. The wolf didn't budge. It just watched the pendant as it changed from the fireball to a tiny spinning galaxy. And then the galaxy got smaller and smaller, until it shrank back into a small dot and then completely disappeared.

The wolf tilted its head to one side. It sat quietly for a while, watching the necklace curiously, but nothing more happened. The wolf nudged the necklace again, but the pendant hardly moved. The wolf whined, lifted its paw, and slapped the necklace. The necklace swung on the branch for a while until it came to a complete stop.

The wolf stood up and carefully pushed its snout through the branches until the necklace slid onto its neck. Then it pulled back. The necklace stuck to its fur and remained hanging around the wolf's neck. The wolf looked down and then hurried to the water. The wolf watched its reflexion for a while, tilting his head from side to side. A few seconds later, it stepped away from the river and started to do a little dance on the bank. It jumped up and down and mimicked trotting in place.

A twig cracked behind the wolf. It turned around in a swaying motion and froze with its right front paw lifted from the ground and stretched forward, and its left hind paw lifted from the ground and stretched backwards. A look of utmost shock appeared on its face.

An extremely hideous wolf that smelled like a human was a few steps away, approaching the wolf. The werewolf didn't wait for the young wolf to figure out what was happening. He jumped immediately. The young wolf jumped as well, and both beasts clashed in the air and heavily fell to the ground. The wolf went for the werewolf's throat, but the werewolf was faster and bit the wolf below the left shoulder blade. The wolf whined and bit the first thing it could reach. The werewolf whined as well and let go. The wolf immediately jumped into the air and landed on the werewolf, biting his throat with all the strength it could muster.

The werewolf fell to the ground and stayed still. The wolf stood above the werewolf with its jaws buried in the werewolf's throat for a while, and only after what felt like ages, it let go. It seemed the werewolf was dead, but the young wolf couldn't be really sure. It looked at the river and then at the werewolf. It grabbed the werewolf's throat with its teeth and dragged the lifeless body to the river. The cold water stung the wolf's wound, but it didn't pay it any attention. It just hoped that the beast would drown and be dead for sure.

The wolf pulled the werewolf underneath the water and let go. The lifeless body slowly floated to the surface, his blood colouring the river. The wolf looked up and froze. It saw three men nearby watching it with their mouths hanging open. The wolf felt weak, and it could smell its own blood. It knew it had to get away immediately. The men seemed to be in shock, which would give it an advantage, but there were three of them. The wolf would stand no chance if they attacked, especially since it was injured.

The wolf spun around and hurried to the heart of the river. Its paw hurt with every movement, and the more water got to the wound, the more it stung. A few painful jumps later, it reached the middle of the river and let the current do the job. The pain and exhaustion made it very difficult for the wolf to stay awake, but the young animal managed to control its movement in the current.

Two long minutes later, the wolf reached another shallow and climbed ashore. It got completely out of water and threw itself to the ground. It was extremely sleepy, but it knew it couldn't just go to sleep right away. Humans would look for it. It had to get to safety.

Suddenly, it realized something was different ... something was strange, maybe even wrong. Why was it thinking of humans? It had never thought of humans before. Well, come to think of it, it had never *thought* before. It had always followed its instincts. This was an entirely new experience for the wolf. It seemed as if it was using some parts of its brain that he had never even known about. Thinking of its brain was also strange; several minutes ago, it hadn't even known it had one!

It shook its head to get rid of distracting thoughts and staggered to its feet. It shook water from its fur and waddled alongside the river splashing water all around. It knew the humans couldn't follow it without dogs. As long as it stayed near water, the dogs wouldn't be able to track it. All it had to do was to find a place to rest and lick its wounds.

Ethan Philipson sat down on the marble throne and leaned back. Even though he was sitting on a red cushion, he could still feel the coldness of the stone. He felt very tired, and he knew he had to look very haggard. With a sting, he realized that he had just become the next king. King Philip had died two hours ago, leaving Norene to Ethan.

Lord Adrian walked in circles around the throne with a little book in his hands, reading out loud. The room was very spacious with tall ceiling, multiple frescos depicting the latest events of Norene, and beautiful tall windows on both sides brightening the room. Below the windows stood statues of various pagan gods that were no longer worshiped but were part of the culture of Norene.

"The chorus," Lord Adrian read while walking, "will be singing for about three minutes. You should restrain from any waving or nodding at the crowd."

"Wait! What? Why would I wave and nod?" Ethan asked, baffled. Lord Adrian looked up from the book in his hands and stopped. He looked at the book again and then at the prince. "I'm just reading the instructions," he said defensively. "I suppose that one of your ancestors waved at people, so the note was added to the instructions."

"Maybe it was one of your ancestors, your lordship," Ethan said snidely. He leaned against one armrest and hung his leg over the other armrest.

"Ehm," Lord Adrian said, not sure how to react. "Your Majesty, you do realize that any of my ancestors that were on the throne are also your ancestors, right?"

Ethan's smile froze as his brain started to process this information. "Oh, yeah." Ethan nodded at last and rubbed the bridge of his nose. "It's been very long three days, Adrian. I am not even sure what I'm saying anymore."

"If you want to take a rest, to have some sleep, we can continue tomorrow," Lord Adrian said quietly. Ethan looked at Lord Adrian and saw a concern on his face.

Ethan had refused to leave his father's bedside for the last three days and was with him till the very end. King Philip had died in Ethan's arms that very morning. His last words, addressed to his son, were: "You are the best thing that ever happened to me. You are the best thing that can happen to Norene."

Ethan was devastated and wished to be alone, but he couldn't leave people of Norene. They too were grieving the king's death and needed Ethan to be strong.

The prince sighed, put his leg down, leaned forward, and put his head into his hands. His father's last words were still echoing in his head. Lord Adrian looked over his shoulder and, when he was sure that no one else was in the throne hall, he crouched. The prince looked at him through his fingers, and Lord Adrian noticed that his eyes were red and little swollen from the lack of sleep. "Look … Ethan," Lord Adrian said softly, "you really need some sleep. It's been very noble of you to stay at your father's side for three days and nights, but now you need some sleep. And maybe a little bath."

Ethan watched Lord Adrian silently and then looked around the hall in front of him. He shook his head, leaned back, and straightened up. He grabbed the arms of the throne and took a long breath. He wondered if he could actually fill the shoes of his father, but he knew he had to try. "Tell me about the coronation," Ethan said as he lifted his chin a little.

They looked at each other for a moment, and then they both burst out laughing. Ethan relaxed and put his left leg over the left armrest. They laughed for a while, and then Lord Adrian sat down on the marble floor.

"You remember when we used to play coronation when we were kids?" he asked. Ethan nodded, still laughing silently. Laughter helped him release the pressure around his chest, and he welcomed it. "I always had to put a crown on your head," Lord Adrian continued. "We never switched sides."

"Oh, yeah … I was a little brat back then." Ethan nodded gloomily.

"No, I just wanted to find some nice way to tell you that you cannot sit like this during the coronation."

They both laughed, and Ethan put his leg down from the armrest. He was very tired, but it was still the throne, and he didn't want to cause a scandal before he even became king.

The door to the throne hall opened, and Brian, his father's most trusted advisor, entered. He seemed a little nervous when he joined them, and Ethan noticed that he was twisting a piece of paper in his hands. Lord Adrian didn't stand up from the floor, but Ethan straightened up on the throne.

"Sorry, gentlemen, for my interruption," Brian said. He nodded slightly to Ethan and Lord Adrian.

"You are not interrupting," Ethan said wearily. "We were just going through the basic protocol for the coronation."

"Oh." Brian nodded and looked at the letter in his hands. "Well … I know that you will officially take over the state duties in two days' time, but I thought that you might want to know … I mean, you might find it useful to know that a werewolf was spotted in Norene."

Both Ethan and Lord Adrian stood up. Brian smiled nervously and looked at his hands. He was still twisting the letter, looking more and more anxious every second. "According to the report from a little village Samforest, which is located just below Mornhill," he continued, "a werewolf was spotted in the forest. He attacked a wolf, and it seems that he changed for that purpose only. The villagers burnt him." He looked at Ethan and Lord Adrian. "Well, he drowned in the river, so they had to drag him out of the river, but they burnt him anyway, just in case."

"How did they manage to drown him?" Ethan asked, confused.

Brian opened his mouth and straightened up the letter in his hands. "Well, they didn't," he said after he consulted the letter. "Apparently, the wolf killed the werewolf and then dragged the body to the river. It then swam down the river and the villagers lost its track."

Ethan opened his mouth to say something and closed it again. He looked at Lord Adrian to see if he understood everything, and when he saw the same confused expression on his face, he turned to Brian.

"Once more," he said as he rubbed the bridge of his nose. Now that he had to process complicated information, he felt way more tired. "A werewolf attacked a wolf for no apparent reason, but the wolf killed him, dragged him to water to drown, and then swam away?"

Brian thought about this for a moment and then nodded.

"It had to be a werewolf," Lord Adrian said as he turned to Ethan. "No wolf would carry the corpse of another wolf—not even a werewolf—to a river. That's too much thinking. And how would it know that would be effective?"

"I thought so too." Brian nodded. "Especially since the report says that the wolf danced on the shore—"

"Danced?" Ethan and Lord Adrian asked at the same time.

"Well, it made strange dance-like movements before the werewolf attacked it. However, the anatomy of the animal suggests that it was a wolf, not a werewolf."

They all stood in silence. Ethan wasn't even sure when he had heard the word *werewolf* the last time. They hadn't caused any trouble for a whole century, and suddenly they had now appeared in his country uninvited on the day of his father's death.

"Call the council," he said at last in a firm tone. "We will meet day after tomorrow," he added, and he stepped away from the men and the throne.

"Ehm …" Lord Adrian said, raising his finger, but before he could say anything else, Ethan stopped and turned around.

"Yeah, yeah, I know." He nodded with a frown. "The coronation. Well, make it the day after that."

Mors barged into Bess's room, slamming the door against the wall. Bess didn't even look up from a book he was reading. He was sitting in a chair with his feet resting on a table. For the last three days, Mors hadn't spent a lot of time with Bess. He hardly ever saw the man. As Mors had anticipated, Bess had decided to stay. He didn't really have a choice—there wasn't anywhere else for him to go. But instead of joining the werewolves, he had gone directly for the library and had been reading one book after another.

Mors stopped in front of Bess and waited for him to acknowledge his presence. Bess turned the page and kept on reading. Mors threw his arms into the air and started to pace the room. "This is outrageous!" he screamed.

"I agree," Bess said calmly without taking his eyes off the book.

Mors stopped near the window and turned to Bess. "You don't know what is outrageous," he said indignantly.

Bess turned another page. "I thought you meant your theatrical arrival."

Mors stood there for a moment, shaking all over, unable to find words strong enough to express his anger. He watched Bess for a few seconds and then ran out of the room, slamming the door behind him.

"One ... two ..." Bess counted under his breath, "three ... four ... aaaand five."

The door opened once again and Mors marched back inside. He stopped by the table and leaned against it. "Axel is dead," he said.

Bess froze for a moment, digesting the information. He knew Mors was watching him intently, and he definitely didn't want to let Mors know how surprised he was. "That is unfortunate," Bess said at last in an even voice. He turned another page.

"That's all you're gonna say?" Mors barked at Bess.

"Did you kill him?" Bess asked calmly. Mors just shot Bess a black look and paced to the window. Bess looked up from the book and watched Mors with some curiosity. When Mors just stopped in front of the window with his hands behind his back and didn't answer, Bess sighed and closed the book. "So, how did he die?"

Mors didn't answer right away. He watched the horizon pensively, biting his lip. A moment later, he sighed and turned to face Bess. "He was killed in Norene by some bloody wolf, which actually survived."

Bess sat there quietly for a while with one eyebrow raised and watched Mors. He blinked and then opened the book again. "This is more interesting," he said, and he continued reading. Mors jumped to the table, grabbed the book, and threw it across the room. The book hit the opposite wall with a loud thud and fell to the floor.

"I haven't finish it," Bess said calmly.

"I don't care," Mors said way too calmly.

Bess knew that Mors was only seconds away from attacking him. He pressed his lips together and put his feet down. "Okay, you have my attention," he said with a sigh.

Mors walked to a chair near the window and threw himself onto it. He rested his left leg against his right knee and slid a little lower in the chair. "As I said, Axel was killed in Norene," he said.

"I think you know my next question."

"I sent him there," Mors said with a little nod. "I needed him to recover a certain necklace for me. But he ran into a wolf and got killed."

"I'm still new to this whole werewolf thing," Bess said. He leaned against the table for effect, "but aren't werewolves sort of supposed to survive any attack a wolf could possibly make?"

"The wolf dragged him into the river after it bit off his throat."

Bess furrowed his brow. He hadn't expected this piece of information. He opened his mouth and closed it again. Then he managed to ask, "Why would it drag Axel into the river?"

"Beats the hell out of me," Mors said. "I suppose it has something to do with that necklace."

"Okay." Bess nodded and stood up. "What is this necklace? And could it somehow make the wolf aware that drowning Axel was one of the few ways to kill him? Because—and I'm no expert here—I don't think that wolves normally kill something and then drag it into a river."

"No, it's not normal for a wolf. And I don't know anything about this necklace. This guy came and offered me a lot of money to get it. It's an inheritance from his mother."

"And you accepted? Are you crazy?" Bess asked. He didn't believe his ears. "Did the guy pay you anything? Who is he? What is this necklace? Why didn't he go after it himself?"

"That one I know," Mors said happily. "He didn't know where exactly it was."

Bess stood there with his mouth gaping open. The only sounds were the guards' steps echoing in the hallway. Bess watched Mors as if he was seeing him properly for the first time, while Mors patiently waited for Bess to break the silence. A few seconds later, Bess finally closed his mouth and turned away. "I stand corrected," he said. He walked over to the fallen book. "The stranger is obviously a nice guy with no hidden agenda," he added sarcastically as he bent down and picked up the book.

"That's right," a deep voice said calmly from the door. Bess spun around with the book in his hand and looked at a tall man in the doorway. The man had the greenest eyes he had ever seen.

A smell of fear reached Bess's nose, and he looked at Mors, who stood up nervously. Whoever the man was, Mors had more than respect for him. Bess looked at the stranger, who watched Mors calmly. Bess didn't like the guy at all. There was just something not right about him. And it wasn't just the eyes.

The man stepped inside the room and looked around. The room was spacious, but a little untidy and crowded with furniture and books. A woman stepped in after the man and wrinkled her nose. Bess knew that the place wasn't tidy, but he was sure it didn't smell. He looked at Mors who stepped forward fretfully. He looked like a little school boy called upon by a teacher.

"I just received the news," Mors said to the man. Though his voice was calm, his hands shook a little. Rex looked at the pile of books on the table and opened the one on top.

"I know." Rex nodded and flipped through the pages. "I just heard myself."

Amy remained in the doorway and folded her arms. She leaned against the doorframe and watched Mors intently. Mors opened his mouth and nodded. He looked at Bess and back at Rex. Bess couldn't help it; he had to speak up. The man was in his room, going through his stuff, yet he hadn't even had enough decency to introduce himself or acknowledge Bess's presence.

"What do you want?" Bess snapped.

Rex closed the book he had been looking at and picked up the one underneath it. He didn't even look at Bess. "I just wish to know the latest news," he said calmly, scanning the book. "I believe you didn't retrieve the necklace."

"No," Mors replied timidly. "Unfortunately, Axel got his throat bitten off. Then he was drowned and then burnt."

"Well, that's what I call overkill," Rex said calmly. He put the book down and turned to face Mors. "Do you have any other plan?"

"Why do you want that necklace?" Bess asked. "And what exactly is that necklace?"

"My grandmother gave it to me," Rex said calmly without taking his eyes off Mors. "I lost it and just want it back."

"Interesting," Bess said calmly and stepped closer. "First I thought it was supposed to be an inheritance from your mother, not a gift from your grandmother, and second, it seems that we are not talking about an average necklace. Why should we help you get it?"

"Because I can help you get Norene," Rex replied, addressing the words to Mors. Bess groaned and shook his head. He knew right away that he had lost. He didn't need to see the greedy look on Mors's face, or realize that the smell of his fear was fading away.

"How?" Mors asked eagerly and stepped closer.

"I can give you money for the attack."

"Money is not a problem," Bess snapped. "Wolfast doesn't have army strong enough, and no money will change that. A century ago, John Mathewson destroyed our army, and we have hardly rebuilt half of it. Norene, however, created a strong army that is the pride of their nation. Their soldiers are driven by the desire for freedom. We cannot possibly attack them and survive. We are actually lucky that Norene doesn't attack us."

"I can get you an army worthy of your leadership," Rex said, not even glancing at Bess.

Bess was really annoyed with this man. Not only did the intruder never look at him, but he was also delusional. Even Amy widened her eyes for a brief moment, which was proof to Bess that the man was bluffing. But what he hated the most was how easily Mors was manipulated by the man.

And there was nothing he could do or say to stop Mors from accepting such ridiculous offer.

"What's in it for you?" Bess asked, but Rex ignored him. He watched Mors, who bit his lip and finally nodded.

"Get me an army, and then we can talk," he said and reached out his hand.

Bess groaned and turned away from Mors and Rex. He didn't like the idea of attacking a strong country. For the last century, Norene had put everything into their army. The king's army, called the Royal Guards, was very strong, and in combination with the army of Lord Blake's family, it was impossible to defeat. This attack would be the end of Wolfast.

"I know you disagree," Mors said as Bess turned around. The man and the woman were gone. The palace was quiet, and the hallway was empty. Only he and Mors were there.

"You do realize that there is no upside for you in this?" Bess asked hotly, stepping closer to Mors. "You cannot possibly win that fight. Do you really think that that man—"

"Rex," Mors said.

Bess blinked. "I beg your pardon?"

"That man's name is Rex," Mors explained. "I just thought it would be better than just calling him 'that man'."

Bess hesitated and then continued as if there had been no interruption: "Do you really think that he has an army? He doesn't even look like he has money. And why would he be doing it? Did you stop and think about that?"

"Yes. He wants that necklace. The victory will be our payment."

"What if it's lost forever? What if there is no necklace at all and he just wants the war? What if that necklace is very dangerous and he shouldn't have it? You know nothing about this Rex person."

"I know I can get into history books as the leader who reunited Norene and Wolfast!" Mors snapped. He turned on his heel, left the room, and marched down the hallway with his hands clutched into fists.

Bess stood there for a while looking after Mors unbelievingly. When Mors disappeared behind the next corner, Bess pressed his lips tight together. "You will get into history books all right," he said as he put his book on the chair near the window, "as a maniac who slaughtered twenty-five thousand soldiers for nothing."

Amy followed Rex out of the palace. She didn't say anything for a while, but once they walked through the gates, she could no longer hold her tongue: "Why do you want Wolfast to invade Norene?"

"Because I cannot go to the king of Norene and ask him for help. He's not so easily bought, and I don't want to draw too much attention to that necklace. So, I need to get the werewolves into Norene. That way, they can find the necklace, and since everyone will be talking about the invasion, no one will notice anything."

"Why can't you go for it yourself? You know where it is. Let's just go there and—"

"And what?" Rex asked sharply. He stopped and turned around so abruptly that Amy nearly crashed into him. "You want to kill the wolf? How? That stupid werewolf bit it before he got killed, which means that the wolf will be more than difficult to kill, and in combination with the necklace ..." his voice trailed off, and he took a deep breath. "I cannot kill it without the necklace," he continued more calmly, "and I cannot get the necklace without killing it. However, the werewolves are strong enough to kill another werewolf ... or wereman, or whatever. Besides, I don't care how many werewolves die for that necklace. I do know that, for Norene, they would slaughter every wolf in the country just to get that necklace for me."

"Okay, but where do you intend to find an army? That other guy was right. Wolfast's army isn't strong enough. It wouldn't be strong enough even if they doubled their numbers."

"Don't worry," Rex said with a nasty smile. "I know a guy ..."

Lord Blake left the room in Royal Castle where the council that had been planned for the day after the coronation had taken place. He walked through the castle's corridors to the yard. He wasn't thrilled with the idea of reinforcing the borders. Young King Ethan had made it clear that he expected some trouble, but Lord Blake didn't share his paranoia. Why should Wolfast attack? Their army wasn't capable of such a massive attack. Yet, he had to send his part of the army to the borders. What a waste of time!

He reached the yard and walked to his coach, which was waiting for him by the castle walls. He stopped by the coach and signalled his coachman that they should be on their way. He stepped inside and closed the door behind him just as the coach moved forward. He sat down and froze. Opposite him sat a tall man with way-too-green eyes that were emitting light.

"Who the hell are you?" Blake snapped as the coach rattled forward on the castle's stone roadway.

"Your fairy godmother," Rex said with a smile. "I'm here to make you king."

"Really?" Blake asked with a blank expression on his face. "Will that charm end with the last stroke of midnight?"

"Maybe, maybe not," Rex replied calmly. "That depends on your ability to defeat the newly crowned king of Norene. You have an army, right?"

"My army isn't big enough for an attack like that. If it were, I would be already on the throne, trust me. As it is, I would need ten thousand men just to come out even."

"What if I could give you twenty-five thousand?"

Blake sat quietly for a while and then leaned forward. "I'm listening."

CHAPTER 4

Captain Stuart looked at the hills in background. He had already travelled through a huge part of Norene and recognized the path to the borders. There was only one place where two armies, one from Wolfast and one from Norene, could have met. That place was a logical choice for any attack. And they would approach that place soon.

A vague curiosity made Captain Stuart watch the mountains. This was most likely the place where King John camped before they moved to face the Wolfast army. And now Lord Blake's army camped in the same place. Hundreds of tents stood on a huge swathe of grassland. Fireplaces appeared every few meters, and thousands of soldiers moved between the tents like ants on an anthill. The excitement was building up in the air as they awaited the order to continue to the rendezvous with the king.

Lieutenant Sven appeared among the soldiers, and when he spotted Captain Stuart, he hurried towards him. Captain Stuart knew that he was quite small for a soldier, but what he lacked in height, he more than made up for in width. He wasn't fat at all. He was big and heavy, but all that mass was pure muscle. He made sure that his figure wasn't a subject for jokes, and really, no soldier would dare to make fun of Captain Stuart.

His dark hair was short, but he thought it way too long. His favourite length was about the thickness of his finger, but it was at least four times as long at the moment. Since he was far away from the city, he didn't have time to go to a barber, though he planned on visiting the city as soon as possible because the hair was slowly getting into his eyes and on his nerves.

He patiently waited for Lieutenant Sven come to him, not willing to move an inch closer. The lieutenant finally reached Captain Stuart and saluted. Captain Stuart didn't return the salute.

"Sir," the lieutenant spoke as Captain Stuart looked at him with a blank expression on his face. "Lord Blake requests your presence."

Captain Stuart nodded and hurried through the camp towards Lord Blake's tent. Lieutenant Sven followed him, having trouble keeping up. The soldiers in the camp saluted as the captain and the lieutenant nearly jogged by. Captain Stuart ignored them, but out of the corner of his eye, he saw that Lieutenant Sven returned every salute.

Captain Stuart reached the tent and turned to Lieutenant Sven. "Wait here and make sure no soldier eavesdrops," he snapped, and the lieutenant jumped to attention.

Captain Stuart pulled aside the cloth hanging over the entrance and entered. The tent's interior was very dark, but even in the dimmed light, Captain Stuart could see a table in the middle. Lord Blake was leaning against it, looking at a map stretched over the top of it.

"You sent for me, sir," Captain Stuart said, looking at the point somewhere above Lord Blake's right shoulder. Lord Blake looked up, and Captain Stuart saluted immediately. Lord Blake straightened up and motioned towards the map.

"Look at the map and tell me what you think," he said, not taking his eyes off the table. Captain Stuart walked to the table and looked down. At the first glance, he realized that the map depicted the area near the southern borders not twenty miles away. This was the spot where King John had fought the Wolfast army. By the borders stood black chess pieces, by the mountains stood white chess pieces.

"The white pawns are the Royal Guards, and the king is Ethan and other lords," Lord Blake said, pointing at the pieces on the table. "Our part of the army is the rest of the white pieces."

Captain Stuart nodded, looking at the map. He noticed that the white pieces had been positioned in a peculiar manner. The king and its pawns were in the centre of the area surrounded by the other white pieces from the mountains and the black pieces from the borders.

"Are we supposed to be the backup or are we trying to cut the king and the Royal Guards off at the mountains?" he asked pointing at the line by the mountains. A satisfied smile appeared on Lord Blake's face.

"You are very observant, Captain," Lord Blake said with a smile. "Yes, we are actually attacking Ethan. Wolfast will help us to make this little change. Afterwards, I will be crowned."

"Are you sure you can trust Wolfast?" asked Captain Stuart. He realized that his voice could have sounded accusatory and quickly added, "Sir."

"After the battle with King John, their economics suffered a lot. There are a lot of natural resources in Norene, which they lost overnight. And all kings since King John refused to open a trade with Wolfast, which is, in my opinion, a bad decision. Wolfast is very rich. It's actually richer than most countries we trade with. Our kings were actually robbing Norene when they were not selling our resources to the highest bidder."

"You may wish to open the trade, and Wolfast may be willing to help you get the throne so that you could do so," Captain Stuart said, "but what makes you think the people of Norene won't rise up once you join forces with the werewolves?"

Lord Blake looked up at Captain Stuart, who was standing in attention, watching a spot somewhere above lord's shoulder. "Yes, you are right," Lord Blake said quietly. "The people of Norene hold great grudge against the werewolves. That's why the Wolfast's army will return after the battle to their country—to make us look like heroes."

Captain Stuart raised his eyebrow slightly, momentarily looking at Lord Blake. "You wish to make it appear," he said slowly, looking once more at a spot somewhere above Lord Blake's shoulder, "as if the Wolfast attacked and you saved the day by pushing it back behind the borders. Of course, the king would die in the process. Such a great loss for Norene, but luckily, there is one lord who survived and is willing to step up."

"You catch on quickly," Lord Blake said, nodding. "And now we get to your role in all this. I need a future captain of the Royal Guards to help the Wolfast army to close the line."

Captain Stuart flicked his attention to Lord Blake's face. Was he serious? Did Lord Blake really plan to promote Captain Stuart to his dream job after this?

"Yes, sir." Captain Stuart nodded. Lord Blake smiled and waved him out of the tent. Captain Stuart saluted and turned on his heel. He walked out of the tent and immediately hurried through the camp. Lieutenant Sven set off after him. He eyed the captain nervously, but didn't dare say anything. They were too close to the soldiers and others who could overhear them.

Captain Stuart hurried through the camp, once again ignoring the saluting soldiers. He headed towards the forest in silence with a determined look on his face. When Lieutenant Sven was sure that they were not within earshot of anyone, he increased his speed so he could catch up with the captain. "Permission to speak, Captain?" he asked looking directly in front of him and not slowing his pace.

"Granted," Captain Stuart replied sternly. The lieutenant had to run to keep Captain Stuart's quick pace.

"Are the rumours true, sir? The soldiers whisper that, after this battle, Lord Blake will be the new king. Did Lord Blake confirm this?"

"You know perfectly well that I cannot reveal that information," Captain Stuart answered, "but I can advise you to get ready for the attack. A lot of things will change afterwards."

He looked over his shoulder at the lieutenant and noticed a satisfied smile on the lieutenant's face. Captain Stuart immediately understood that the lieutenant was aiming for the soon-to-be-vacant position as captain of Lord Blake's army. Captain Stuart could use an ambitious young man by his side. All he had to do was to be careful to not reveal any weakness to the lieutenant. It was possible that the lieutenant would aim much higher. "I need to deal with the preparations," Captain Stuart said and stopped.

The lieutenant understood right away. He saluted and hurried through the camp, returning to his tent, leaving Captain Stuart alone.

Ten hours later, King Ethan arrived at the borders with his army. He met the enemy there and was really glad when Lord Blake's army joined him. That meant that the werewolves' army was much smaller than his, and everything seemed to be in his favour. His cavalry attacked first. The riders galloped towards the horizon when an attack came from the back. Ethan hadn't expected that at all.

Lord Blake and two lower-ranked lords betrayed him and attacked the high command. Suddenly, Ethan's army was surrounded by the enemy.

Though the Royal Guards responded quickly, the defeat was inevitable, and what was worse, the king himself was pulled into the heart of the battle, fighting amongst the other lords and soldiers. He was really angry. Almost half of his army had gone to the other side. Two of his lords were dead, three had betrayed him, and he himself was on his feet fighting in the crowd like a common soldier.

He stabbed one of the Lord Blake's soldiers and looked around. It was mostly his soldiers who were still fighting around him, which was a good sign, but the enemy army was visible all the way to the horizon. That was a bad sign. He knew he'd lost this fight. He knew they needed to retreat. He wasn't sure what to do after the retreat, but he would deal with that after they got to the mountains. Right now, they needed a plan—something simple, something fast, something that would save their necks. Nothing came to his mind.

He heard a horse's neigh above the cries of the battle. Ethan spun around with his sword at the ready, prepared for any possible attack that he could imagine. Amongst the fighting men, he saw Lord Adrian galloping towards him on a horse. He was leading a riderless horse by reins, and Ethan couldn't even express how happy he was to see him.

"Your Majesty, Lord Jonathan has been killed," Lord Adrian said as he stopped by the king. He handed Ethan the reins. "Lord James is retreating with his cavalry towards the mountains. It seems that the army of Blake and Wolfast had some trouble, and their ranks became weaker in the north. Lord James used that opening immediately."

Ethan climbed onto the horse and looked over his shoulder at the mountains. From the back of the horse, he could see much further, and it looked much worse. The cavalry was indeed moving towards the mountains as mounted archers covered their retreat, and part of the infantry and the archers moved to the mountains by the river.

"Well, Lord James always took a different approach," Ethan said as he looked to the other side at the approaching soldiers. There were way too many of them. The infantry would be able to hold them off for a while, but they were outnumbered. "And I'm glad that he is keeping to his true self even now. Pull everyone to the mountains."

"Yes, sire." Lord Adrian nodded and moved into the heart of the battlefield. Ethan turned his horse around and spurred it. As he galloped through the fighting soldiers, he heard a hissing noise. He looked at his horse in surprise and then he realized that the horse didn't make the sound. Before he could look around, something close to him exploded, and he was thrown off the horse. He hit the ground really hard, and then everything went black.

The young, injured wolf woke up in a cave two days after it had been bitten. At first, it couldn't remember where it was or why it was there, but then the memories flashed back. Its paw didn't hurt anymore. It couldn't check it properly, but it felt as if its shoulder blade had also healed. The wolf wasn't sure how that could be possible, but it suspected that it had something to do with that strange human-smelling wolf.

After it was sure that everything was all right and its paw could not only hold its weight, but was also sound enough so he would be able to flee from any danger, the wolf set for the forest. It spent next few days walking around the forest because it wanted to know the place well. It needed safe places to hunt, eat, and drink water. It didn't feel like looking for other wolves, but it became very much interested in humans. While it was watching people from a safe hiding place, it realized that it understood their speech. The wolf could even form answers in its head, but its vocal cords didn't allow it to voice them. Strange feeling, thinking of vocal cords ...

Very occasionally, the necklace shone. It emitted a little light, but every time this happened, the wolf realized something new. On one of these occasions, it realized that it was actually a *he*. Well, it wasn't exactly ground-breaking discovery, but it was new to it ... him.

He spent a lot of time by a crossroad, but had to flee at one point when humans went by with their dogs. Before he ran for the forest, he noticed that humans named their dogs. When he was sure that no dog followed him, he stopped and thought about this strange habit of naming things. Humans had names, their dogs had names, their homes had names, and it seemed that even their body parts had names. The strange thing for him was that he could even remember the name of the village that was near the forest where he had grown up. He wondered what the purpose the names served and came to the conclusion that it was to enable people to recognize and talk about friends and family members. He wondered how it would feel to have a name.

The sun set, and an owl hooted somewhere above him. He looked into the dark trees, but he couldn't see it. When he looked down, a beautiful she-wolf stepped onto the road. It seemed very curious about him. He lifted his head to make himself look bigger, and he stepped closer. Another wolf followed the she-wolf and stopped when it saw him. He decided to name them. The male wolf was obviously the Alpha, and the female would be the Hot She-Wolf. Then another wolf appeared. He decided to name him Other Wolf. And then the rest of the pack arrived. Very quickly, he ran into a problem because he couldn't distinguish between all of the she-wolves.

One male wolf approached him and sniffed the air around him. There was something unnerving about it. It looked at him as if he was a freak of nature. It growled and moved closer. He stepped back, but the male wolf didn't follow. It just eyed him suspiciously, growling. The rest of the pack looked on curiously. He stepped back some more, and when the male wolf didn't follow him, he left the road and the wolves behind. He decided to name that wolf Hate Wolf.

He looked over his shoulder, but the wolves didn't follow him. On the one hand, he was glad; on the other, he really liked the she-wolves. Maybe he should name them properly—like Susan or Joan. He had also heard some nice male names during the day—Timothy, Damon, Daniel, although they all sounded strange when he tried to use them to name himself. What would be the point anyway? He couldn't tell anyone his name.

The next day, he was more careful to avoid the wolves, and they were obviously avoiding him. He figured out where their den was and stayed away from the place. He went to his cave for the night when the wolves walked the forest. He found out where they went for water and where they hunted, and he chose another part of the forest to make his home. This part was closer to the village and was therefore not so interesting to the rest of the wolves. For him, it was perfect.

The next day, he walked to the river to have a drink. Suddenly, he heard a beautiful voice. It was a woman's voice, singing a song. He hesitated and then stepped towards the river. A breeze blew from the river and brought with it the smell of water, trees, and the woman.

Slowly, and as quietly as possible, he walked between the trees. He reached the bank and crawled behind a bush. Fifty feet away, there knelt a beautiful young woman. She was washing some clothes in the current, singing softly as she soaked the clothes in the water.

He watched her from behind the bush, wondering what the song was. How did he know it? He couldn't remember hearing it before. He couldn't remember a lot of details from before four days ago, and he assumed that the necklace was helping him with the memories. Carefully, he crawled deeper into the bush and watched the woman through the branches. Her voice was very soothing. He lay on the grass and listened to her for a while.

She turned her back on him and continued to sing while she fiddled with a large basket. The wolf lifted his head and turned his ears towards the woman, but she was too far away, and her voice became lost in the noise made by the river.

Cautiously, he stood up, left the safety of the bush, and crawled closer to the river. The woman suddenly turned around and froze, holding a white shirt in her hands. Her eyes met his for a brief moment. He froze, still crouched down with one paw stretched in front of him as he prepared for another slow step forward. He started to wonder if he should turn around and run away, but he wasn't scared of her. She seemed nice.

The woman screamed at the top of her voice, threw the shirt to the ground, and ran towards the village. The wolf straightened up and tilted his head to one side. He was puzzled. This definitely wasn't the reaction he had expected. True, he hadn't found the woman dangerous, but he had forgotten to take into an account the fact that he was still a wolf in a forest. She had every right to feel threatened.

In the last few days, he had become very curious about humans, and the more he learned about them, the more curious he became. Therefore, he didn't even hesitate. He hurried to the river. He stopped by the woman's basket and peeked inside at the clothes. It was more than interesting. The smell was a strange mixture of fruit and sweat. He buried his snout into the basket and took a long sniff. He pushed aside some clothes, burying his head deeper into the basket, and sniffed again. He flicked his ears and lifted his head from the basket. Something strange followed him. He jumped back, and a pair of trousers fell to the ground. He tilted his head to one side and stepped closer. He sniffed the trousers and sneezed. He sneezed some more and quickly stepped away.

He walked around the trousers, making sure he didn't touch them while he checked the basket from the other side. Suddenly, he heard male voices—screams, actually—spreading through the forest. He looked up from the basket and listened to the sounds. The echo of the voices made it difficult for him to detect the direction. All he could do was to guess that the voices came from the path the woman had chosen for her flight.

He turned towards the river, but the voices seemed to be coming from that direction. He turned away from the river and felt as if the voices were following him. He twirled around, but the voices were everywhere. He started to panic. He hadn't meant to scare the woman, but that would be difficult to explain, since he couldn't express his thoughts in words. He could think them, but humans were not mind readers. The worst thing was that they had weapons. He realized that a lot of humans were coming after him with a lot of weapons.

Suddenly, the humans were the least of his problems. A strange feeling ran through his body. He retched, and then weakness overcame him. He wasn't sure what was happening, but he couldn't move. His front paws started to shake, and when he looked at them, he could see that they had changed. They were a strange shape. They were actually changing in front of his eyes. The claws were getting smaller. Fingers were growing, and the fur was receding into his skin, which was changing colour as well. A few seconds later, he realized that he was turning into a human.

He tried to focus on changing back into a wolf, but nothing happened. He knew that, as a wolf, he didn't stand a chance against the humans, but he could at least try to run away. He shook his head, and the necklace hit him in the chin. He looked at it. He looked down and saw his new body. Well, he was definitely human. He stood up and fell to the ground immediately. His legs refused to keep him up. He wasn't even sure how to stand properly. And he was getting cold.

The shouts were getting closer. He grabbed the shirt that the woman had left by the basket, and the smelly trousers. Partly dragging his body across the ground and partly crawling on all fours, he retreated from the river. He reached the bush he had used for cover earlier and quickly hid behind it.

Once more, he tried to focus on changing back to wolf, but he didn't feel any different. All he could think of were the approaching humans. He was shaking with the cold and, though he wasn't sure how to work with the body, he managed to put the trousers and the shirt on. He had to wait for a while, but finally he stopped shaking. He hid the necklace inside the shirt and watched the river through the branches of the bush. He didn't dare to run away. He wasn't sure how much time he had before the humans would come to the river, but he was sure it would not be enough time for him to get away, especially in this form. He really wondered how humans managed to keep their bodies upright.

A few seconds later, the humans arrived on the bank of the river. It was quite a crowd. It seemed that a lot of men from the village had hurried to the forest. Most of them carried axes and hay forks, but two of them held swords. The wolf in the boy's body didn't dare to make a sound.

And then he heard a slow and low growl right behind him. He gulped and very slowly and cautiously looked over his shoulder. There stood Hate-Wolf, but this time it wasn't cautious. It just saw a weak human behind a bush. And the worst part was that it was correct in its assessment.

Hate-Wolf bared its teeth and stepped closer, but the boy didn't move. He didn't know what to do. He couldn't defend himself, and he couldn't run away. He moved closer to the bush, and the wolf bared its teeth some more. Its growl deepened, and the hair on its back stood up. The boy jumped to his feet, but before he could even find out if they would support his weight, the wolf attacked. It bit his calf and started to drag him away from the bush. The boy fell heavily to the ground and screamed. He grabbed everything in the path: the dirt, the leaves, the branches.

He lifted a heavy branch from the ground and turned around, ignoring the pain in his leg. He swung the branch at the wolf but missed completely. The wolf bit his leg further up and shook it hard. The boy screamed, and the branch fell out of his hand. He tried to kick the wolf with his other leg, but he was too weak to make an impact.

The wolf let go off the boy's leg and jumped for his throat. The boy instinctively lifted his hands and managed to stop the wolf two inches from his face. The wolf tried to get around the resisting hands, snapping its teeth in the air, but the boy managed to keep it at bay.

Screams came from behind the bush, and the wolf jumped away. It turned around, completely ignoring the boy, and ran to the forest. The boy watched it disappear between the branches, and then his head hit the dirt. The adrenalin, the pain, the change, and the exhaustion had caused the boy to faint.

CHAPTER 5

Mors entered the king's office in Royal Castle with Bess at his heals. Mors stopped in the middle with his mouth gaping open. Bess looked around and whistled. It was even more spectacular than he had imagined. It was spacious, well furnished, and full of ancient books. Together, this made a great effect. He scanned the covers of the books and then tore his eyes off.

"I like this table," Mors said happily and sat down, placing his hands on the surface. "It's elegant and stylish."

"And doesn't smell of blood," Bess added. Mors nodded and leaned back in the armchair.

"So," he asked with a happy smile. "Do you like it here?"

"No," Bess said calmly and stepped towards the desk. "I smell trouble."

"What are you talking about? It went well!" Mors threw his arms in the air and beamed at Bess. Bess walked to the table and stopped in front of Mors.

"First," he said calmly as he extended his index finger, "you won the battle, not the war. That was one battle, and we know for sure that Lord James survived."

"So?"

"You don't want to mess with Lord James. His history is certainly to his advantage. Second," Bess continued as he extended his middle finger as well, "you have no proof that Ethan is dead. I just talked to Captain Stuart, and the soldiers didn't find his body. Until the previous king is dead, no one can be crowned. It's their law, and our plan requires that we keep their laws."

"I know," Mors nodded. "But we can change that law."

"Only the king can change that law. And it has to be approved by the

46

majority of the lords. We have three lords on our side. Three lords who didn't change sides are dead, and I seriously doubt that their heirs would be thrilled to help us. And four lords are nowhere to be found. It's very likely that they survived along with the king. Our odds for changing that law legally are not good."

"The only reason we didn't find Ethan Philipson's body is that it's buried under other bodies," Mors said. Annoyed, he folded his arms. He glanced at the corner behind the door and noticed a small chest.

"I seriously doubt that." Bess shook his head, put his hands onto the table, and leaned against it. "Third, that Rex guy made this happen for a reason. And that reason is a necklace. We don't know where it is or how to get it. How do you think he will react?"

Mors froze for a brief moment and then put his hands down. He nodded slowly and scratched his chin. "The last known location of that necklace was in Danforest—"

"Samforest," Bess corrected.

"Yeah, yeah." Mors waved his hand impatiently and stood up. "So, you can go there—"

"Hell no!"

Mors looked at Bess, surprised. They stood facing each other for a while in silence. Bess straightened up, folded his arms, and waited, determined not to break the silence. After what felt like an eternity, Mors sighed. "Fine. I will send someone else," he said, and he walked over to the chest in the corner. "As for Ethan Philipson, I am sure we will soon find his body."

"And if not? What is your plan for that scenario?"

Mors stopped next to the chest and stood still for a while. He gazed at the chest with a faraway look as Bess patiently waited for him to gather his thoughts. Finally, Mors shook his head and opened the chest. It was empty. "I will deal with that once it's clear that he survived," he said, and he let the lid fall back down with a loud thud.

Ethan jerked awake and groaned. His head really hurt, his body ached all over, and he felt a little confused. Wherever he was, it was dark and a little cold. The first thought that came to his mind was that he was dead, but that was very unlikely. If he was dead, he wouldn't hurt; or in any case, he wouldn't care about the pain anymore. And if this was an afterlife, it really sucked.

He sat up and massaged the bridge of his nose. His vision got somewhat better, and he could make out some shapes around him. He was sitting on some blankets, but when he touched the makeshift bed, he found that it was actually made of many coats. This ruled out a prison. Even if the werewolves didn't kill him right away—which was very unlikely—they wouldn't make his stay in prison comfortable.

He swung his feet off the bed and groaned again. His whole body hurt, and every movement made it even worse. He wondered what had happened. He remembered wanting to ride away from the battlefield. There was some strange memory inside his head about an explosion, but that made no sense. The werewolves didn't know how to blow things up … well, he definitely hoped that they didn't.

He touched his left arm and felt bandages. There was something sticky and dark on them. He suspected that it was his own blood. The wound would certainly explain the pain. Gingerly, he touched his head, but didn't feel any bandages. This was a little comforting—only a little, because his head still hurt like hell.

Out of the corner of his eye, he noticed a dim light that was slowly moving closer. It seemed that there was a tunnel leading from the place. As the light approached, more and more of his surroundings were illuminated, and Ethan could see that he was in a cave. He watched the entrance, hoping for a friendly face. Since he wasn't manacled, it was very likely that whoever was coming was a friend.

Lord Adrian walked out of the tunnel holding a torch high above his head. Ethan heaved a sigh of relief and smiled. Of all the people in the world, there was no one he would rather see at the moment. Only now Ethan realized that Lord Adrian was more than a subject to him. Ethan really looked at him as a friend.

"How are you feeling, Your Majesty?" Lord Adrian asked as he came closer. "I'm really glad that you are finally awake. You had me really worried."

Ethan stood up, winced, and fell back down on the makeshift bed. He tried to smile through the pain, but the look on Lord Adrian's face made it clear that he wasn't doing a very good job. "I am glad to see you," he managed to say. "I have a somewhat fuzzy memory of the battlefield, so I have a few questions. Well, the first one would be: Where the hell am I?"

"In a cave, sire."

"Really?" asked Ethan sarcastically. "I wouldn't have guessed that."

Lord Adrian chuckled and nodded. He looked around at the dark cave walls. The cave was rather spacious with some stalagmites here and there. Some items were stocked inside the cave, including armour, weapons, and some clothes.

"We are in the Simels Mountains," Lord Adrian said as he looked at the king. "There is a complex of caves leading to sort of a clearing between the summits. Lord James brought us here after the retreat. All the entrances are guarded, but I don't think a lot of people in Norene know about this place. And I seriously doubt that the werewolves know about it. Or Blake."

Ethan nodded, looking at the dark wall opposite him with a faraway look. He had to ask another question. He was tempted to postpone it, but the sooner it got out, the better. "How many soldiers are here? And which lords?"

Lord Adrian took a deep breath and said quickly, "We have twelve thousand foot soldiers, over two thousand cavalry soldiers, and about one thousand archers. Lords James, Erik, and Thomas are setting and overseeing the camp. We believe that some part of the Royal Guards is also outside the mountains. Lords Jonathan, Robert, and John are dead."

Ethan nodded slowly, not taking his eyes off the dark wall. It was easier to face the wall than the look on Lord Adrian's face. The news was even worse than Ethan expected. They had started with ten lords and sixty thousand soldiers. The remnant was a small fraction of the previous army. There was no way he could face the combined armies of Wolfast and Blake.

"What is the news of the enemy?" he asked with a lump in his throat. His voice came a little higher, so he coughed to release the pressure. The pressure remained.

"Not much. We know that they also experienced severe casualties.

Wolfast's army was a big help to Blake, but they weren't trained well in combat. Unfortunately, we're not sure what their next plan is. Luckily, it seems we have allies. For example, there is a leaflet of unknown origin, which spreads like wildfire. And it spreads the truth about Wolfast's invasion and about Blake's betrayal. It's usually glued over the official news of *The Royal Messenger* and it's called *The Freedom Speaker*. The official news is that Wolfast attacked and Lord Blake bravely beat them back. The Wolfast army, or the remnant of their army, returned to Wolfast. Part of Blake's army remained by the borders to 'keep guard.'" Lord Adrian made quotations in the air when he said the last two words. "The rest moved to Royal Castle.

"Blake is feeding people of Norene with false information: his army fought bravely, but even though they pushed the enemy back, they couldn't save you and most of the lords. We assume that, from now on, Wolfast will take advantage of Norene's resources via Blake who will have power and money in return. Yet, for obvious reasons, they don't want to make this conspicuous. That's why they keep the official news circulating. However, the coronation still wasn't announced, which means that they either know that you survived or are still not sure."

"How do you know all this?" Ethan asked furrowing his brow and looked up at Lord Adrian.

"Someone sent us leaflets. We don't know who or even how. We call him by the name he gave himself: Blackbird."

"What do you mean you don't know how he managed to send you the information? We are not really in a known area, are we?"

"No. We suspect that there is a messenger here. It's difficult to notice someone new with this many soldiers in one place."

"And how do we know we can trust this Blackbird?"

"We don't trust him," Lord Adrian said in a matter-of-fact tone of voice. "We're just taking the information into a consideration. And we are very careful about the information we spread amongst the soldiers. We are actually spreading some misinformation, just to be sure."

Ethan nodded, deep in thought. This approach sounded a lot like Lord James's way of putting things, but then again, Lord Adrian was no angel either. A pain shot through his left arm and he winced. "And …" He hesitated and looked at the bandage on his left arm, which was illuminated by Lord Adrian's torch. Ethan had been right; the sticky dark fluid was blood. Under the circumstances, he was more than sure that it was his own. "Can … ehm … Do the werewolves know how to blow things up?"

Lord Adrian furrowed his brow. A concerned look appeared on his face. "Oh," he said, and his expression brightened. "No, that was only a stone. Wolfast's army was using catapults. The stone landed very close to you and threw you off your horse. There wasn't any actual explosion."

Ethan nodded with relief. He could almost deal with the werewolves, Blake's army, and the loss of his lords and throne, but he definitely wasn't ready to deal with witchcraft.

Lord Adrian continued: "We really didn't think that you survived. It wasn't until we got back here in the cave that we realized that you had only been knocked out."

"Back in the cave?" Ethan asked. "You mean you took me off the battlefield even though you thought that I was dead?"

"No." Lord Adrian shook his head. "We took you off the battlefield fearing that you might be dead. First, we didn't want the werewolves to get possession of your body, and second, there was still some hope that you had survived."

Ethan nodded slowly. He had quite a lot of information to process, and no matter how he looked at it, it seemed more than bad. "So," he said as he scratched the bridge of his nose, "to sum up: We have approximately fifteen thousand soldiers, yet we started with sixty thousand. Twenty-five thousand joined the enemy along with three lords. Three lords are dead, and there is a possibility that their heirs will join Blake. Four lords are in hiding, and the werewolves probably suspect that I survived. Unfortunately for them, the law requires that the old king must be dead before a new king can be crowned, which they cannot prove right now. If they want to keep up the charade, they have to obey the laws or they will have a difficult time explaining the situation to the people of Norene, who have already proven that they can be very dangerous when united. I am currently bleeding, and we probably have no food because we fled the battlefield. Did I miss anything?"

Lord Adrian thought about the list for a while and then shook his head. Ethan stood up and nearly fell down again, but Lord Adrian grabbed him by his healthy shoulder.

For Ethan, everything went blurry for a moment, and he stood quietly until his head stopped spinning. "To tell you the truth, Adrian," he whispered, "I wish I had died on that battlefield."

"Really?" Lord Adrian asked with a smile. "I don't think that the history books will record a lot about that battle. I'm more than sure that there are a lot of things that you have in stock for the werewolves and Blake. And don't forget that we have Lord James on our side."

Ethan looked at Lord Adrian, who winked at him. Ethan couldn't help it but smile. Another light appeared in the tunnel, and muffled voices came their way.

"Speak of the devil." Lord Adrian sighed. The voices came closer, and two men stepped out of the tunnel. They couldn't have been more different from one another. One was a tall, well-built, middle-aged man with long black hair, yellowish smooth skin, and almond-shaped black eyes. The other was a short, very skinny, over-seventy-years-old man with bright blue eyes and white hair and beard.

They were arguing about something, but it was difficult to decipher their words, which echoed through the cave. Another man, who carried a torch, stepped out of the tunnel with an annoyed look on his face. He was nearly as tall as the first man, but was nowhere as slim. He was bald but wore a very rich chestnut beard. He walked around the arguing men and hurried towards Lord Adrian and Ethan.

"Your Majesty," he said over the echoed voices, and he bowed. Ethan nodded and gently freed his shoulder from Lord Adrian's grip. He felt all right, and he was sure he didn't need the support anymore. Lord Adrian stepped back and set the torch into a jug that stood near the bed. The jug obviously served as a torch holder.

"Lord Thomas, I'm glad to see that you are all right," Ethan said with a smile, but his words got lost in the echoes of the risen voices nearby. He looked at the arguing men still unable to recognize the actual words. "Gentlemen!" he shouted.

Both men stopped arguing and looked around. The younger one shot the older one a black look and stepped towards the king. A big smile appeared on his face. "Your Majesty," he said jovially with a little bow of his head. "I cannot express how great it is to see you are feeling better. I am sorry about the ruckus, but Lord Eric wouldn't shut up."

"Hey!" the older man shouted as he hurried after the man. "Excuse me, *Lord* James, but I wasn't the one making the ruckus."

"*Lord* James? What's that supposed to mean, numbnuts?" Lord James asked and turned to face Lord Eric.

Lord Eric puffed himself up and poked Lord James in his chest. Even with his head raised up high, Lord Eric was smaller than Lord James. Lord James raised his brow and looked at his chest. He brushed at the front of his tunic theatrically and looked back at Lord Eric.

"Gentlemen," Ethan said calmly. But neither Lord James nor Lord Eric heard him.

"That means," Lord Eric said with his chin lifted high, "that I don't think you know what it really means to be a lord."

"Well, neither do you. And I also don't think you know what it really means to get your ass kicked. And I don't mean that in a metaphoric sense."

"You can try to attack, but I think you wouldn't even know what hit you," Lord Eric hissed back as he rose up on his toes. Their noses were almost touching.

"Oh, that's true," Lord James nodded. "Because you hit like a little girl, so I wouldn't even notice that you touched me."

"They've been having this conversation for almost an hour now," Lord Thomas said to Lord Adrian. "And it's really getting on my nerves."

"Gentlemen, please," Ethan said with a sigh, just as Lord Eric pushed Lord James. Lord James stepped back a little and was about to charge when Lord Adrian jumped between the men and raised his hands to keep the distance between them. Lord James's expression hardened.

"Lord Eric, that was uncalled for," Ethan said. Lord Eric tore his eyes off Lord James and stepped back. Lord James watched him intently, but didn't follow him or say anything. He glanced at Lord Adrian and then walked over to Lord Thomas. He stopped behind him with his arms folded.

It was no surprise to anyone that they had never warmed up to each other. Lord James was the only man in the history of Norene who had been given the title despite the fact that it had been proven that he had committed crimes in his past. Lord James had started off as a pirate known as Flying Jimmy. His targets had usually been ships and fortresses that belonged to Lord Eric. Later, he had helped king Philip with another group of pirates. It was for this work that, years later, the king rewarded him with the title.

Lord Eric had always been against this, and therefore always showed an open hostility towards Lord James at any opportunity. Lord James always claimed that he never wanted to return to piracy, and he had proved a loyal subject to King Philip on many occasions. His actions during and after the battle had proved to Ethan that he could trust Lord James.

"So," Ethan said as Lord Adrian put his hands down. "Let's try a more productive discussion, shall we? We need a plan."

"We must strike back!" said Lord Eric in a strong voice that made an echo in the cave.

Lord James snarled and sat down on the makeshift bed. "That's really worked well for us so far," he said.

"Lord Eric is right," Ethan said, nodding. "We need to strike back, but not directly. We need a plan of attack. Actually, that's where you come in," he added and turned to Lord James.

"Him?" Lord Eric shouted. Out of the corner of his eye, Ethan saw Lord Thomas slap his forehead with the palm of his hand in exasperation. "He has no education in battle or tactics. He doesn't even know how to fight!"

"You want to see me fight?" Lord James asked as he stood up. Ethan put his palm on Lord James's chest to stop him from walking to Lord Eric.

"Right," Lord Eric snarled over Ethan's shoulder. "That's your answer to everything—empty threats and ridiculous stories afterwards."

Lord James stepped closer to Lord Eric with an angry look on his face. Ethan was sure that Lord James would punch Lord Eric. Lord Eric stepped closer too.

"Gentlemen," Ethan said louder than all of them. He raised both his arms to stop them from approaching each other. A sharp pain shot up his hurt arm, and for a moment everything dimmed. He was partly aware of voices around him, but it took him a moment to focus again. He knelt on one knee, with the other leg bent for support, and Lord Adrian was steadying him by his healthy shoulder. He helped Ethan to stand up and led him to the makeshift bed.

"Thanks," Ethan whispered as Lord Adrian lowered him onto the coats. Ethan turned to the lords. After a long sigh he said, "I know I was supposed to die on that battlefield." He ignored the shaking of heads around him. "But I didn't. And I don't plan to just hide from the werewolves for the rest of my life. I don't plan on letting the werewolves get very comfortable here. However, for that I need your help. Each of you—and I really mean *each* of you—has some strengths, and each of you has some knowledge that can helps us win Norene back. But for that I need you to cooperate with each other. I don't need bickering lords."

"Yes, Sire." Lord Eric nodded and hung his head low. Lord James ran his fingers through his hair. Ethan was glad to see that they both had decency to look ashamed.

"Until we kick the werewolves out of Norene and get rid of Blake," Ethan continued, looking from Lord James to Lord Eric, "I need you to put your differences aside. After we get our country back, you can go back to hating each other to your hearts' content."

"I promise I will behave myself, though I cannot speak for all of us," Lord James said, ignoring the black look Lord Eric shot him. "I actually have a plan," he added with a nasty smile. "And it's a good plan. Lord Eric won't like it at all."

"I'm listening," Ethan said.

The wolf in the boy's body slowly regained consciousness. He didn't open his eyes; he just enjoyed the peacefulness around him. He understood right away that he was not in the forest anymore, but he didn't feel that he was in danger. He was lying on something very soft and very comfortable. His leg was throbbing slightly, but he didn't pay it any attention. He knew it would heal within a day or two. He could smell some people nearby, but he didn't care.

Someone grabbed his wrist, and he reflexively jumped up. He hit the wall and dragged blankets with him, freeing his wrist. His heart pounding, he pushed away an old balding man.

"You're safe," another man said and leaned in. He was a small, middle-aged, chubby man with red hair, two-day-old ginger beard, and some freckles. He smiled at the boy. "I'm Charles. You're safe now. You're in my house. What's your name?"

The boy looked at the old man and back again at Charles. Charles nodded encouragingly. The boy opened his mouth, but no sound came. He mustered all his strength and tried again. "Daniel," he said finally, choosing the first name that came to his mind. His voice was soft and weak. He didn't like it at all.

"This is Maxwell," Charles said, nodding in the direction of the old man. Maxwell waved at Daniel. "He's our doctor. He was just checking up on you. May he continue?"

"No need," Maxwell said, picking up his bag. "He got startled, so his pulse will be off the charts anyway. Well, I'll be going now. If that leg hurts or anything happens, just send for me."

He smiled at Daniel, shook Charles's hand, and left the room. Daniel watched the man leave. Instinctively, he pulled the blanket higher to cover himself, and he leaned his head forward to have a better view of the door. Charles turned back to Daniel and smiled. Daniel relaxed a little but didn't smile back. "You are lucky, you know," Charles said. "If Samantha hadn't seen that wolf and called us, it would have torn you apart."

"Did you find it?" Daniel asked. His voice sounded so weird to his ears.

"No." Charles shook his head. "That wolf ran away. Samantha just got scared because, a few days ago, we killed a werewolf near that spot. She doesn't know the difference between a wolf and a werewolf, so she was very nervous. But how did you get there? Where are you from?"

"I'm from Solhill," Daniel said. It was true, partially anyway. He just had never stepped into the village that was behind the forest he grew up in. "I was just passing through the forest when that wolf attacked me."

Charles nodded and stepped towards the door. "I will bring you something to eat," he said. "You need to gain your strength back." He smiled again and left the room.

Daniel moved to the edge of the bed, dragging the injured leg behind him. He leaned over the edge to have a better look through the doorway but couldn't see the corridor properly. He leaned some more and suddenly felt that the top of his body was leaning too far forward. He grabbed the edge of the mattress but couldn't stop his body. The floor was slowly but inevitably approaching. He landed on the floor face first, taking the blanket with him.

He sighed and sat up. He checked his nose and face, but luckily, all seemed to be unharmed. Using the bed as a support, he carefully stood up. He was glad to see that his legs could finally support him. He straightened up and looked around.

The room was quite small. Apart from the big bed and a big wardrobe, there were two doors leading out of it—the one through which Charles had left, and another one, which was closed, on the other side of the room. Daniel limped through the room towards the other door. It would be too risky to run away through the first door because he might run into Charles, so the second door was the only possibility for a quick getaway.

As he moved to the door, he saw a second room. A young man suddenly appeared there. Daniel jumped back and hit the wall. Breathing hard, he looked around, but there was no place to hide. The wardrobe was on the other side of the room, and there didn't seem to be enough space beneath the bed. He didn't dare to run away through the other door because there were people there for sure. He stood pressed against the wall for a while when he realized that the man still hadn't crossed the threshold.

Once his breath and heartbeat slowed down, Daniel decided to check the second door again. Leaning against the wall, he moved slowly towards it. Thanks to the adrenalin in his blood, he completely forgot about his injured leg. When he approached the door, he stopped, took a deep breath, and quickly peered to the other room. The face of a young man appeared in his view.

He quickly jumped back and hit the wall again. He waited for a while, but when nothing happened, he risked another look. With his back to the wall, he leaned to the side and peered into the room. The man appeared again, but this time Daniel didn't jump back. The man was looking him in the eye with his mouth agape. After a while, Daniel stood up straight; the man in the doorway stood up straight. Daniel bent his knees; the man bent his knees as well.

"It's me!" Daniel said with relief. He stood back a little to have a better look. The mirror definitely made a much better reflexion than flowing water in the river. He was seeing himself as a human for the first time. His eyes were dark brown, which was a bit surprising to him. He expected his eyes would be orange, the same as they were when he was in wolf form. His hair was quite long and dark, and he had weird lumps on his shoulders and arms, which made him look swollen. His waist was thinner than his chest, which he considered weird, since the widest body part of the men in the village was usually their waists. The most surprising thing was that he didn't have a beard or a moustache. He had been expecting to be more … hairy.

The sound of footsteps broke his focus. He spun around and winced at the pain in his leg. For a moment he lost his balance, but he managed to stay on his feet. He started to panic. He had wanted to run away, but he'd been so caught up in the mirror that he completely forgot about his plan for the moment. He looked at the window, but immediately dismissed the idea of jumping through it. He hesitated for a moment and then jumped onto the bed. He grabbed the blanket from the floor and pulled it up after him.

A girl entered the room with a tray in her hands just as he covered himself up. She stopped and looked at Daniel in the bed. She had a long red hair and freckles, and Daniel suspected that she was Charles's daughter. She was very pretty. She smiled nervously at him, and Daniel smiled back. Her scent reached Daniel's nose, but was overpowered by the smell of the food immediately. His stomach growled.

"I brought you something to eat," she said as she put the tray on the bedside table. "My father asked me to bring it to you. My name's Lucy."

Daniel nodded and peeked at the tray. "I'm Daniel," he said.

"I also brought you some pie. I made it myself just this morning. It was my granny's recipe. I'm the only one in Samforest who knows how to make it properly," she said proudly.

"Thanks," said Daniel. He didn't know what else to say. He realized that he was still holding the blanket all the way up to his neck, so he released his grip and tried another smile. He wasn't sure if he was doing a good job, but Lucy didn't run away screaming, so it was probably not that bad.

"Well, enjoy your meal," she said after a short silence, and she turned on her heel. She flashed him a smile from the doorway and closed the door behind her.

Daniel looked at the dinner. They had given him a nice piece of chicken with some potatoes. He knew people had been cooking meat. The first time he'd seen them make fires close to the forest, he had searched the place when they left. Sometimes he got lucky and found some leftovers or bones. He rather liked cooked meat. However, he had no idea what potatoes were.

He sat up on the bed, pulled the plate closer, and grabbed the chicken. He was so hungry that he gulped pieces of meat as quickly as he could. Occasionally he had to stop and take a deep breath to avoid suffocation, but even this didn't slow him down. When he got his hunger under control, he slowed down. He finished the chicken and put the bones down. He decided to leave them for later. He wiped his mouth with the back of his hand and looked down at his shirt. He was dirty, but happy, and really glad that he hadn't run away before the meal.

He looked at the fork and decided to try it. He knew people used them a lot, and now he had a chance to try it himself. He picked it up carefully and prodded a piece of potato. He looked at it critically and picked it up with the fork. He smelled it. He smelled it again and bit. The fork hit the plate with the loud clang, the spit-out bite of potato followed it nearly immediately. He reached for a glass of water and drank it in one go. Then he looked down at his plate. Once again, he picked up the potato with the fork and looked at it from all sides. *What do they see in this?* he wondered. *They taste awful.*

He put the fork down and pushed the plate away. He yawned and looked at the soft bed. He knew he had to sneak out and find some place to sleep and possibly change back to his wolf shape. He didn't want to linger at Charles's, but he didn't see any harm in putting his head down on the pillow for a minute or two.

He lay down. As soon as his head hit the pillow, he fell asleep.

CHAPTER 6

E than crouched behind a bush and looked at the road. A breeze rustled few leaves on the bush behind which he was hiding, but nothing else moved. He motioned for the Royal Guards to approach. Several guards approached the bushes and stationed themselves by the road. They were very careful to take the wind into the consideration, since there could be werewolves anywhere.

A deer appeared from behind the trees on the other side of the road and walked all the way towards Ethan. He motioned for the soldiers to wait. This was a good opportunity to determine if his theory about the wind and motion was true.

The deer stopped at a raspberry bush. It checked the road thoroughly and then stepped closer to the bush. It picked up a raspberry and chewed it slowly. It took its time with the raspberry, moving its jaws in slow circular motion. It swallowed and took another raspberry from the bush. It was still chewing when the guard to Ethan's left moved slightly. The deer stopped chewing and looked around, its ears flicking from side to side. The breeze moved some leaves at its hooves, but nothing else happened.

The deer relaxed, finished the raspberry, and took another one. As it was chewing, Ethan heard a cracking of a twig to his right. He looked at the guard who crouched a little deeper with a pained look on his face. The deer turned its head towards the guard and flicked its ears. It took a step back from the bush and watched the trees intently.

Another noise came through the forest, and the deer turned around. A cart appeared on the road, and the deer ran to the other side of the road and disappeared between the trees.

Ethan motioned to the guards, who lifted bows, nocked arrows, and aimed through the trees without firing. The cart was slowly approaching the raspberry bush. It was surrounded by two dozen mounted soldiers wearing Lord Blake's crest on their chests: six were sitting on the cart around the cargo, eight were galloping behind the coach, eight were in front of it as a vanguard, and two sat on the top of the cart. They all looked nervous. They drove in silence, constantly checking the forest around them.

When they approached the raspberry bush, Ethan motioned to the guards, and a swarm of arrows flew from the forest. Some of Lord Blake's soldiers screamed, and the birds in the trees flew away. The soldiers in the rear managed to draw their swords, but before they could do anything else, more arrows flew through the air. Several of the horses stampeded down the road, but most of them remained by the cart, surrounded by dead bodies. The horses in the harness neighed and stopped. The entire attack lasted only a few seconds, and then everything went dead quiet.

Ethan stood up and nodded at the guards who came out of the forest and started to collect arrows from the dead bodies. Ethan followed with Lord Adrian, stepping over the dead bodies as they made their way towards the cart. They jumped onto the cart. Ethan walked to the boxes while Lord Adrian looked around. Ethan threw aside a dead soldier and opened the box nearest to him. Lord Adrian looked down at the box. "Well," he said, "it seems that Blackbird was actually telling the truth, Your Majesty."

"Not necessarily." Ethan shook his head and picked up a sword from the box. "We were expecting a trap, so we were careful. But it could still be a snare. Maybe we just found the bait, and the trap is about to be released."

He looked at the sword from both sides and threw it back into the box. Lord Adrian opened another box and whistled. "It seems they are really re-arming the army. This box is full of bows. And nice bows, too."

"Maybe we shouldn't linger," Ethan said, and he looked at the road behind him. "Hide the bodies in the forest. We'll take the whole cart with us, and the horses too."

Lord Adrian nodded and motioned to the two nearest guards. Meanwhile, Ethan opened another box and picked up an arrow. There had to be hundreds of arrows in the box. They could definitely be put to use. Lord Adrian opened another box that was full of arrows, and then moved to the last box. This lid was stuck, and he had to use force. He finally pushed the lid up and froze. He picked up a silver cup and turned to Ethan. Ethan took the cup from his hands and turned it in his hands, scanning it thoroughly. "Why would the army want silverware?" Lord Adrian asked. "They don't need silver arrows or anything. The werewolves are on their side."

"The werewolves probably want to control the silver," Ethan replied, and he threw the cup into the box. "However, we can melt these and use the silver for arrowheads."

"Good thing we have two blacksmiths," Lord Adrian said with a nod. "They will know what to do with this," he added, and he kicked the box.

Ethan nodded, slammed the box closed, sat on the spring-seat of the cart, and took the reins. Lord Adrian sat next to him and motioned to the guards. Ethan spurred the horses and drove the cart into the forest. The first part of their plan had definitely been more than successful.

Captain Stuart walked between the soldiers in the yard of Royal Castle deep in thought. Royal Castle was a magnificent complex of buildings surrounded by high walls. Part of the castle was carved into the mountain. A lot of windows were currently lit, and the vast yard was full of soldiers.

The castle was very alive these days because it served as a main camp for part of the remnant of Blake's army. The rest of his army remained by the borders. Though they had officially won, no one had seen Mors or Blake lately. Bess spent most of his time in the library reading everything he could find. The rest of the werewolves spent their time in the main dining room, playing various games. A lot of betting took place in that room. The games were not that important.

Captain Stuart walked by a few soldiers who were sitting around a fire. The soldiers saluted him as he walked by, but he hardly noticed them. He saluted back absentmindedly and realized that fewer soldiers saluted him these days, and those who did only slightly raised their hands to their foreheads. He wasn't bothered by that. He wasn't really that keen on saluting in the first place, and he preferred to be feared than loved.

Captain Stuart entered the castle and wondered what Blake was doing. If Blake became king, Captain Stuart would be promoted to the captain of the Royal Guards immediately. The only rank that was higher was that of the lords, and of course, king. Captain Stuart had wanted to be the captain of the Royal Guards ever since he saw a parade as a little boy. He had joined Lord Blake's ranks fifteen years ago and had systematically worked his way up. He had the trust of the lords, and everyone in the castle knew that he was the logical choice for the post, especially since the last captain of the Royal Guards had died in battle earlier. The only thing that kept Captain Stuart from the post was Ethan's unwillingness to join his father in the afterlife.

He was walking up the stairs when the sound of dishes being smashed brought him back to reality. He stopped for a moment and then hurried up the stairs. He was on the top of the stairs when a voice halted him, "I wouldn't go in there if I were you."

Captain Stuart looked around and spotted Amos, Lord Blake's advisor, leaning against the wall nearby. More smashing was audible in the corridor, but Captain Stuart didn't even blink. A group of soldiers entered the corridor, but stopped when they saw their captain at the top of the stairs.

"Why?" Captain Stuart asked as he looked at the far door. It led to the gallery where all the precious works of art were stored. There were more sounds of pottery being smashed, and Captain Stuart wondered how many things remained undamaged.

"His lordship is upset," Amos said with a sigh. Captain Stuart looked at him with one eyebrow raised. The unmistakeable message of that look was: *Really? I wouldn't have guessed that.* Amos straightened up and stepped closer. "Mors just said that Lord Blake wouldn't be king until Ethan is dead. He said something about a snag in the plan. I was there when Mors gave him the news."

They heard the sound of canvas being torn to pieces. Captain Stuart waved the soldiers away and watched them leave. When all the soldiers were gone, he turned to Amos. "I thought he would be able to handle that information better," he said. "He knows we didn't find Ethan's body, and he also knows the laws. If he wishes to keep the appearance of the hero who saved Norene, he needs a burial, and for that he needs Ethan's body. Besides, it would be safer if Ethan was out of the picture."

"Well, I suppose he didn't expect this turn of the events," said Amos in a bored voice. "Some strange guy came to him and offered him help.

He promised Lord Blake that he would be the new king. He gave him the army his lordship needed, yet the old king is still alive. And we don't have much of the army left. Wouldn't you be pissed?"

"Yes." Captain Stuart nodded slowly. More smashing came from the gallery, and he looked at the closed door. "But why is he destroying the gallery?"

"I think he just needs to filter his anger, and there is nothing better than destroying the collection King Philip spent his whole life accumulating. I am just surprised that you are taking that news so well."

Captain Stuart slowly turned his face and looked at Amos. "Why shouldn't I?" he asked with a dangerous look on his face. There was a warning in his voice, but Amos either didn't hear it or decided to ignore it.

"With King Ethan alive, there is no chance for you to become the captain of the Royal Guards. Everyone knows how much you want that post. With Ethan out of the picture, the post was as good as yours—maybe even the lordship, since four lords remained with the king, but now ..."

Captain Stuart's expression hardened, and Amos's voice trailed off. Captain Stuart stepped closer to Amos, who became obviously nervous, but didn't step back. Captain Stuart looked at the gallery door and then back at Amos.

"True," he nodded. "Ethan is still alive. And, yes, with him in the picture, I cannot become the captain of the Royal Guards. But the war isn't over. That was just one battle, and Lord Blake won that battle, didn't he? This is just a minor setback. We will win. I feel it in my bones."

"You sound confident."

"I am." Captain Stuart nodded. "I will make sure that this is over, even if I have to go out there and find Ethan myself. However, I doubt that he will remain in hiding. He *will* come here. And when he does, I will be ready."

"Do you know why the werewolves sent Hans away?" Amos asked suddenly in a shaky voice. Captain Stuart blinked in surprise. He knew that Mors had sent another werewolf called Hans away on some mission, but he hadn't expected Amos to know this or to change the topic so suddenly.

"I don't know. Don't you?" he asked at last.

"I thought you were the one who knew about everything that happened around here," Amos said. "I'm just a humble servant of Lord Blake. I am in no communication with the werewolves."

Captain Stuart looked at Amos for a while and then stepped back. "Well, have a nice evening," he said with a forced smile, and he hurried up the corridor before Amos had time to react.

Amos watched the captain for a while and then turned around and entered his new room.

As the corridor became empty once more, a slim feminine figure stepped out of the shadow and looked around. She was dressed in tight black clothes with a black mask covering her face, which made her blend in with the shadow perfectly. She sighed and pulled a little notebook out of her cleavage. She marked down the information she had just heard and put the notebook back.

Amy wasn't that keen on staying in the castle, but Rex wanted her to keep an eye on the werewolves. He wanted to know how they were progressing with their search for the necklace. Yet, all the information she was currently gathering suggested that the werewolves were trying harder to get Ethan than they were to get the necklace. This was understandable. Lord Blake was claiming that he was the hero who had saved the country, but unfortunately couldn't save the king. The werewolves wanted Lord Blake on the throne, and having the king parade himself around was very dangerous, especially since Lord Blake had joined forces with the werewolves. People of Norene really hated the werewolves.

Amy was getting curious about how Lord Blake was planning to establish trade with the werewolves once he became king. Since the official news was that the king, along with most of the lords, had been killed while fighting against them, Amy was sure that the people of Norene wouldn't appreciate trading with them. But then again, there was no reason for official trade. All Lord Blake had to do was to sell the werewolves weapons and armour and pretend that they were never made or that they were stolen, in case someone wanted to look closer at the transaction.

Amy sighed and stepped after Captain Stuart. Her goal was to find out if the werewolves had got hold of the necklace, and then to steal it back if they had. She could sniff out a lot of information, and she could move without being seen. But with the werewolves in place, she had to move without being smelled which was much harder. Her scent could jeopardize her goal. Yet she felt proud because Rex thought that she was the best for that job.

Lord James stopped and waved at the Royal Guards behind him. Lord Thomas and twenty men walked up to him, stopped, and crouched behind the bushes. The breeze blew some leaves in their direction, and the bushes rustled. Lord James motioned to the guards and Lord Thomas to wait on the spot, and then he hurried up the road. He crawled to the bushes higher up the road and hid in the foliage. He pulled an arrow out of his quiver, nocked it into his bow, and got ready. Slowly, he rose and peeked over the bush. He quickly hid back and then blinked. He put the bow down and crawled closer to the bush. He pushed aside the branches and watched the clearing for a while.

Out of the corner of his eye, he could see that the guards had readied themselves for an attack, but he ignored this. He stood up abruptly and put his hands on his hips. Lord Thomas crawled after Lord James, keeping his head down.

"What's going on?" Lord Thomas whispered, staying hidden behind the bush.

Lord James didn't look away from the camp. "Huh," he said. "I don't think you need to hide anymore."

Lord Thomas peeked over the bush carefully and then stood upright. He folded his arms and watched the camp in front of them, his lips pressed tight. They both stood there for a while, and then Lord Thomas motioned for the guards to get closer. The men stood up hesitantly and carefully approached the lords. The lieutenant stopped by the lords and whistled.

The camp was empty. The clearing bore some marks showing that men had camped there a few hours ago, but no one remained. The fire had been put out, some bones had been left behind, and cart tracks disappeared into the forest.

"We are too late," Lord Thomas said at last. "They have already left."

"Maybe if we hurried after them," the lieutenant suggested, just as Lord James walked towards the fire pit. Most of guards followed him, checking the clearing.

Lord James placed his hand above the ash and moved his hand lower. He frowned and lowered his hand. He stopped for a few seconds and then lowered his hand some more. He knelt and touched the ash. "They left some time ago," he said as he picked up a piece of charcoal. He threw it back to the fireplace, dusted his hands off, and looked at the tracks. "Even if we went after them, we wouldn't be able to catch them in time. I think we should return."

Lord Thomas eyed Lord James and then motioned for the guards to leave. Lord James watched the clearing. He was deep in thought while the guards slowly returned to the forest. He really hadn't expected the soldiers to leave that early. He had had a bad feeling about the situation that morning but hadn't been able put his finger on the reason. Now he knew. Subconsciously, he had known he was running late.

"I will inform the king of the situation," Lord Thomas said quietly. Lord James nodded gloomily. "I will try to keep the information from Lord Eric as long as possible."

Lord James raised his eyebrow and looked at Lord Thomas, but there was nothing but honest concern in his look. Lord James smiled and shook his head. "That won't be necessary," he said, and he walked out of the clearing. Lord Thomas sighed and followed him. The guards waited for them on the road and followed the lords back to the caves in silence. No one dared to break Lord James's concentration.

Two hours later, they reached the caves. Lord James stopped by the entrance, but the guards hurried inside, saluting him as they went by. He nodded to them and watched them vanish into the darkness of the cave. Once he was all alone, he turned to face the trees around the caves and leaned against the stone. He really couldn't just let that go. If Lord Eric succeeded, he would never hear the end of it. That thought was the worst he could face. He just couldn't let Lord Eric be better.

A cart drove from the forest with Ethan at the reins and Lord Adrian sitting beside him. Ethan brightened up when he saw Lord James, but his smile froze when he saw his expression. He slowed down in front of Lord James and then stopped. The Royal Guards behind him stopped as well.

"Did you succeed?" Ethan asked quietly. Lord James opened his mouth, sighed, and shook his head unable to find proper words to express his anger.

"What happened?"

"We were too late," he said gloomily. "The soldiers left hours ago."

Ethan looked at Lord Adrian, who stroked his chin, lost in thought. Ethan turned to Lord James and smiled. "Well, these things happen," he said. "The most important thing is that we have weapons and some silver for arrowheads. Maybe Lord Eric will succeed in getting the other cart with the food."

Lord James's features hardened, and he looked at the forest. Ethan handed the reins to Lord Adrian and motioned for them to continue. He jumped down from the cart and waited until Lord Adrian and the guards had vanished inside the cave. "I understand that it bothers you," he said quietly to Lord James, who looked at the ground, "but don't do anything stupid. We can get food some other way. It wasn't your fault. We all thought there was more time. You saved our lives when you broke through enemy lines and got us to these caves. Even if Lord Eric got a hundred carts with weapons and food, he couldn't beat that."

Lord James looked up, smiled, and nodded. Ethan smiled back, patted him on the shoulder, and walked into the cave. Lord James watched after him, thinking hard. Then a nasty smile appeared on his face, and he stepped towards the forest. He walked slowly at first, but then he quickened his pace. By the time he reached the trees, he was running.

CHAPTER 7

Daniel didn't dare to try to change back to wolf shape in the room. He still wasn't sure if he could even do it. He had to get back to the forest, but he still couldn't figure out the best way to leave. He came to the conclusion that he needed to get away in the dead of night. However, the first night, he slept soundly till the next afternoon. During the second night, Charles had some visitors. Daniel tried his best not to fall asleep, and he managed to stay up way after midnight. When he got the feeling that the house was very quiet, he sneaked out of the room, but nearly ran into Charles and his friends, who were in the kitchen talking and drinking beer. Daniel quickly returned to the room and decided to wait for them to leave. Suddenly, however, he woke up next morning, lying on the covers.

His leg didn't hurt at all, and he was getting more and more nervous. If the doctor came, he would be very surprised at the fact that the wound had healed in two days. And this was a wound that should have left a scar. Daniel decided that it was time to leave. He prepared for his departure thoroughly. Since leaving during the night hadn't worked, he decided to go during the day. He practiced all possible outcomes of the conversation he could think of. He was grateful to Charles for saving him. Charles didn't know that Daniel didn't need medical attention, but his effort to get a doctor still counted for a lot. For this reason, he decided to say thank you and goodbye.

When lunchtime came, he got out of the bed, descended the stairs, and entered the kitchen. Charles, his wife Mary, and Lucy were sitting at the table eating. Charles was the first one to notice Daniel. He looked up from his plate, and a big smile appeared on his face. "How are you feeling?" he asked happily as he stood up.

Daniel smiled back and hesitated. He hadn't expected this start of the conversation. All the scenarios that he had practiced started with something similar to "How is that you can walk?"

Charles motioned to an empty chair by the table, and Daniel sat down nervously. "I'm much better, thank you," he said. The smell of roasted goose came to his nose, and he lost his focus.

"How's your leg? Does it hurt?" Mary asked as she hurried to the cupboard. She took a clean plate from a shelf and put some potatoes on it. Daniel still hadn't warmed up to potatoes, though he had actually eaten several of them the previous day.

He realized that they were all watching him, and then he remembered he had a question to answer. "It's much better, thank you," he replied, feeling like a parrot. Time to continue with the planned conversation.

"There is a fair today," Charles said suddenly, and Daniel completely forgot what he wanted to say. "Since you can walk, you can join us."

"Oh, Charles," Mary said. "I don't think Daniel wants to go. He needs some rest." She put a big chunk of meat on Daniel's plate. Daniel followed each movement of the meat with his eyes. He didn't even blink. "You can eat this here and then go back to bed, or you can take it with you to bed," she added to Daniel in a much nicer tone of voice.

"I actually wanted to thank you," Daniel said, unable to take his eyes off the goose.

"You're welcome, sweetie," Mary said with a smile. "So, do you want to take it upstairs with you?"

Daniel hardly paid any attention to the conversation. His stomach growled. Mustering all his willpower, he tore his eyes off the plate and looked up at Mary. Then his brain caught up with the last part of the conversation. "I meant that I wanted to thank you, but I should continue on my journey."

"Nonsense!" Charles shook his head and cut a piece of meat. "You are still too weak, and your leg needs more time to heal. You can stay here even a few weeks if necessary. My son, John, is with his aunt in the south, studying for his exams, so that room is available. Besides, where would you go now? Everyone within twenty miles radius is coming here, and you would walk the other way? No, you can postpone your departure. Come with us to the fair."

"I would love to, but no thanks," Daniel said carefully. Mary put the plate in front of him and sat back at the table.

"Why not?" Charles asked baffled. "If you feel all right for travelling, you can spend five hours with us."

Daniel wasn't sure what to say to that. He wasn't trained in argumentation and had no idea how to get out of the fair and yet manage to leave that evening. After a short moment of internal torment, he decided to go with them to the fair. He had two reasons for this. First, he had a strange feeling that Charles was getting very suspicious of him, and second, the fair was quite a big event, and he could use the crowd as cover while he disappeared into the forest. Once in the forest, he would try to figure out how to change back into his wolf form. He had to acknowledge that the conversation hadn't gone as planned.

Two hours later, Daniel stood in the doorway and looked at the square in the distance. There was already quite a crowd over there, and he wondered how many more people would come. Charles had been right. The fair in Samforest was one of the biggest summer attractions in this part of Norene. Hundreds of people came to the village and spent several hours there.

He heard a quiet yelp by his feet and looked down. A small furry dog was sitting next to him, looking up. It was wagging its tail on the ground creating a little dust vortex. It seemed very curious about Daniel, but Daniel had no idea what to do with it. "Hello there," he said at last and leaned down to pat the dog. The dog yelped and ran away. Daniel straightened up, watching after it, and wondered what had just happened. That had been his first encounter with a dog, and it had been weird. He had imagined that dogs were bigger than the small grey-and-white ball of fur he'd just seen. He'd always only heard or smelled them, but he'd always imagined them to be similar to wolves. The only difference was that they listened to humans, whereas wolves attacked or ran away from humans. However, upon seeing this little creature, he had to re-evaluate his knowledge of dogs.

He smelled Lucy approaching rather than actually hearing or seeing her. He spun around and found himself face to face with her. She flashed him a big smile and took his hand. He had no idea what to think of that action.

"You know, this fair is a great occasion," she said as she stroked the back of his hand. Daniel didn't say anything. The touch of her hand was both nice and weird. He smiled at her, suspecting that it was desired behaviour on his part. "You know, there is something strange about you," she said and looked him in the eye.

Daniel's smile froze. "Really?" he asked quietly, but his heart started to pound against his chest. He had a feeling it was so loud that Lucy had to be able to hear it.

"It's nothing in particular," she said. "It's as if you were from an entirely different world."

"Well, I am," Daniel heard himself say, and Lucy laughed merrily. He didn't understand why she laughed. He was serious.

The door behind them squeaked. Lucy immediately let go of Daniel's hand and stepped back. Charles stopped at the threshold with his left hand on the handle and looked from Lucy to Daniel. Daniel felt very uneasy. He felt warmth on his face, though he stood in the shadow. "Can we go?" Charles asked suspiciously. Lucy nodded with an innocent smile and immediately set off for the main square. Daniel wasn't sure what to say. He had no idea what had just happened, but he had a feeling that Charles wouldn't be happy about it. He stepped after Lucy. Charles and Mary followed, and they all walked in silence towards the fair. Lucy didn't even look at Daniel the whole time, and Daniel wondered if her behaviour was normal for humans.

As they approached the square, Daniel noticed stalls around the perimeter. It was difficult to see them clearly through the crowd, but there were dozens of them. The chatter got louder as they came to the square, and Daniel got a little nervous. One part of him—the part that was closer to his true self—wanted to run away and hide, but the other part of him—the part that usually did the thinking—was excited.

The people were walking through the square looking at the exhibited goods. There were some foreigners from much further away than local villages. They wore nice silk clothes that were much more colourful than the local fashion. The local women had put on their best clothes, and even the poorest of the poor had done their best to look noble. The vendors and craftsmen were showing off their merchandise in a very loud manner. Some were calling for people to come and see the wares in their stalls; some were calling for people to try their remedies and ointments.

Daniel wanted to see everything, though he didn't want to purchase anything in particular. He understood the possession principle humans followed and knew that the vendors and the craftsmen weren't giving away their things. He just wasn't sure how he could acquire any of the goods. Even if he wanted something, he didn't have anything to trade that would be interesting to anyone. And he sure wasn't going to give the necklace to anyone for anything.

Lucy took Daniel's hand, and he felt his face warm up again. He wasn't sure how Charles would react, but he knew he didn't want to find out. He tried to let go of Lucy's hand, but she was holding onto him. He looked at her, not sure what to say. She smiled at him brightly. "Would you like to meet my friends?" she asked sweetly.

Before he could answer, he felt a heavy hand on his shoulder. He knew right away that it had to be Charles, because she let go of his hand immediately and looked a little alarmed. "Let him look around the fair, first," Charles said in a calm voice. Lucy nodded with a rather sad smile and departed to meet her friends.

Daniel wasn't sure if he was glad about this or not. One part of him wanted to follow her, but the other part—the wolf part—knew that he should keep away from her. Though there was something hypnotizing about her, she was a little scary, and he wasn't even human. He only looked human, and it would be unfair to Lucy to make her believe that she stood a chance; not that he was sure what that chance would be. Besides, Charles's grip was so strong that it actually hurt a little, and Daniel's instincts told him that it wasn't a good idea to tempt her father.

"So," said Charles as he released Daniel's shoulder. Daniel could feel the hair on the back of his neck stand up. Something about the tone of Charles's voice was scary. "Where do you plan on going from here?"

Daniel hadn't expected this question. And he hadn't prepared or practiced any conversation for this occasion. The truth was that he had no idea where he would go. Somehow, he didn't feel comfortable in the Samforest forest anymore though he knew it would be the first stop on his way. "I honestly don't know," he said at last. "I will probably go north and see where the road takes me."

Charles nodded, and they both slowly walked through the crowd. Daniel's instincts were screaming, but he tried to remain calm on the surface.

"We killed a werewolf here, you know," Charles said in a matter-of-fact tone of voice. Daniel's heart started to beat so hard that it felt as if it was trying to raise the alarm. "It happened a few days ago," Charles continued calmly. "However, we didn't really need to burn him, you know?"

Daniel felt Charles's stare fixed upon him, but he didn't dare to look at him. He quickly scanned the crowd for escape routes but didn't see any, so he walked silently by Charles's side as they walked through the square. Daniel didn't want to break the silence. He didn't know what to say, anyway.

"No, we didn't have to burn him," Charles continued when Daniel didn't say anything. "Funny thing. A wolf was attacked by that werewolf. Normally, a wolf would stand no chance, but this one was fast and strong. It managed to bite the werewolf's throat, which was actually enough to kill him. But then, as if to make sure, it dragged him into the river to drown. If the bite didn't kill the werewolf, the water sure did. We just burnt him to make sure, but that was really unnecessary."

"Really?" Daniel asked quietly. His voice was so strange to him, that he wasn't sure for a moment who had spoken.

"Yeah," Charles nodded. "But the wolf got away. It's been a few days now, but I think it survived. I just wonder what happened to it."

Daniel stopped near one of the stands and pretended he was interested in the apples on display. No one around them paid them any attention. Charles waited for a while, but when Daniel didn't say anything, he continued: "When a human is bitten by a werewolf, he or she becomes a wolf. So, maybe if a wolf is bitten by a werewolf it becomes … a human."

Daniel froze when his hand was halfway to an apple. He stood still for a while then slowly pulled his hand back. He still wasn't sure how to react to this conversation. He hesitated and then looked up at Charles. "Is there a point to this story?" he asked with a blank expression on his face. He had surprised himself by the smoothness of his reaction.

"I just think it's an interesting thought," said Charles calmly, not taking his eyes off Daniel. "And I always wondered what a wolf would look like if it changed into a human. How's your leg, by the way?"

Daniel said nothing. He kept staring at Charles, thinking hard. There was no answer to the last question that wouldn't cause more trouble. He turned his back to the apple stall and to Charles and slowly walked to the centre of the square. On the other side of the square, he noticed the start of a path that led into the forest. If he got close enough, he could try to run all the way there.

"It's an interesting theory, don't you think?" asked Charles who had followed him through the square.

"Yes, it is." Daniel nodded, trying hard to keep the same pace. "I just wonder how that wolf would behave. A werewolf is a human, so they can think, but wolves are animals. Or do you think that a wolf would be able to have some complex conversations or even talk at all?"

Charles was quiet for a while as he walked next to Daniel to the other side of the square. Daniel didn't dare to look at him but hoped that this little question had got Charles off track.

"Well, it's just a theory," Charles said at last. He shrugged. Daniel eased himself, but then he started to think about his situation. What if Charles was right? What if there was no difference between him and a common werewolf? Daniel had at first thought himself to be a wolf that had started to think, but this transformation to human form had changed everything. Maybe he was a werewolf and just didn't know it.

In his memory, he returned to that moment when he was bitten. He had not had any idea that the werewolf was nearby. He had been so happy because he had found this beautiful necklace. Maybe the necklace had something to do with his situation. Charles had said that no wolf stood a chance against a werewolf, but he was obviously different. One thing that was definitely different about him—except brighter fur, longer ears, better hearing, better sense of smell, and better agility and stamina—was the necklace.

He could still remember the shock he'd felt when he spotted the werewolf. It had already been too late to flee, but he still had stood a chance. He hadn't smelled him before, which was weird, because he couldn't get that smell out of his mind. It was something between a human and a wolf. He had never smelled it before, but he would definitely remember that smell for the rest of his life. He could even remember that strange feeling he'd had when he realized that the voices inside his head were his thoughts.

Suddenly, he stopped and took a deep breath. For a while he thought that he was remembering the smell, but no memory could be this strong. He would know that smell anywhere, even in a crowd of humans.

"What do you smell?" Charles asked as Daniel spun on spot, looking around.

"A werewolf," he said absentmindedly, and he took another deep breath. He knew that Charles was suspicious of him, but he didn't care anymore. He wasn't that far away from the forest. He had to be sure where the werewolf was before he decided to run away from him.

"Go and take Lucy home," he said to Charles. "There is a werewolf here."

"Are you sure?"

"I would recognize that scent anywhere."

Out of the corner of his eye, he saw Charles hurry away. Daniel couldn't identify the werewolf. There were too many people in one place, and smells from the stalls made it all too difficult, but he knew that the werewolf was close.

"Where did Charles go?" a voice asked behind Daniel.

Daniel spun around and found himself face to face with one of Charles's friends. He recognized the man from the previous night when he had tried to sneak out of the house. If he remembered correctly, the man was Stuart. Daniel didn't want to have any conversations at the moment, but he knew he had to at least answer the question. "Over there," he said, and he motioned in the direction of Charles's house. He concentrated on the smell again and absentmindedly added, "He went for Lucy."

"Really? But Lucy's over there," Stuart said, pointing to the other end of the fair. Daniel looked in that direction, and his heart missed a beat. By the path to the forest, there stood a tall man who looked a little out of place. He was much taller than anyone around him, and a long, dark-brown leather coat made him look even taller. His long black hair was bit greasy and combed back. The wind blew towards Daniel and brought him the man's scent. There was no doubt about it; the man was a werewolf. And Lucy was not far away from him, looking at jewellery in a nearby stall.

Daniel looked behind him, but there was no sight of Charles. He looked back at the werewolf, and their eyes met for a brief moment. A devilish smile appeared on the werewolf's face and he stepped closer to

Lucy. Daniel was sure that the werewolf didn't recognize him, but then he realized with dread that the werewolf chose to hunt down Lucy.

The werewolf's smile widened to a maniacal grin, and Daniel watched in terror as he took off his coat and threw it to the ground. He stood naked there, his body slowly changing shape. His hands, chest, and legs were getting hairier and smaller; his nose and mouth were elongating, creating a snout. He landed on all fours and stepped forward as the last changes took place. Two steps later, there stood a hideous wolf.

A woman somewhere in the crowd shrieked. It took a few seconds for the fair goers to realize that something was wrong, but very soon the panic started. Daniel didn't pay any attention to the screams or the people behind him. The only thing that mattered to him was the werewolf in front of him. He was wondering how to get the werewolf away from villagers and, most importantly, away from Lucy, but he couldn't come up with any idea that would help him protect his own identity.

Lucy spun around, surprised by the havoc around her. When she noticed the werewolf in front of her, she screamed and jumped back. Her foot slid to the side, and she fell to the ground, smashing against the stall and taking one tray of jewellery with her. The people started to run in all directions, leaving the werewolf behind. The square was quickly emptying. The werewolf slowly approached Lucy, who was lying there on the ground rigid with shock. Daniel didn't care about the forest and getting away anymore. He wouldn't care about anyone else, but this was Charles's family member, and he couldn't let anything happen to his family.

Daniel could feel the wolf inside him roar as he stepped forward. All he could see was the werewolf. For him, the square was empty, and the only creatures were Lucy and the intruder. Someone grabbed his shoulder and started to drag him in the opposite direction.

"Come on!" He heard Stuart's voice by his ear. The werewolf was now six feet away from Lucy, who was pressing her back against the stall. Her eyes were wide with shock as she watched the hideous wolf in front of her.

Daniel fought himself free from the man's grip and started to run towards the werewolf. He could hear some screams, even someone shouting his name, but he didn't care. He threw off his shirt and sprinted forward, the necklace bouncing against his chest. And then shouts changed to shrieks. His forepaws hit the ground, and he tripped a bit on the pants that he hadn't taken off. He shook himself free of them and accelerated his speed. The strange thing was that he just knew he would manage to change. He didn't hesitate for a second, and he didn't wonder about it at all. It didn't matter.

The werewolf looked up from his victim. Shock appeared on his face. Daniel leapt, caught the back of the werewolf's neck, and started to push him away from Lucy. He could feel the werewolf struggling, but he had no problem keeping him down. The werewolf was trying to bite him, but he couldn't turn around. His jaws were snapping in the air in a futile attempt to find their target. Out of the corner of his eye, Daniel saw that Lucy had gone pale and fainted. He could hear some footsteps, and Charles appeared next to Lucy.

Daniel pushed the werewolf away from the stall and thought hard. His cover was now blown. There was no way that he could return to the village after what had just happened. He could keep the werewolf down, but he couldn't kill him with his jaws in the werewolf's back. He needed to get to his throat.

Daniel saw Charles pick up an unconscious Lucy and leave quickly. Daniel was glad that they were safe for now. He could concentrate on finding his way out of the situation he was in. Suddenly, the werewolf started to change to human right in his jaws. The feeling was very strange, and Daniel couldn't hold onto the werewolf's back as it got wider and the skin got tougher. He let go and stepped back. The werewolf changed completely and remained naked on the ground on all fours, blood dripping from his back. He looked up at Daniel and grinned. "And now what?" he asked as he stood up. At that moment, Daniel realized how tall and strong the man was. "Will you kill me? Just like that? Well, if you kill me, the werewolves will come here and kill everyone."

Daniel changed to human form as well and stood up. He felt strange. He wasn't used to these changes. He was standing there naked, but he didn't even notice. The werewolf stepped forward, but Daniel didn't budge.

"I could help you, you know," the werewolf said. "I can teach you how to deal with the changes and how not to be affected by the moon and by emotions. There must be a lot of things that are scary for you, and I could help you with them."

"I am not a werewolf," Daniel said defiantly, "because a werewolf ..." His voice trailed off, and he hesitated.

The werewolf grinned. "Just come with me," he whispered.

"I can't trust you."

"You can't trust *them* either," the werewolf said, motioning in the direction of the village. He changed to wolf form, took his coat between his teeth, and ran for the forest. Daniel hesitated but decided not to follow him. It could be a trap.

Suddenly, he smelled someone behind him. He quickly turned around, but all he could see was a log coming towards him. It hit him hard in the face, and everything went black.

CHAPTER 8

"Are you sure you know what you're doing?" Lord Thomas asked as he looked at Lord James. Seeing a manic grin on his face was not encouraging at all.

"This reminds me of my youth," Lord James said, and he winked at Lord Thomas.

"That's what scares me," murmured Lord Thomas as he peered over the bush that was covering their presence. He could see the enemy's small provisory camp. It was difficult to say how many soldiers were in the clearing, and the worst part was that some of them could be werewolves. He definitely didn't like their odds.

"Are you really sure?" Lord Thomas asked again. "It's great that you found them, but who knows how many of them there are, and there are only two of us. And no one even knows we're here."

"Have you ever heard of the fortress known as Moonshine?" asked Lord James as he sat down behind the bush. He pulled one of his boots off and shook it.

"Is there any chance that you were actually defending it?"

"No, I conquered it," Lord James said with a happy faraway look of someone remembering something pleasant. A little stone fell out of the boot.

"Oh, big surprise," said Lord Thomas sarcastically.

"Those were good old times, you know?" said Lord James ignoring this. He put the boot back on and stood up. "Not that I'm pining or wanting it back. Well, it's time to remind those werewolves who we are," he said. He drew his sword.

"Yeah, but are you sure you want to do this alone? Maybe we should—"

"Hold on!" Lord James frowned. "You didn't have to follow me. I didn't invite you here."

"I was curious to see where you were going," Lord Thomas said, shrugging.

"Okay. But we also agreed that I'm in charge here. Remember?" said Lord James, and he patted Lord Thomas on the shoulder. "You don't worry about a thing here. I know what I'm doing."

"I hope so," Lord Thomas said as he watched Lord James vanish between the trees. He raised himself higher for a better view of the camp. He could see seven soldiers from this spot. Three of them were sitting around the fire roasting some meat, two were leaning against a cart watching the forest, and two were walking in circles, so from time to time they disappeared from sight.

One of the walking soldiers disappeared, and in two minutes reappeared. At first, Lord Thomas thought it was the same man, but on a more thorough look, it was clear that the man had grown a little. He was adjusting his helmet under his chin while walking towards the cart. When the soldier by the cart looked at the approaching soldier suspiciously, Lord Thomas knew that this could never work.

The soldier by the cart straightened up and looked the newcomer up and down. When the newcomer, obviously hiding something behind his back, came closer to the soldiers, even the second one got curious. The newcomer smiled and stabbed the first soldier so quickly that Lord Thomas didn't even see the sword move. Then he fired a crossbow at the second one. The soldiers dropped to the ground dead.

The soldiers by the fire stood up and looked at the cart in surprise. Lord James threw his sword and crossbow onto the cart and jumped up. He grabbed a bow and some arrows that were lying in the cart and immediately started to shoot at an incredible speed. The soldiers by the fire fell to the ground dead, arrows sticking out of their chests. Lord James jumped onto the seat and took the reins. He spurred the horses and drove the cart out of the clearing. He ran over some enemy soldiers on the way and slowed down only long enough for Lord Thomas to jump onto the cart.

Lord Thomas jumped up and sat next to Lord James. Lord James spurred the horses and hurried the cart forward. Lord Thomas looked over his shoulder, but no one was following them. He looked at Lord James with some concern. There were many rumours about Lord James, but he had never thought them true, or at least not completely true. He always thought Lord James had had some incredible experiences in his youth, but he had always thought that the stories were all exaggerated. However, after what he'd just seen, he had to re-evaluate his opinion.

The fact that everyone got right about Lord James was that he used to be a pirate who went by the name of Flying Jimmy. And a damn good pirate, too. He was ruthless and cruel and caused a lot of trouble, mainly to Lord Eric, who controlled most of the land along the seacoast. Flying Jimmy hunted Lord Eric's ships, though these days he diminished this information by saying that Lord Eric was such a big tightwad there was hardly anything interesting to plunder from his boats.

No one knew where Flying Jimmy had come from, but he made the North Sea his home. He conquered the fortress Moonshine with only three of his men and then sneaked into Lord Eric's castle and stole two hundred barrels of rum in one night. He sank five ships belonging to Lord Eric with a single cannon shot. He and his crewmates caused so much trouble that King Philip had to do something.

Everyone expected that the king would send a fleet after the notorious pirate, but instead he sent only one man, a young prodigy, Stuart, who had just finished his training. Young Stuart managed to become part of Flying Jimmy's crew and found out all the information he needed. He then tipped off king's men who waited for the pirate and his crew on a little-known little island the crew used as their haven. The operation went smoothly, and Stuart joined Lord Blake's ranks afterwards. In a few years, he became captain.

Flying Jimmy and his crew were captured. Most of the crew died on the island, and the rest were hanged four days later on the king's orders. Only Flying Jimmy was kept in prison awaiting a big trial for his crimes. And then, luckily for Flying Jimmy, another group of pirates arrived. Suddenly, Flying Jimmy looked like a true gentleman compared to the new pirates. And King Philip offered Flying Jimmy a deal: no gallows in exchange for his help in dealing with the new pirates. He was to join the king's fleet and help them to get rid of the pirates. Flying Jimmy didn't have much choice, so he accepted.

The legend says that, during the fight with the pirates, Flying Jimmy climbed onto the pirates' ship and singlehandedly killed the captain and his first mate, captured and tied up twenty members of the crew, and commandeered the ship. However, he didn't run away; rather, he handed the ship over to Lord Eric's navy. The king kept his word, and Flying Jimmy wasn't hanged. He joined one of the ships he had attacked in the past as a third mate and kept guard in the North Sea.

He served the king for ten years, working his way up to the rank of ship's captain and keeping the north of Norene safe. King Philip granted him freedom, officially releasing him from service, but Flying Jimmy remained in King Philip's service by his own request. He refused to serve under Lord Eric, whom he thought to be an idiot and openly claimed so, and so his ship was the only one that took orders directly from the king.

Three years later, the king made Flying Jimmy a lord and gave him several islands in the North Sea along with a little fleet. Lord Eric protested very much against this arrangement, but the rest of the lords didn't hold a grudge and thought it wise to tie down Flying Jimmy. He changed his name to James and proved to be very loyal servant to King Philip and then to his son.

Lord Thomas had always thought that Lord James had just plundered a few ships and then got caught and made an agreement with the king, but suddenly, he wasn't so sure. However, there was one thing that he was sure about; the current king would be angry if he found out about this little unplanned operation. Lord Thomas wouldn't normally mention it at all, but he couldn't think of a way to explain the presence of the cart when the last information they had given was that they had been too late and hadn't found the soldiers. The whole situation went against common sense, but the worst part was that Lord James had really managed to kill dozen soldiers singlehandedly. Lord Thomas's respect for Lord James rose rapidly.

"You're very quiet," Lord James said a few minutes after their departure from the clearing.

His comment broke Lord Thomas's chain of thoughts. "I just don't have anything to say." Lord Thomas shrugged. "Maybe save for the fact that I am still not sure what happened out there."

"Oh, we just took some provisions and probably weapons from the enemy without risking anyone else's life. I told you I wouldn't need your help or reinforcements."

Lord Thomas nodded. The soldiers hadn't even noticed what had hit them, except for those who had been hit by the cart. And the way Lord James got to the cart was unbelievable. It was so obvious that the soldiers didn't even suspect him despite the fact that Lord James didn't look like a Norenian at all. He had really caught them off guard.

"Oh, how I missed this," said Lord James happily.

Lord Thomas shot him a glance and then focused on the road in front of them. "I seriously doubt that Lord Eric will be happy about this," he said without thinking.

Lord James's smile froze. Slowly, he turned his head and looked at Lord Thomas, who was trying to look very innocent. Lord James narrowed his eyes and watched Lord Thomas intently. They drove for a few seconds and then Lord Thomas cleared his throat. "The road's that way." He pointed forward. Lord James didn't budge. "I was just stating the obvious," Lord Thomas added defensively. "You know Lord Eric doesn't approve of this …" His voice trailed off. He knew he had walked right into the lion's den, and there was no way he could talk his way out of it.

Lord James looked at the road and then back again at Lord Thomas. "First of all," he hissed, "I didn't ask you to come with me. You followed."

"I know." Lord Thomas nodded.

"And second of all, I don't see what was wrong with what I did."

"Nothing," Lord Thomas said quickly. "I just meant that Lord Eric takes the art of fighting and war as a true mark of a gentleman."

"I'm sure it's not his fault," Lord James said calmly as he turned to watch the road.

Lord Thomas relaxed. He knew he had gone too far and hoped that this situation would never be used against him. They drove in silence for a while until the cave leading to the camp appeared.

"Don't tell Lord Eric about how we got the cart," Lord James said suddenly, and Lord Thomas nodded. "And if he asks, tell him I gave them jolly good chance to fight back and kill me."

Hans was sprinting in wolf form through a field in direction of Royal Castle with his coat flapping behind him. He had been wearing some type of coat for almost a century and had some practice with it. The bad thing about the change was that the clothes didn't change with him, so he'd had to figure out this little problem. It wasn't a question of shame or prudence, but of getting cold. Humans had no fur, so they had to wear a substitute for fur. During the decades, he perfected his way of carrying the coat while in wolf form—he carried it as a cape.

Over the centuries, he also learned a lot of other things. He had learned that people never changed, that the best way to kill a man was by sneaking up on him, that there was nothing better than a frantic crowd, and that wolves were really easy to kill.

He had a simple task, but so had Axel who had been killed. Only now Hans understood why. He had to acknowledge that he had found the wolf. However, the problem was that "it" turned out to be a "he". There were several theories about what could happen if a werewolf bit a wolf, but none of them predicted this. Normally, wolves didn't survive an attack from a werewolf, but even if they did, he couldn't imagine that they would be so ... sapient.

The wolf frightened the hell out of Hans. It was quicker and stronger than he was, and Hans had a suspicion that it was also smarter. And it didn't seem to be so easily manipulated. It was only a question of time until the wolf realized all this. Once it would realize that it could actually defeat a werewolf without any trouble, the werewolves would have a serious problem.

And, as a bonus, Hans had to face Mors and explain the situation to him. He wasn't even sure what the situation was.

Charles sat down behind a small table in the village school. In a small village like Samforest, there was no need for separate buildings for school, mayor's office, and the jail. So Charles had come to talk to the mayor and had been ushered into the school's only classroom.

Charles looked around the small room and then at the floor. Beneath the floor, there was the jail. It was just one small, dark, and cold room with a small barred window and one large barred wall that allowed very comfortable entrance to the cell. It was lockable, but it had been locked only twice in the history of Samforest. The first time was when children were playing in the cell and broke the key in the lock. The second time was that very evening.

The mayor had already been in the room when Charles arrived, as were two other villagers, including Stuart. The mayor was sitting behind the teacher's desk. He seemed to be rounder than he was tall, and he hardly fit behind the table. His long beard was of a similar chestnut colour as the table, which made the beard of this really large man appear to be even bigger than it was.

"I know what you came to say, but I had to take an appropriate action," the mayor said. "I know you disagree, but he is dangerous."

"He just saved us," an elderly man pointed out. He was rather short and a little overweight, though he himself just said he had "big bones". He had long, curly, snow-white beard and hair. If there had been a cult of a cheerful old man giving presents to children during winter, he would portray this man at every end-of-the-year party.

"Saved us?" the mayor growled. "Did you see the same situation I did? He caused Charles's daughter to faint with fear. He even had some discussion with that other werewolf. Now they will come for him and kill us all."

Charles put his head into his hands and sighed.

"Don't be so dramatic," said Stuart in a bored voice. He put his feet up on a little table and leaned back. "I don't like the boy either, but Simon is right. He did save us."

"He is a damn werewolf, and I don't know if you noticed, but the werewolves attacked our country. Didn't you see *The Royal Messenger*? The leaflet is on the school's notice board, if you didn't."

"Even if he is a werewolf, it doesn't necessarily mean he's our enemy," Charles pointed out. "He dragged the werewolf away from my daughter. He actually stopped him from attacking her—and then us!"

"Charles is right." Simon nodded and leaned back. He rested his hands on his stomach and burped. "The boy risked a lot to safe us. He could have just stood there and let the werewolf do as he pleased, or run away like most of the people did. This way he actually revealed himself and risked being killed by the werewolf in the process. However, he was our only defence against him. We couldn't have killed the werewolf ourselves."

"He didn't kill him, remember?" the mayor pointed out. "He actually let him go. It was all just an act, nothing more."

"That's ridiculous," Charles hissed.

There was a short silence. The mayor stood up, put his hands on the teacher's desk, and leaned forward. The desk squeaked in protest. "So, what do you propose we do?" he bellowed. "Let the boy go? He could join his comrades, and they would all come back and kill us. Maybe the boy is their spy and came to find some information about us."

"Information about what?" Charles asked. "We are completely uninteresting to anyone. We have no resources, no money, and our village is not even on an important road or close to an important area. There is nothing here that would be of any interest to anyone."

"Yet werewolves have come here twice in less than a month," the mayor replied quietly. "Coincidence? I don't think so. I still think the boy is very dangerous, but I have decided to make this someone else's problem. Therefore, I have sent a messenger to Lord Michael's soldiers."

"You did *what*!" shouted Charles and stood up so quickly that his chair hit the floor.

"Soldiers will come for him some time tomorrow," said the mayor, and he waved his hand vaguely. "You don't have to thank me."

"Thank you?" snapped Charles. Stuart's chair made a quiet thud sound as he leaned forward. "Are you out of your freaking mind?"

"No," snapped the mayor. "You are! All of you! That ... that ... *thing* could kill us all, and we could not even fight back. And you want let him go free?"

Charles watched him with his mouth hanging open. The mayor walked around the table, pushed his way among the tiny chairs in the room, and walked to the door. The other men watched him in silence. He stopped in the doorway and turned around. "If the boy is not in his cell tomorrow when the soldiers come," he said, "you will all replace him." He gave them a meaningful look and left.

They all remained silent for a while, looking after the mayor. Stuart stood up and left the room without even saying goodbye. Charles picked up his chair and sat down gloomily. "He saved Lucy." He sighed as Simon walked towards him. "He could have left. He could have run away or hidden, but instead he attacked that werewolf. I owe him my gratitude. I feel as if I let him down. He wanted to leave after lunch, you know. I persuaded him to stay for the fair. And now he's paying for that."

"Well, you can pay it back, if you want," Simon said quietly. Charles looked up at the old man. "That is, if you want to make sure that Lord Michael's soldiers don't abuse or hurt him."

Charles nodded and watched Simon leave the room. He then reached into the leather pouch on his belt and pulled out the necklace that Daniel had been wearing around his neck. It was a beautiful light-blue stone, and Charles had taken a great risk to get it before the villagers put Daniel into the jail. Luckily, they were so scared that most of them vanished when the werewolf attacked and didn't know that Daniel was wearing any jewellery. Charles had a feeling that they would not have hesitated to confiscate the gold.

Only now he had to figure out how to give it back to Daniel.

The camp was slowly growing. Lord Adrian and Lord Thomas were in charge of the new soldiers, and Ethan didn't want to step on their toes. He trusted Lord Adrian, and Lord Adrian really tried to keep records of all soldiers to make sure that no outsider or spy made his way in. However, Ethan doubted that they could prevent a spy amongst their ranks.

As he walked through the system of the caves, Ethan thought about their plans. Lord Eric was still out there getting the last cart. The fact that he still hadn't returned made Ethan a little nervous. Lord Eric's cart was supposed to be guarded the least, but further south, so the reason he was late could be anything. It didn't necessarily mean that he had encountered trouble.

Ethan had warned all the lords that the information about the carts could be a trap, but Lord Eric might have underestimated this information. He was very old fashioned in some ways, and more importantly, he preferred doing everything differently from the way Lord James would, so Ethan was surprised when he had agreed to the plan. Though the fact that Lord James had sneaked out of the cave and searched the cart all by himself was a little annoying to Ethan. He was glad that Lord James had procured the weapons and food, but the risk had been completely unnecessary. The good thing about Lord Eric was that he would never do anything so suicidal.

As Ethan walked to the edge of the cave, the sunlight fell on his face. He was in the heart of the cave complex—a beautiful and vast space completely surrounded by rock walls. There was no ceiling, so it looked like a clearing. It was their haven hidden between tall walls which made an impression of a chimney. The ground was covered in soil and grass, and Ethan wondered if they would be able to cultivate anything in that soil. Even the small amount of sun didn't bother the grass, which probably meant that the soil was very nourishing.

He noticed a box of apples on a table nearby and walked towards it. He had really liked apples ever since he was a little boy, so it was difficult for him to resist. Besides, three groups of soldiers had gone hunting and brought back enough food for the guards for two days, so no one would mind one apple. He picked up an apple and brushed it against his tunic. He had just lifted it to his mouth when someone barked behind him: "Put that back!"

He turned around with a surprised look on his face. Behind him stood a sergeant with a very stern look that turned into a shock when he recognized Ethan's face. Little drops of sweat appeared on his forehead.

"Y—Your Majesty," he stammered nervously. "I'm s—sorry. It's just … Some men are stealing apples and I thought … I—I didn't mean to … I didn't recognize—"

"As you were," Ethan said wearily. The sergeant saluted and hurried away. Ethan watched him as he left and had to smile when he saw him break into run halfway through the clearing and then into sprint at the mouth of one of the caves. He chuckled and lifted the apple to his mouth once more, but just then another guard stopped in front of him. With his hand still raised and his mouth partially opened, Ethan lifted his eyes. The guard saluted and held out some papers to him. Ethan sighed, put the apple down, and took the papers. There was another leaflet called *The Freedom Speaker* and a letter. He suspected that the letter was from Blackbird.

"Where did you get this?" he asked. The guard, still keeping his right hand by his head in a salute, pointed to the cave behind him with the other hand. Ethan looked at the cave but didn't see anyone suspicious. There was darkness in the tunnel, and there were plenty of guards.

"Lord Eric's men arrived moments ago," the soldier said as he put both hands down. "They found it not far away from the entrance."

Ethan nodded, still looking at the cave. Well, he was glad to hear that Lord Eric was back, but what had caught his attention more, were the words *not far away from the entrance*. That could mean anything. That could mean that whoever was bringing this news knew where they were, and they needed to leave their hiding place immediately, or it could mean that Blackbird was just sending these to their proximal location and the guards found it and brought it back in. The last letter had been moved from one man to another so they couldn't trace its origin, but this time it was easier. This could also mean that the first letter had come from outside the camp.

He realized that the guard still stood in front of him. He looked at him and waved him away. He wanted to check the documents and didn't need any company for that. The guard saluted again and left. Ethan watched him for a while and then leaned against the table.

First, he scanned *The Freedom Speaker*. There was some news, but it was all old news to him. The leaflet described once again to the people of Norene how Ethan had survived and was therefore still the rightful king. Ethan read the notice with a smile on his lips. He could imagine how furious Blake had to be when he read this, and it made his day. The leaflet also informed of a possible promotion of Captain Stuart and the author found this highly infuriating. Whoever wrote the notice wasn't very fond of Captain Stuart. Well, neither was Ethan.

He opened Blackbird's letter and read it. It contained much more information than the leaflet did. Blackbird wrote down the routes for the search parties that were supposed to find Ethan and the Royal Guards. It seemed that another group of the Royal Guards was causing trouble in the south, and the werewolves didn't know where to look. All the necessary information was written down including the numbers of soldiers on each route and planned dates and hours. Blackbird also warned that the schedule might change, but the routes would not. Ethan was glad to see that no route came even close to their hiding place, though he still wasn't sure if he should believe the secret informer.

The letter also mentioned another, more private, search conducted by the werewolves. Blackbird wrote of the wolf that had survived the werewolf's attack a few days before the Wolfast attacked. It seemed that the werewolves were very much interested in it; however, only to find and kill it.

Out of the corner of his eye, Ethan noticed Lord Adrian. He looked up and watched Lord Adrian in the distance. Lord James appeared in the clearing as well, walking from a cave on the other side. He stopped by Lord Adrian. They started to discuss something, and Ethan got very curious. He stepped towards his lords and headed for the centre of the clearing. "What's up?" he asked as he came closer. Lord James turned around and stepped back.

"Lord Eric just arrived," Lord Adrian announced while Lord James left them with a little bow towards Ethan. "We just received the news from his men. He's still sorting the food he brought."

"Was there any trouble?" Ethan asked. "Did Lord Eric manage this 'bandits' fight' as he calls it?"

"No, Lord Eric didn't have any problems with the bandits' type of fight, Sire," Lord Adrian said with a smile. "His men didn't even have to fight."

"Really? Why is that?" Ethan asked suspiciously.

"Well …" said Lord Adrian hesitantly, "according to Lord Eric's men, his lordship grabbed two battle-axes and ran towards the approaching cart without giving an order to attack. The men didn't know what do to, so they waited, but then one sergeant sent them after Lord Eric to help him. However, they didn't need to do that because, by the time they approached the cart, Lord Eric had killed all of the enemy soldiers."

Ethan listened intently to Lord Adrian, trying to process the information. Then he realized that his mouth was gaping open. He closed it and cleared his throat. "Lord Eric," said Ethan in a hollow voice. Lord Adrian nodded. "We're talking about a small, skinny, seventy-year-old man who looks as if he is already dead and just hasn't noticed?"

"Actually, he's only sixty-five, Sire," said Lord Adrian with a grin.

"Is he injured?" Ethan asked with a little concern in his voice.

"No, Sire," Lord Adrian shook his head. "He has only a few scratches; nothing serious."

"Right. Well, at least we have food and weapons." Ethan sighed and handed Blackbird's letter to Lord Adrian, "Now we need to figure out what to do with this."

CHAPTER 9

B ess sat in the library going through the king's journals. At first, he had looked for Ethan's journal, but there either was none or he had it with him. However, in the other journals, he found some interesting information on history of Norene. Bess learned that, in the last hundred years, Norene had made much bigger progress than anyone had suspected.

He finished the last page of King Michael's journal and closed the book. Only significant events were usually described in kings' journals, and King Michael had had a short and rather boring reign. Someone else wrote at the end of the journal the date of the king's death and the official reason. King Michael had been overweight and had had a heart attack during dinner. Bess thought that very suspicious, but then again, maybe it was really only a heart attack. Not all rulers were ruthless like the werewolves.

He tossed the journal on top of others that he'd already read and rubbed his eyes. He sighed and picked up another journal. He hoped this one would be more eventful than the previous one. It looked very old and very used. It seemed that the owner probably carried it with him everywhere he went. He opened the journal and looked at the first page. The name was written in a beautiful handwriting. His tiredness faded away immediately. He straightened up and leaned over the journal with raising excitement. The name John Mathewson stared back at him. He flipped through the pages. The beginning was about Mathewson's desire for Norene's freedom. After that, he had written about the preparations. All successes and failures were recorded. It seemed as if King John really wanted to record everything as it happened, not as he wished it to be remembered.

Bess flipped some more pages and stopped in the middle of the journal.

He read the recollection of the battle between Norene and Wolfast. It seemed surreal, and Bess suspected that King John made it sound more romantic than it actually was. In Wolfast, there weren't many records on the battle for Norene's freedom, and no precise description existed. Therefore, Bess had no frame of reference when he read King John's diary.

Ten pages later, King John described the first coronation in thousands of years. It was really grandiose. Bess suspected that it was done to anger Wolfast. He turned another page, read a few lines, and froze. King John had written:

> When I returned to the castle's office, a man stood by the window, a stranger who had got through the guards and inside the most guarded room in the castle without anyone seeing him. The stranger was very tall and big, but what frightened me were his eyes. I had never seen glowing green eyes like that before.

Bess read the last sentence three times, still not believing his eyes. It had to be about Rex, or whatever his name was. He continued reading:

> He talked of some stone that was most likely in Norene. He offered me a lot of money and weapons if I would help him to find it, but I refused. No money or any other bribe would make me help him. There was something wrong about the man. He left without any problem, and I hope I will never see him again. Those weird eyes of a murderer will haunt me in my dreams. I just hope that he never finds that stone. My gut tells me that he should never get possession of it. Ever!

Bess put down the diary and looked at the opposite wall where the shelves containing hundreds of books on the history of Norene stood. Since the werewolves could live for centuries, Bess didn't really wonder how the man could still be around after one hundred years. The man could actually be around much longer than that. Bess returned to King John's journal and continued reading. He was determined to find out more about this stranger and the stone.

Lord Michael walked onto the balcony of Royal Castle and looked at the camp inside the castle's walls. He could see many tents below him, but not as many as he would like to be there. The battle had been really devastating for them, and the worst part was that Blake didn't seem to realize it. Wolfast's army camped further south, but their numbers were even smaller than Blake's. A rumour had spread that the ranks were getting even smaller because the Royal Guards were attacking them on regular bases.

Lord Michael hadn't seen Blake at all since the battle. He had met Mors only twice and really didn't like the man. Bess was easier to find, since he was always in the library, but he was very secretive and gave away hardly any information. Captain Stuart wasn't ranked high enough to be given any important information, though it seemed that he always knew the best of what was going on in the castle. However, even if he had any relevant information, he would not give that information away. All in all, Lord Michael didn't have any information on the current status. All he could work with were some rumours.

Lord Martin joined Lord Michael on the balcony and stopped by the railing. He leaned against it and scanned the camp below them. They stood in silence for a while, and then Lord Martin sighed. "How many soldiers?" he asked.

"Thirty-eight, so far," Lord Michael answered quietly, not taking his eyes off the tents. "There is a gossip that Lord James survived. It's dangerous talk. I'm afraid we can expect more deserters."

Lord Martin nodded, leaned further down, and placed his chin on top of his hands, which were resting on the railings. The camp was full of life in the evening. The soldiers usually started multiple fires and entertained themselves by the firelight while they ate their dinner. The sun was setting, and soon the fires would be the only source of light in the yard.

Lord Michael started to wonder where everything had gone wrong. He no longer believed that Blake would become king. There was no way for them to find Ethan in Norene. It was a small country, but not that small. They were supposed to leave the castle and search for Ethan and his lords on Blake's orders, but Lord Michael couldn't see any sense in that. It would be easier to find a needle in a haystack. The fact that Blake had suggested the search and the werewolves approved it showed that they were very nervous. The rumours circulated that Captain Stuart had protested against this action, but he hadn't changed their minds.

"I thought that no one would dare to desert Captain Stuart's ranks." Lord Martin broke Lord Michael's train of thoughts.

Lord Michael sniggered a little. "Maybe that heartless bastard is the reason they desert," he said, looking at Lord Martin, but Lord Martin didn't even smile.

"He might be a heartless bastard," whispered Lord Martin hoarsely, "but he's not stupid. It seems we have a spy in our ranks, and I'm sure he already knows who it is."

Lord Michael eyed Lord Martin nervously. It was very dangerous to talk about spies in the same castle where Captain Stuart was. True, there were rumours amongst the soldiers. The fact that the resupply carts hadn't arrived didn't help the matter at all. But to discuss this was very dangerous. Captain Stuart had ears everywhere and could sniff out even the smallest piece of dirt. Lord Michael looked over his shoulder to make sure that they were still alone. It wasn't a good idea to badmouth the man because he could be their equal one day. At least the rumours suggested as much.

"It's not working," Lord Martin whispered. "Blake was supposed to be king already, and Ethan was supposed to be dead. We were supposed to be out of here. I sometimes wish I had never agreed to all of this."

"I'm sure it's just a matter of time." Lord Michael shrugged. He wanted to be positive about their situation, but it was rather difficult. He looked at the camp below them and sighed. "It will end soon, one way or the other."

Daniel jerked awake and sat up abruptly. He looked around ignoring the pain in his head. He wasn't surprised by the pain; he knew he'd been knocked out. He only hoped that everyone was safe. The last thing he could remember was the werewolf running away, but he had no other information. The fact that his head still hurt meant that it was the same day, or the next morning. The pain didn't bother him. It was annoying, true, but it was of no concern to him. He knew he would heal soon.

He was in a cell, though he didn't know the word for it. The barred door and window made it clear that he was not a welcomed guest there. A low sun shone inside and illuminated the very sombre space. He wasn't sure if it was a sunrise or a sunset because he had no idea which way the window faced.

He was naked, lying on a wooden bench. Though he was covered with a warm blanket, he was a little cold. He looked down at his chest, and a panic rose inside him. The necklace was gone. He hoped that he'd lost it in the village, and that the villagers hadn't taken it. He had to figure out how to get out of the cell and then find the necklace. He looked at the door and noticed that his shirt and trousers—or, to be precise, Charles's shirt and trousers—lay on the floor nearby.

He swung his legs off the bench and winced at the pain in his back. He straightened a little, and a sharp pain shot up his back. At first he was surprised that his back hurt, but then again, he probably had hit the ground hard when he was knocked out.

The blanket slid off, and he immediately felt cold. As he grabbed his shirt and trousers, something fell to the ground with a soft clinking sound. He looked down and saw the necklace by his feet. Surprised, he picked it up. He couldn't believe his eyes. It was clear that he had an ally outside the cell.

Quickly, he put the necklace around his neck and gingerly put on the clothes. His head really hurt, and the pain shot through his back every now and then, so he tried to move as little as possible. Once he had his shirt on, he hid the necklace inside, hoping that no one would notice it.

He looked around looking for the shoes, but didn't see any. Well, he had shaken them off along with the trousers on the square. Maybe they'd got lost, or whoever put him in the cell didn't think he would need them. He covered his feet with the blanket to keep warm and leaned against the cold stone wall. He closed his eyes and sighed.

So, he was as good as dead. There was no way they would listen to him. He had changed to wolf form, and they had seen him. No one would believe that he was not a werewolf. Even he had his doubts. He could try to plead his innocence. He had attacked the werewolf and tried to protect the villagers, and though he had been knocked out and was not sure how the whole situation had ended, he was more than certain that no one had been hurt. All that thanks to him.

He heard some voices approaching and opened his eyes. He didn't want to attack anyone, but he was determined to use the first opportunity to run away from Samforest. He just needed to get to the borders of the village. He couldn't outrun everyone, but once he was close to the forest, he could try to get away.

A loud snore drowned out the footsteps. Daniel straightened up and looked at the door. He noticed a man sitting outside the cell. The guard snored loudly and jerked. He looked around with a bewildered look on his face and quickly stood up. He dusted himself off and then looked at the stairs. The footsteps echoed in the underground dungeon, and the mayor and three soldiers entered into view. They all came to the bars and stopped. Daniel's and the mayor's gazes met, and the mayor looked away with an uneasy look on his face. The soldiers looked Daniel up and down with disgust.

"Open the cell," one of the soldiers commanded while the other two lifted their crossbows and took aim. Daniel pulled the blanket off his feet. Watching the arrow points, he slowly stood up.

"Stay where you are!" snapped the first soldier. "If you try anything, we'll shoot you."

Daniel nodded slowly to make it clear that he understood. The guard fished a key out of a bag that hung from his belt and handed it to the mayor, who was still looking at the ground. The guard stood there for a while with the key in his shaking hand and then coughed softly. The mayor jumped up, startled, and looked at the guard wide eyed. His gaze fell to the key in the guard's hand, and he took it with a shaky hand. The guard hurried towards the stairs immediately while the mayor unlocked the cell.

The mayor opened the barred door and quickly stepped away from the range of the archers. The first soldier entered the cell and pulled handcuffs from behind his belt. Daniel wasn't sure what the handcuffs were for, so he just stood there, awaiting some instructions. The soldier stopped in front of him and hesitated. Eyeing Daniel, he took Daniel's hands one by one and quickly handcuffed him. Only when Daniel's hands were cuffed did he seem a bit at ease. He looked into Daniel's eyes and grinned. "So, this is the famous wolf that killed a werewolf," he whispered. Daniel turned pale. Maybe the humans were more intelligent than he had given them credit for.

One soldier, who was still standing outside the cell, put the crossbow down, entered the cell, and grabbed Daniel's shoulder. He led Daniel out of the dungeon, carrying the crossbow in the other hand. Daniel didn't resist nor say anything, though he had a little trouble keeping up. He knew he stood no chance in the dungeon, so there was no point in attacking the soldiers there. He had to plan his escape carefully. Attacking the soldiers inside the building would be suicide. He needed better odds.

They walked out of the dungeon and into the bright blinding daylight through a room that was full of little tables and chairs. Daniel saw the forest in the distance and could immediately tell that it was early morning. The sun was still rising, and the village was very quiet.

He realized that his escape plan had a major flaw. There were too many soldiers outside. Then he noticed Charles in the crowd. He and an elderly man were talking to one of the soldiers, who was sitting on a horse. The soldier's uniform was different from those of the rest of the soldiers, and Daniel understood that he was leading the other men. He looked at Daniel and nodded. Whatever that meant, it was a signal for Charles, who hurried towards Daniel. "How do you feel?" he asked as soon as he got within an earshot. Daniel thought that Charles would be angry and was very relieved when he saw a smile on his face.

"I'm handcuffed, my head and back really hurt, and I am a little cold. Oh, and I don't know what's going on. But other than that, I'm fine."

"It could be worse," said Charles.

"Yeah, I could be dead!" Daniel nodded. "One can't have everything. Who's that fellow?" he asked, looking at the old man.

"That's Simon. He used to be a teacher here when he was younger. These days, he just sits and reads in his garden. He helped me to persuade the lieutenant to let us go with you. The mayor called Lord Michael's soldiers yesterday after he locked you up in the jail."

"I don't blame him," said Daniel, and he looked at the mayor who quickly looked away. "The entire village saw me change."

Charles didn't say anything. He followed Daniel's gaze and shot the mayor a black look. Simon slowly walked towards them, but before he could come closer, one of the soldiers grabbed Daniel's left arm and dragged him to the horses. Daniel hadn't expected that at all. He lost his balance and fell to the ground. The soldier pulled him to his feet and tossed him to another soldier, who grabbed him and pushed him onto a cart.

The horse pulling the cart got very nervous, flipping its ears in all directions. It neighed and stepped back, pulling the cart with it. Another soldier grabbed the reins and tried to ease the horse, but it was getting more and more nervous. Other horses around them had similar reactions to the new arrival, and the soldiers had some trouble calming them down.

"This will be an interesting ride," Charles said to Simon as he mounted his horse.

Captain Stuart stood by the entrance to the castle and went through the list of available food. Since the food supplies hadn't arrived, they needed some other way of getting food. He was just trying to calculate the remaining number of days, when Lieutenant Sven appeared next to him. "Sir, please, come with me," he said in a shaky voice, and he stepped back expecting Captain Stuart to follow him.

Captain Stuart hesitated. He was in no mood to follow a lieutenant without knowing the reason. He outranked the man and deserved to know all the information beforehand. On the other hand, this could be important. "Why?" he asked as he stepped forward. The lieutenant looked over his shoulder at the gate and then back again. That gave Captain Stuart the willies. He wondered if the Royal Guards might be standing in front of the castle.

"Ehm … We caught a deserter," Lieutenant Sven whispered.

Captain Stuart looked at the tents around him and decided to follow the lieutenant without any more questions. The situation in the camp had been very difficult in the last few days, and the less information that passed to the soldiers the better. He stepped forward with the list of food in his left hand and followed Lieutenant Sven to the gate. As he followed the nervous lieutenant, he wondered why so many soldiers had deserted. Though the Royal Guards were better soldiers than Lord Blake's, Captain Stuart expected more professional behaviour from his men.

Since the Royal Guards were currently scattered somewhere in the mountains, Lord Blake wanted to create new Royal Guards from the soldiers he already had and then train new soldiers as part of his former army. Unfortunately, even the number of current soldiers was getting smaller with each day. The more Captain Stuart thought about this, the more he was sure that the presence of the werewolves in the castle had something to do with it.

As they walked through the yard, the soldiers watched them curiously. Captain Stuart tried to look as disinterested as always, but the lieutenant was obviously nervous. By the time they reached the other end of the yard, a few hundred soldiers were watching them.

Lieutenant Sven led Captain Stuart to the castle walls. There was a little tower by the gate which contained the drawbridge mechanism and stairs to the top of the walls. They entered the tower and stopped in the semi-darkness of the room. Captain Stuart had to wait a few seconds for his eyes to adjust, and then he noticed one of his sergeants. He was handcuffed and held by two soldiers. The sergeant looked up, and when he saw Captain Stuart, he narrowed his eyes.

Captain Stuart didn't have to say that the feeling was mutual; the emotion appeared on his face clear and loud. "What do we have here?" Captain Stuart asked, not taking his eyes off the sergeant.

"We caught him below the drawbridge, sir," Lieutenant Sven said from behind Captain Stuart. The sergeant tried to shake off the soldiers, but they held him tight.

Captain Stuart looked at him with his eyebrow raised. "What do you have to say for yourself?" he asked the sergeant.

Instead of an answer, the sergeant spat at Captain Stuart's boots. Captain Stuart looked down at his polished boots and then back up at the sergeant. His jaw tightened as he stepped closer to the sergeant. The sergeant lifted his chin and looked back defiantly. Captain Stuart curled fingers of his right hand into a fist and took a deep breath. The sergeant kept looking into the captain's eyes. They stood silently for a while facing each other.

"Lock him up," Captain Stuart ordered through his teeth, and he stepped back, releasing his fist. "He will be executed tomorrow morning in the yard—just to remind everyone what happens to deserters."

The sergeant's expression didn't change as the soldiers took him away. He shot a last glance at Captain Stuart from the door and calmly went with the soldiers. Captain Stuart stepped out of the tower and watched them from the door all the way to the entrance to the dungeon. He noticed that the soldiers in the yard stopped and watched them too. There would be some rumours soon, but they should be cleared by the next morning. The execution would be public and official.

When they had vanished into the castle, Captain Stuart turned to the lieutenant who immediately jumped to attention. "Prepare some simple gallows in the yard, maybe underneath the tree that is next to the stables," he said calmly. "Nothing fancy, just use a barrel from the warehouse and a branch of the tree. Prepare it now, but set it up tomorrow morning before the execution. I don't want the soldiers to have too much to discuss during the night."

The lieutenant nodded, saluted, and hurried through the yard to the warehouse. Captain Stuart watched him for a while and then slowly walked through the yard to the castle. He looked at the papers in his left hand and pretended to be studying them. Out of the corner of his eye, he noticed that a lot of his soldiers stopped and peeked at him as he went by, trying to be inconspicuous.

He entered the castle and walked up the stairs to his office deep in thought. The desertion of soldiers was one thing. The desertion of officers was something else altogether. He had already banned trips to the city two days ago, but that had only sped up the desertion rate. The soldiers found their way out of the castle. And he was determined to find out how they were doing it.

CHAPTER 10

E than crept between the trees to the spot where Lord James stood. Lord James was leaning against a tree trying to have a better look at the road in front of him. Behind a bush next to the tree, Lord Adrian squatted, peering through the branches.

"How many?" Lord James hissed toward Lord Adrian as Ethan reached them and crouched next to Lord Adrian.

"Twenty soldiers, two civilians, and one prisoner," Lord Adrian whispered. Lord James nodded slowly. He readied his bow and motioned to five archers who were stationed behind another bush. They got ready and awaited the signal.

"The civilians seem to be important," Lord Adrian said. "They are not handcuffed and are travelling by cart. They seem to belong to the cart, or to the prisoner."

Ethan looked at the approaching cart and soldiers over the bush. The Royal Guards were well situated, and twenty soldiers would be no problem for them. It was all just a matter of timing. The only thing that bothered him was that Blackbird hadn't even mentioned the cart and the soldiers. Did it mean that he was leading them on and didn't want them to get to this particular cart or that he just hadn't known about it?

"Twenty soldiers escorting one prisoner and two civilians," Lord Adrian whispered to Ethan. "That's highly suspicious."

Ethan nodded and studied the prisoner. It was a boy—maybe sixteen years old, maybe a little older. He was handcuffed and under constant surveillance. The fact that twenty soldiers escorted one boy could mean the boy was dangerous or very important.

"I wonder," Lord James whispered and leaned closer, "why so many soldiers for one prisoner. Are they scared that something will happen to him or are they scared of him?"

"You want to ask them, my lord?" Ethan asked with a grin on his face. There was a snigger from Lord Adrian.

"Maybe we should send out Lord Eric," Lord James added as he watched the cart approaching. He raised his hand to give a signal for attack. Ten more archers further down the road got ready.

Ethan and Lord Adrian exchanged glances. Ethan was really curious. What would Lord Eric do if they told him to go there and sort it out? On the other hand, none of the soldiers he had attacked earlier had survived, and Ethan wanted the prisoner and the civilians alive.

"The boy might be important," Ethan said at last. He signalled for the rest of the archers to get ready. Fifteen bows were aiming on the unsuspecting soldiers on the road.

"Or a werewolf," added Lord James. Ethan thought about that for a while. He noticed that the wind was blowing towards them, which should have kept their position hidden in case a werewolf was indeed on the cart. He suspected that his lords hadn't chosen this side of the road by accident.

"Well, let's find out which it is, shall we?" he said at last. "Prepare for the attack. But—I want the civilians and the prisoner alive and, if possible, unharmed," he added and looked at Lord James. Lord James nodded and quickly joined the archers.

Daniel looked at the treetops. There were no birds in the trees, or even in the sky. This was unusual for this part of the country. Norene was full of birds and wildlife. The cart hit a little indentation in the road, and Daniel was thrown to the side of the cart for the millionth time that morning. He winced at the pain and pushed himself away from the wooden boards.

The scarcity of birds could be explained by the noise the soldiers and the cart made. The soldiers were very cautious, but they didn't bother to be very quiet. After three hours of driving, they had to pass a village, and they chose to go through the forests over uneven ground, which was a torture to Daniel, who couldn't use his hands to steady himself.

Suddenly, Daniel realized that the forest was also lacking any animals, yet it seemed to him that there were some sounds and some motion between the trees. All his senses were screaming for him to run away. There was something strange going on nearby.

The cart hit another indentation, and Daniel was once more thrown to the side. He hit the same spot and yelped from the pain. "We should stop for a rest." He heard Charles's voice. He looked at Charles, who had a concerned look on his face. Simon, behind him, was dozing off on the horse's back and hardy paid any attention to the road. Daniel tore his eyes off Charles and scanned the trees and branches. For a moment, he thought he saw a flash of blue colour between the branches, but when he focused on the spot, he couldn't see anything. He wished the wind was blowing the other way. It would enable him to smell any danger. Unfortunately, the wind wasn't kind enough.

Charles spurred his horse a little and approached the cart. Daniel didn't take his eyes off the forest; he only motioned his head in the direction of the bush they were approaching. "There's something there," he whispered.

Charles followed his gaze and shrugged. "Probably just some wild animal. This forest should be safe. No bandits are in these parts. Besides, only a mad man would attack twenty soldiers."

Daniel still watched the bush where he had seen the blue flash. He hadn't seen anything recognizable, but he had that strange feeling that something was watching him. He knew Charles was right. No bandits, solitary madman, or animal would attack a convoy like the one they formed, but maybe there was something else hidden in the forest. He was tempted to warn the lieutenant in charge, but his dislike for the man stopped him.

"Oh, don't worry, Danny," Simon said encouragingly. "There is nothing in these woods more dangerous than twenty soldiers escorting a werewolf."

Daniel slowly turned around and looked at Simon. He hadn't thought about his situation in that way, and it was no picnic for him. Simon flushed and looked at Charles, who was angrily frowning at him.

"I was just trying to put him at ease," Simon said with a nervous smile.

Daniel looked back at the trees as they passed. Even though the forest made him nervous, Simon's words, which were echoing in his head loudly, made him forget about the forest for a while. He knew Simon had every right to think that Daniel was a werewolf, but that didn't make it any better. Daniel couldn't help but admit that he had to be a werewolf—a strange one, true, but still a werewolf.

"What makes you think there is something?" asked Charles, who was watching the forest as well. Everything around them looked peaceful and quiet.

"Well, there are no birds here," Daniel answered.

"Probably flew away when we came." Charles shrugged. "We are making quite a ruckus. Animals don't like that."

"True." Daniel nodded deep in thought. "However, the forest is way too quiet. Besides, I saw something blue over there."

Charles followed Daniel's gaze and looked at the bush that was now only a few feet away. He nodded slowly. There really was something behind the bush that seemed out of place. Suddenly, arrows flew from the deeper part of the forest with a hissing sound.

Daniel stood up, surprised, and the cart horses stopped abruptly. They took a step back, and the cart rattled in protest, throwing Daniel back. He hit the planks on the side and fell off the cart, hitting the wheel on the way. He landed heavily onto the ground, and the landing knocked the breath out of him. He felt as if his lungs were painfully trying to absorb the shock of the fall. His entire chest hurt, and the only thought in his mind was that he needed air—at least a little bit. He wasn't even sure what was happening around him, and he didn't care. He hardly noticed that Charles was leaning above him saying something.

It felt like ages, but Daniel finally managed to draw breath. He looked to the side and stared into the dead stare of one of the soldiers. Charles pulled Daniel to his feet and gently shook him. Daniel didn't take his eyes off the arrow that was sticking out of the dead soldier's chest. His arms were spread, and his face was frozen in an expression of utter shock, his glassy gaze turned to the cart.

Charles shook Daniel once more, but Daniel didn't pay him any attention. Charles let go of Daniel's shoulder and raised his arms into the air. Daniel looked at him, baffled, and then followed his gaze. He turned around and took a step back. A soldier was aiming an arrow tipped with silver at him. He gulped and raised his handcuffed hands.

"The royal coat of arms," Simon breathed out somewhere behind

Charles. Daniel didn't even notice him there and didn't care. All his focus was on the arrow in front of him.

"Does that mean they're the good guys?" Charles whispered nervously, eyeing the arrows around them.

"I think the good guys are those who don't kill us," said Daniel.

"Why shouldn't we kill you?" a voice from the forest asked. Daniel looked up from the arrow and turned to see the man. All he could see was his silhouette because he was hidden among the trees. Charles was squinting into the forest as if he couldn't see anything.

"Well," Daniel said and hesitated. It was hard to focus with a silver arrow in front of him. "Maybe the right question would be why you should."

The silhouette leaned against the tree and folded his arms. Charles nervously shifted from foot to foot. The man in the forest didn't move a muscle. Daniel gulped and looked at Charles.

"You know what they say," Charles said at last with a trembling voice looking at the forest in general. It seemed that he really didn't see the man at all. He just answered in the direction of the coming voice. "The enemy of my enemy is my friend."

The man in the forest didn't move; neither did the bowmen who were obviously waiting for his orders. Daniel could hear his own heart beat in the silence. "Bring them with us," the man commanded at last, and he disappeared into the forest.

"Come on," one of the bowmen snapped, and he grabbed Daniel's shoulder. Daniel winced at the pain in his back. The adrenalin was slowly leaving his body, and he realized that the fall from the cart would most likely have some after effect. It was a miracle he hadn't broken his neck in that fall.

The soldier took Daniel back onto the cart and pulled him up. Charles and Simon followed without a word. The attackers took away the dead soldiers and covered the puddles of blood on the ground with dirt and dry leaves. As the cart moved forward, Daniel saw that some of the guards were digging a big grave. He was really glad he wouldn't be in that grave. Even a werewolf—or whatever he was—wouldn't survive being buried alive.

The cart rattled through the forest until they reached the mountains. Two hours later, they entered a huge cave. Daniel was really nervous, but he didn't dare to say or do anything. He just looked around the place. There were many soldiers who walked around them. Daniel noticed a tall man in the corner who was talking to another much younger man. The first man seemed to be out of place because of his different skin and eyes. He was well built, and his dark hair seemed almost black.

"Look, look, look," Simon hissed as he watched the men as well. Charles turned around and looked at the men in the corner. "That's the king and Lord James!"

Charles nodded slowly, watching the men. Daniel wasn't sure what that meant for him. He had seen a picture of King Phillip once, and he had assumed that all kings had white beards, yet one of the men seemed to be too young, and the other too foreign.

"Do you realize where we are?" Simon asked excited as he looked at a frowning Charles. Charles slowly nodded and looked sideways at Daniel. And then Daniel understood. He knew that the werewolves had attacked Norene. The people in Samforest had been discussing it. The official news was that the king had died on the battlefield, and Lord Blake had to turn back the attack and save the kingdom. Seeing the king here meant that the news was false. And the king would probably consider that Daniel was another werewolf who could have interesting information about the situation or was too dangerous to be around.

The king listened intently to whatever Lord James was saying and then nodded. Lord James made a little bow and departed. Another soldier came to Ethan and handed him a key. Ethan took it and walked to the cart.

The soldier who had put Daniel onto the cart climbed up and helped Daniel down. Charles and Simon followed. They all stood by the cart and watched as the king approached them. When Ethan came closer, he handed the key to one of the soldiers. The soldier used it to unlock Daniel's handcuffs. Daniel could smell that, though Ethan acted relaxed, he was a little nervous. He also knew that the soldiers around them were obviously ready for an attack. Daniel wouldn't dare to attack them, but he doubted that they would believe him even if he told them so.

"What are your names?" Ethan asked as the soldier stepped away from Daniel with the handcuffs in his hands. Daniel massaged his wrists silently, not daring to speak.

"I'm Simon. This is Daniel, and this is Charles," said Simon politely, motioning towards each man.

"Fascinating," said Ethan in an even voice as he fixed his gaze upon Daniel. "What were you accused of?" he asked quietly.

Daniel looked up at him and shrugged. "I don't know. They didn't tell me," he said. This was true. The mayor had called the soldiers because he thought Daniel was a werewolf, yet the soldiers had been informed that he was the wolf. No one had ever mentioned any official reason.

Ethan put his head to one side and smiled. He looked at Charles, who took this as a quiet order to explain the situation. "It all happened yesterday, Your Majesty. There was a fair in our village. Everything went well until the moment three drunken guys started to cause some problems. Daniel, here, knocked them out, but since Daniel was new to our village and the guys were born there, the mayor accused Daniel of riotous conduct and called Lord Michael's soldiers. With Simon, here, we went along to explain everything to his lordship."

Ethan looked from Charles to Daniel and back again. Daniel's mouth gaped open at this explanation, but he quickly realized he'd better close it. Daniel had a suspicion that Ethan didn't believe the story.

Ethan looked down at Daniel's bare feet and raised an eyebrow. He looked up and said something to one of the guards. The guard nodded and left.

"Are you hungry?" Ethan asked suddenly, addressing the question to Daniel. Daniel opened his mouth to answer, but his stomach answered for him with a loud growl. Ethan smiled and motioned for them to follow him. Though Ethan seemed relaxed and very calm, Daniel couldn't help but notice that the guards around them were on the alert. Most of them had bows or crossbows with silver-tipped arrows at hand, and Daniel suspected that he was the reason.

They walked through the cave. It was filled with men who were cleaning their swords and getting ready for a battle. Ethan led them to the clearing surrounded by the mountains, and Daniel looked around in awe. He loved the place at first sight. It seemed so safe and peaceful even with hundreds of armed men walking around. In the middle of the clearing were some fires. Ethan led them to the one in the middle.

"M'lords," he said as they came closer, "meet our guests, Daniel,

Charles, and Simon." He pointed out the men around the fire as he said to the newcomers, "These are Lords Eric, Thomas, James, and Adrian."

"Sit down," said Lord Adrian, motioning towards a vacant log. Daniel sat down next to Lord James and smiled nervously at him. Lord James handed him a piece of bread. Daniel thanked him and took the bread. Somehow he had a feeling that the situation had been staged, but he wasn't sure what to expect.

Ethan sat down as well, and they all listened to Simon's explanation of the situation. Simon, as Charles had, altered some information. Daniel felt like a big hero. He listened to the discussion, slowly chewing on the bread and watching the flames in fascination. While Simon and Charles were talking about the rumours they'd heard, the meal was cooked. After a while, Daniel stopped listening to the conversations around the fire and got lost in his thoughts.

Lord Adrian poked the fire with a stick, and several sparks flew into the air. Daniel watched them with interest, but then something else got his attention. He smelled a sudden change around him. The guards and the lords became a bit nervous. Lord James handed a plate over to Daniel who took it absentmindedly, still focusing on the smell.

"No!" screamed Simon suddenly, and Charles sprang to his feet. Plenty of arrows were suddenly pointing in Daniel's direction, and Ethan quickly lifted his hand to prevent the men from shooting. Daniel looked around, dumbstruck. Everything around them went dead silent, and everyone in the camp was watching them.

Daniel looked down at the plate in his hand. There was a chicken leg and a piece of bread. He didn't understand what the fuss was all about, but then he noticed that the plate was silver. His heart started to beat very fast, but he tried to keep his calm and looked up. "Ehm ... what's wrong?" he asked innocently. Ethan waved the guards away, and the arrows were lowered one by one.

"It didn't burn you?" asked Lord Adrian, and he leaned closer to have a better view.

"Why should it burn me?" asked Daniel. He was shaking a little and was really glad when Simon took the plate from his hands.

"We thought you were a werewolf," explained Lord James, watching

Daniel's unharmed hand suspiciously. Daniel's heart missed a beat. Did this mean that he wasn't a werewolf after all?

"Why would you think that?" Simon asked surprised.

"Some interesting news reached us even here in this cave," Ethan said, not taking his eyes off Daniel. "About a huge group of enemy soldiers escorting a werewolf."

"He's not a werewolf," snapped Charles as he sat back down.

"You two seemed to be pretty surprised yourselves when that silver didn't hurt him," Ethan retorted. He looked from Charles to Simon, awaiting some explanation.

Simon shrugged and gave Daniel sideway look. "Well, I don't know about Charles ... But I was obviously wrong," Simon admitted. He set the plate aside.

Daniel eyed the plate. He was very hungry and wanted to take the plate, but it was too far away, and he didn't dare to stand up to reach for it. The chicken looked very inviting, and the smell was making his stomach growl.

"You thought he was a *werewolf*?" Lord Adrian asked in an even voice. His eyebrow rose. "You forgot to mention that little piece of information."

Simon shifted uneasily. Daniel tore his eyes off the plate and focused on the conversation. The situation was turning worse.

"I didn't want you to judge him before you got to know him ..." Simon tried to explain, but his voice trailed off. There was a silence around the fire for a while. Ethan looked from Simon to Daniel, and their eyes met. Daniel wasn't sure what to do, so he smiled at Ethan.

"Will you tell us why you thought he was a werewolf?" Ethan asked without taking his eyes off Daniel. Daniel's smile froze. "Our mistake could be simply misinformation, or we apprehended a wrong man. What is the reason for your *mistake*?"

"Well ..." Charles hesitated and looked at Daniel. Daniel had a huge urge to stand up and run away, but he knew it would do him no good. The caves were full of armed men with silver-tipped arrows who knew how to kill a werewolf. Charles hesitated and then put down his plate. He looked into the fire, and Daniel could smell fear coming from Charles.

"I don't think that Daniel is a werewolf. Never thought that," Charles said, not taking his eyes of the fire. Daniel could feel drops of sweat on his forehead. "A few days ago, a werewolf came to the forest and attacked a wolf."

Daniel looked down. He felt warmth creeping into his face. Unlike the last time, when Lucy was the reason, this time the feeling was not agreeable at all. He could feel the stares fixed upon him.

"The wolf survived, but the werewolf got killed," Charles continued. "Then three days ago ..." Charles hesitated and looked at Daniel, "Well, we found Daniel in the forest. A wolf had attacked him. He was unconscious, and we took him to my house. Yesterday he felt much better, so he went with us to the village fair, but another werewolf came."

"The name of that village wouldn't happen to be Samforest, would it?" Ethan asked calmly.

Charles opened his mouth in surprise and slowly nodded. "How did you know?"

"We have some information on the situation as well," Ethan replied. "Please, continue. What happened after the second werewolf came?"

"He ... he changed and attacked, but Daniel ... well ... he ... he stopped him. The werewolf then ran away."

A stunned silence filled the air. Though Charles hadn't said *how* Daniel stopped the werewolf, it was clear that everyone had come to the same conclusion. Especially since Charles and Simon had suspected that Daniel was a werewolf.

Daniel risked a glance at Ethan, who was watching him with a furrowed brow. He was slowly stroking his chin, and when their stares met, he smiled at Daniel. Daniel felt a little relief and smiled back. Ethan picked up the plate that Simon had placed nearby and walked over to Daniel. He handed the plate to him.

Daniel looked at him wide-eyed and hesitantly took the plate, his stomach growling loudly. He wanted to say something, but his voice was suddenly too weak to produce a sound. He smiled at Ethan, hoping that the message was clear, and he was relieved when Ethan smiled back. Ethan glanced at Lord Adrian and walked away from the fireplace. Lord Adrian put aside his own plate with a little sigh and then followed the king.

Ethan walked through the clearing deep in thought. Lord Adrian followed at his heels as he wiped his hands and face in a piece of cloth. They stopped by the entrance to the southern cave, and Ethan turned to face the fireplace. Daniel was quickly eating the chicken, and the rest of the men by the fire were talking among themselves. Ethan had to smile when he watched Daniel. The boy reminded him of a hungry puppy with something very tasty.

"What do you make of this, Your Majesty?" Lord Adrian asked as Ethan still watched the fireplace in silence. "Do you believe them?"

Ethan's smile froze. He chewed on his cheek for a while, watching the fireplace in the distance. He wasn't sure what to think. "Well, though it was implied, they didn't say that he changed to wolf during that fight," he said after a while. "The boy held the silver plate without getting hurt, which technically rules out the werewolf theory. And if he really is that wolf from the forest, I doubt that he would be smart enough to have all these conversations with us."

"He didn't say much," Lord Adrian pointed out.

Ethan thought about this for a second and then nodded slowly, trying to sort all the information. "The fact that twenty soldiers went with him indicates that the story is true. I mean *twenty* soldiers for *one* boy!"

"Maybe they too thought that he was a werewolf," Lord Adrian said.

"Maybe." Ethan nodded hesitantly. "There's another thing that puzzles me. If this Blackbird sends us all the necessary information and he didn't notify us about this supposed werewolf in our vicinity, does it mean that he didn't know or that the rest of the information is part of a trap, and he didn't want us to find out about the boy?"

"I honestly don't know. There is a possibility that he didn't know. According to their story, the whole situation happened quite fast."

Ethan reached into a bag hanging from his belt, retrieved a piece of paper, and handed it to Lord Adrian. It was small and rather dirty, yet the writing on it seemed fresh. There was a short notice:

A wolf in human form is taken by twenty soldiers from Samforest to Royal Castle. They will pass the main path around noon. Don't let them get him!

Lord Adrian read the note and then looked towards the fireplace. Lord Eric gave Daniel another piece of chicken, and Daniel wrenched it from his hands. Everyone by the fire laughed.

Lord Adrian looked at Ethan mystified. "How did you get this? And when?"

"When we returned with the boy, one of the soldiers gave it to me. He had found it near the entrance."

"You just said that Blackbird didn't notify us about—"

"This isn't the same handwriting," Ethan said, interrupting Lord Adrian. "And there is no signature. Besides, the note was found *after* noon. It could have been sent too late to make sure we didn't get to the boy, yet to create impression that the informer was trying to help us. Also, it's unclear to whom it is addressed. 'Don't let them get him!' Did the author mean that we weren't supposed to let the werewolves have the boy, or that we are the ones who weren't supposed to get him? If the second is the case, to whom was the notice sent?"

"I think it was meant for us to find and read," Lord Adrian said slowly. "Another question is, What are our plans for the boy? Do you want to leave him here or take him with us?"

"I am not sure," Ethan said. "It may be dangerous to take him with us. He could still be with the werewolves ..." His voice trailed off. There was no way that the werewolves wanted him as a partner. The boy seemed a bit confused, but otherwise very nice. He reminded Ethan of a dog. And if the information they had was correct, the boy was much stronger than any werewolf. That was probably the reason the werewolves wanted to kill him. That was why they had sent two werewolves to Samforest. They were probably scared of him, and for a good reason. Daniel had managed to deal with both werewolves, killing one with ease. "It would be great if he could join us," Ethan said at last.

Lord Adrian looked at Ethan with his eyebrows raised. Then he looked towards the fireplace and watched Daniel gulping the chicken. "I'm not sure about this," he said. "We cannot trust him, and we don't know if he would be willing to help us even if we could trust him."

"True." Ethan nodded. "Let's leave him to his lunch for now. We have some preparations to make, and a lot of things can change before we have to leave." He took the note from Lord Adrian, and while he was putting it inside his bag, he turned to leave.

"Are you sure about the attack?" Lord Adrian asked after him. Ethan stopped on the spot and thought about the question. "If Blackbird is right, the castle will be almost empty with only Blake and Mors inside," he replied, not turning around. "And if he is wrong, we can try to attack anyway. We know the way in, and we have weapons and armour. Besides, I don't think that waiting is an option for us."

CHAPTER 11

B ess entered Mors's office and closed the door behind him. The castle was getting quieter with each hour. In two hours, all troops would be out of the castle and on their way to find Ethan. Captain Stuart, with four hundred men, had been left to keep the castle.

Mors was in the office most of the time. Even now he sat there with his head in his hands. Bess looked at the paper in his hand and sighed. He waited for a while, but when Mors didn't react, he came closer. "This is madness, Mors," he said, and he threw the paper on the table.

Mors looked up surprised and frowned. "How dare you to speak to me like that?"

"I have always spoken to you like that," snapped Bess. He put his hands on the desk. "That's the reason you couldn't let me go. And now I am telling you once more: Leaving the castle without an army is madness. What do you want to accomplish?"

"What do I want to accomplish?" Mors asked quietly as he leaned back. "I want Ethan dead. And I hope to accomplish that."

"The only thing that you will accomplish is the complete destruction of Wolfast. Let's leave now. Leave this place to Blake. We already have the treaty, so we don't need to remain here."

"We do!" Mors sighed. "First of all, the treaty will be valid only if Blake becomes king. Second of all, Rex wants that necklace, and I still don't have it. I have to wait for Hans to return."

Bess straightened up and folded his arms. Mors was looking really tired, which was very unusual. Bess was still new to the whole werewolf thing, but he believed that werewolves could handle much more stress than this. And then there was that strange guy with the way-too green eyes. "What would happen if you didn't give him that necklace?" he asked curiously. Mors shrugged. "Then leave the necklace and let's go. I don't trust this Rex. There is more to him than meets the eye."

"Replacement supplies are on their way—"

"Actually, they're not," Bess said. Mors frowned and then looked at the paper in front of him. "That's the report," he explained. "Since the supplies didn't arrive, we sent some soldiers to check the situation. The supplies vanished; three groups with food and weapons—all gone. And it's very probable that the weapons and food are now with Ethan."

"Well, I have to deal with that."

"Let Blake deal with that. We've lost most of our army. Blake's army also suffered great losses and is losing more and more soldiers every minute. Almost two hundred soldiers deserted just in the last three hours. They are now deserting in hordes. I believe that most of the soldiers who went to search for Ethan won't even bother to come back. If they find Ethan, they could actually join him. And Lord Blake probably doesn't believe any longer that he will be king. By the way, did you know he just left?"

"Yes," snapped Mors.

Bess was stunned. He really believed that Mors didn't know. "You sent him away?" he asked in a calmer voice.

"He left of his own accord." Mors shook his head. "He went to his castle to tend to the matters. And I need to tend to mine."

Bess put his hands on the desk again and brought his face closer to Mors's. "You bit me in order to turn me into an advisor, so now listen to my advice. Leave. Let the lords of Norene have a civil war if they want to. Just pull back. The army is getting smaller, and we've been here for only a few days. Who knows how many soldiers we'll have left at the end of the week? And if this Rex wants that necklace so much, let him find it on his own. Maybe he won't be able to get it, and maybe that will be for the best. Or do you want it for yourself?"

"What would I do with it?"

"I don't know. I don't know what that necklace is, but I know that it is no ordinary necklace, and I doubt that it was a gift from his grandmother or heirloom from his mother. I have some doubts as to the origin of that necklace. I actually found out that—"

"I don't care!" Mors shook his head. "Rex wants it, and my payment for it was Norene. He gave me an army and money. I *have* to get that necklace."

Bess sighed and straightened up. He could see that there was no talking to Mors. He watched the man in front of him for a moment and then turned around and walked to the door. When he opened the door and stepped outside, he looked over his shoulder and noticed that Mors had his head in his hands once again.

Bess closed the door and walked away, thinking hard. He was getting more and more curious about the necklace, especially since the necklace was the reason for the war. It seemed it had some powers. That could be the only explanation for why Rex would be looking for it.

He turned around the corner and crashed into Hans, who was running through the corridor. The impact surprised him, but not as much as it surprised Hans, who fell heavily to the floor. Bess stood still for a while, and when he had processed the situation, he stepped to Hans and offered him hand. Hans shot Bess a black look and stood up without accepting his help. He brushed off theatrically and walked around Bess to the next corridor, bumping into him on the way. Bess looked after him with his eyebrow raised and then followed him to the Mors's office.

Hans opened the door and entered, closing it after him. Bess sped up and grabbed the handle, pushing his way inside. Hans turned around, surprised, and when he noticed Bess, he narrowed his eyes. They eyed each other for a moment, and then Hans let go the handle. Bess entered the office and closed the door behind him, watching Hans curiously.

Mors looked up. When he noticed Hans, he slowly stood up with hope in his face.

"I met him," Hans said instead of a hello. Puzzlement crossed Mors's face. "I met the wolf in that village up north."

"What do you mean by 'met it'?" Bess asked perplexed.

"Not it, *him*," Hans said over his shoulder to Bess, and then he turned Mors. "The wolf can change to human form. He can even talk."

"That's not possible." Mors shook his head. "It's a wolf. It cannot talk and communicate, no matter who bit it. There's no way that a wolf could evolve like that. It had to be another werewolf."

"No, he was no werewolf." Hans shook his head. "He didn't smell right. When he changed, he looked like a wolf. You wouldn't be able to notice the difference between him and other wolves. He just smelled different. And he was incredibly strong. I couldn't move. I felt like a puppy when we clashed. I was lucky to get away, considering that he'd already managed to kill Axel. Maybe even three werewolves would have problem killing him."

"Did he have the necklace?" Bess asked suddenly. Hans looked at him, obviously puzzled, and hesitated. "Yes, he did." He nodded at last. "I could see it when he changed back to human form. It hung on a chain that was around his neck."

Bess looked at the sky that was visible through the window and slowly nodded. He wasn't sure what the necklace was, but he was sure that it had to do something with this miraculous evolution of the wolf. Then, without a word, he spun around and hurried out of the office.

As the sun sat lower, a shadow fell onto the clearing between the mountains. The Royal Guards were running to and fro preparing for their departure, and the lords were with the king organizing all the necessary arrangements. This left Daniel, Charles, and Simon by the fire. Simon and Charles were deep in conversation. Though Daniel tried to pay attention, the topic was of no interest to him, and he was soon really bored. He played with the fire, but this too became boring after a while. He stood up and slowly walked to the walls of the clearing. He was fascinated by the caves in the mountains around them. The wall was very steep, and in some places seemed sharp. He reached out and touched the cold rock.

"They say that it's a crater," a voice said behind him. Daniel turned with a start and hit the wall as he stepped back. "Sorry," Lord Adrian said with an apologetic smile. "I really didn't mean to startle you."

"That's all right," Daniel said, feeling silly for jumping like that. "I just find this place fascinating. I didn't mean to cause any trouble."

"You caused no trouble at all," Lord Adrian said with a smile. As he stepped closer, Daniel noticed that he was hiding something behind his back. "It feels like a haven," Lord Adrian continued and looked up at the sky. "I'm really glad Lord James knew about this place. By the way, I brought you these," he added, and he pulled a pair of shoes from behind his back.

A wide smile appeared on Daniel's face when he spotted them. He looked up at Lord Adrian and then took the shoes eagerly. He looked at them thoroughly and then quickly sat down on the grass and immediately put them on. "Thank you," he said happily, and he stood up, trying them out. Human feet weren't made for walking without some covering. He was getting cold too quickly.

"Do you want to go for a walk?" Lord Adrian asked as he watched Daniel walking in little circles around him.

Daniel stopped and looked up. He was a little scared. He glanced at Charles and Simon, but they were both so deep in the conversation that they didn't even notice that Daniel was no longer with them.

"Don't worry," Lord Adrian said encouragingly. "I will just show you around and then bring you back to the fireplace. You are in no danger here."

Daniel didn't want Charles out of his sight, but he was getting very curious. Though he wasn't sure if he could trust Lord Adrian, he decided to follow him. Maybe he would learn something new. And if they wanted him dead, there wasn't much he could do about it anyway. He nodded, and Lord Adrian motioned for him to follow. They stepped towards the closest cave and, in silence, walked inside. Daniel kept looking left and right, fascinated by nature's design and the way the humans had managed to turn it into a comfortable living place. A man walked by Daniel with a bowl full of water and a straight razor in his hands, and Daniel looked after him fascinated, nearly crashing into a soldier who carried a crate of potatoes to the clearing.

Lord Adrian led Daniel deeper to the cave, occasionally pulling him out of way, until they came to a little chamber with one makeshift bed. There was no hole for the daylight, only torches on the wall. On the bed sat Ethan. He was reading some papers. He looked up, his glance briefly stopping on Daniel, and then he looked back at the papers in his hands. "It seems that the werewolves are really scared of you," he said with a little admiration as he put the papers down. He stood up, smiled at Daniel, and handed the sheet of paper from the top to Lord Adrian.

Lord Adrian took it and scanned its content. "Well, well, well," he said as he lowered the paper. "It seems that the werewolves are getting desperate. According to this, they are sending fifty soldiers tomorrow to find you."

"Why are they after me?" asked Daniel, looking from Ethan to Lord Adrian. He hoped that at least one of them could explain that to him.

Ethan stepped closer and folded his arms. "I was hoping you could explain that to us," he said solemnly. "We know of a wolf that got bitten by a werewolf, and now the werewolves are after that very wolf. And it seems that the wolf can change form too, like a werewolf only the other way around. And then we have you. There is really something strange about you, and I would wager that the wolf and you are one and the same pers ... being."

Daniel looked behind him, but the escape route was blocked by Lord Adrian. He looked at Ethan and decided to remain silent. Technically, there wasn't any question in the air. Ethan glanced at Lord Adrian. "I'll be frank with you," he said, and he stepped closer. Daniel had an urge to step back, but he suppressed it. "I have no idea what to do with you."

Daniel gulped and peeked at the opposite wall. He couldn't see any escape route there either. Ethan suddenly focused on Daniel's chest. He reached out and picked up the necklace that was hanging from Daniel's neck. Daniel looked down and back up at Ethan.

"What is this?" Ethan asked curiously, studying the necklace.

Daniel wanted to pull away, to tear the necklace from Ethan's hands, but he decided against this. He could feel the hair on his back standing up. "I don't know," he said, and he looked at the necklace. He hesitated as he studied the little pendant. He had never really thought about it before. He'd just liked it, so he had taken it. And he didn't feel like parting with it.

Suddenly, the necklace flashed for a fraction of a second. The light was very brief, but very bright. All Daniel's fears faded away, and he looked up at Ethan. Ethan was still studying the necklace, lost in thoughts.

"Your Majesty?" Lord Adrian said quietly. Ethan didn't look up from the necklace. He seemed a little frozen in the moment. Daniel noticed that a little strange light appeared in his eyes. It reminded Daniel of the fireball he had seen in the necklace the first time he encountered it. Lord Adrian stepped closer and frowned. "Your Majesty, Sire," he repeated. Ethan didn't react. He seemed completely consumed by the necklace as if the necklace was controlling him. For the first time, Daniel wanted to throw the necklace away. He wanted to tear the necklace off his neck and drop it right there and then. Lord Adrian coughed loudly, watching the king with raising concern. "Ethan!" he shouted and stepped closer.

Ethan looked up with startled and baffled expression. He blinked and looked back at the necklace. He let it go and stepped back. Daniel heaved a sigh of relief. Ethan looked from Lord Adrian, who watched him with apprehension, to Daniel, who watched him with interest. "Sorry," he said, massaging the bridge of his nose. "I was just wondering … I mean … I just lost the … What was I talking about?"

"You just started by saying that you have no idea what to do with me," Daniel replied, surprised by his own boldness. "I think I can help you with that."

Ethan looked at Daniel. Lord Adrian stepped back to his original spot and folded his arms.

"Given that the werewolves are scared of me," Daniel continued, "because I am obviously stronger than they are, but on the other hand they are after me probably for that very same reason, I believe that the only possibility for me to get rid of them is to get rid of them—literally. So I will help you get back your kingdom. That is, if you let me."

Ethan peeked at Lord Adrian and then back at Daniel. He watched the boy for a while, thinking hard. He nodded slowly. "I will accept your help on the matter because I could really use your help. You will accompany me, Lord Adrian, and Lord James with a few of our soldiers to the secret tunnel. Our goal is to open the gates for our army and get them inside Royal Castle."

Bess walked through the castle with a carrier pigeon in his hands, thinking hard. The sun was already very low, and the evening was approaching. The castle was very quiet and felt deserted, which helped him to focus. Only his footsteps echoed in the empty corridors as he paced the place.

The more information he found about the necklace, the more curious he was. The fact that a wolf could behave as a standard werewolf, yet be much stronger was no coincidence. Bess would be prepared to bet his left hand that the necklace was responsible for that.

He walked onto a balcony and checked left and right. No one else was in the corridor, and since the army already left, there was no one below the balcony either. He checked the letter that was secured on the pigeon's leg once more, and when he was satisfied that it would not fall off, he threw the pigeon into the air. The pigeon fell several inches before it managed to spread its wings and then fly into the night.

"Sending a love letter?" a familiar voice said sweetly behind Bess. Bess spun around, and his eyes narrowed when he spotted Captain Stuart. Captain Stuart folded his arms and leaned against the doorframe.

"My private correspondence is no business of yours," Bess said calmly.

"On the contrary," Captain Stuart replied in a sing-song tone of voice as he stepped onto the balcony. "There is a spy in this castle, and I am trying to find out who it is. And then I find you alone on a balcony sending a letter to someone, when all the werewolves are here with you."

"Are you trying to imply that I am that spy?"

"I'm not implying it; I'm saying it."

"That's nonsense." Bess spit the words out and folded his arms. "Who would I spy for? Ethan?"

"Why not?" Captain Stuart replied calmly. He shrugged. "You've been a werewolf for only a few days or so, and you didn't want to be one in the first place. And then you were dragged here. You are against this war and want Mors to return to Wolfast. If Ethan regained the throne, Blake would be overthrown, and you could *flee* home. Mors wouldn't have any other option."

"Really?" Bess asked and raised one eyebrow. "In the same logic, I should want Blake to get the throne because then we wouldn't need to *flee*. It would make much more sense for me not to spy for Ethan."

"I know." Captain Stuart nodded. "But there is another man who may be playing some interesting game in the background. If the country has no king, he could be the ruler in the shadows. I believe he calls himself Rex, and he's the reason you are here and Blake is so close to the throne, yet so far away."

Bess's jaw dropped. He hadn't expected to hear that name from a Norenian. He watched Captain Stuart for a while, unsure what to say. He tried to see through that mask of his but wasn't sure what he was looking for. "You know quite a lot for a captain," he hissed at last. "You know so much that I wouldn't be surprised if you were that spy."

"I didn't know about Lord Michael's men," Captain Stuart replied calmly. "Only someone very close to Mors could have this information and pass it on. And if you think that I will let you spoil this for us, you are mistaken."

"I don't care if Blake becomes king. I don't care if Ethan stays king. But I hope you will meet your end here because boys who play with fire get burnt."

"Really?" Captain Stuart asked and smiled derisively. "That's all you can come up with? *Boys who play with fire?* Here's another thought—maybe I should arrest you right now, just to be sure."

"You wouldn't dare," Bess hissed, and he stepped so close to Captain Stuart that their noses were almost touching.

"You can bet that I would."

"You have no proof, no—"

"To whom did you send that letter?" Captain Stuart barked. Bess pressed his lips together and leaned back a little. "Why did you suggest to Mors to look for Ethan?" Captain Stuart continued. "Did you want him to send all the troops away?"

"I didn't suggest something so stupid," Bess snapped. He turned to leave the balcony. Captain Stuart grabbed his arm and stopped him. Bess turned around and slowly looked at the captain's hand.

Captain Stuart hesitated and then let go off Bess. "I will find out the truth," the Captain said quietly.

Bess shot him a glance and marched off the balcony. He hurried through the corridors, marched into the library, and slammed the door behind him. He paced the room for fifteen minutes until he calmed down. Then he walked over to the table and leaned against it. His stare fell on the documents he had been studying before, and he picked up a drawing that was lying on top of the kings' journals. A small, round, light-blue gem was pictured there. He looked at the image for a while and then put it down.

The anger was slowly fading away, and curiosity replaced it. There was something strange about the necklace, but he couldn't figure out what it was. He knew that Rex had wanted it for a long time, but the really annoying part was that he still couldn't find out why. All he could trace were the drawings of a necklace made from the gem. It had been ordered in a little Norenian town near the borders with Wolfast, which explained why Rex had come to King John for help.

The jeweller had received a simple request—to turn the little round gem into a necklace. However, after he finished the job, he hadn't been able to continue with his work. The necklace was still on his mind, and even weeks later, he couldn't forget about it. When his thoughts were no longer bearable, he wrote down everything he could remember. And if the drawings and descriptions were accurate, he definitely remembered a lot.

Bess turned the drawing of the gem around and read hastily written sentences:

> When I picked up the necklace, I felt the urge to throw it away, to get rid of it. Yet I wanted to protect it. Now that it's gone, I still wonder if it was cursed. I cannot forget that bright blinding light that flashed when I placed it into the golden setting for the necklace. It felt like a warning. I only wish I knew what the warning was about.

Bess put down the paper and leaned against the table. He sighed and shook his head. There was obviously something about this necklace, and he felt as if Rex should have been the last person to have it. He had created this war just to get to it. To what limits would he go to get it? How far would he go to get what he wanted? And what would happen if he didn't get it? Or, more importantly, what would happen if he did?

They were nowhere even close to finding it. Mors was looking for the necklace, and at the same time, they were trying to find Ethan, who was hiding successfully in the country, killing off their soldiers and stealing their food and weapons. Then another thought came to Bess. He had just realized something and needed to test his hypothesis.

He spun around and hurried out of the library, slamming the door behind him.

CHAPTER 12

E than climbed a steep rock, followed by Lord Adrian, Lord James, Charles, Daniel, and twenty guards. He had planned their arrival carefully. It was few minutes after midnight, which would give them the advantage of darkness and hopefully the advantage of surprise. With Lord Adrian, he had planned the routes carefully to ensure that they did not meet Blake's troops, and Ethan hoped that Blackbird was really on their side and his information was true.

The odds were actually very good: Royal Castle was nearly empty; Ethan's archers had silver-tipped arrows along with the regular ones; plenty of Blake's soldiers had deserted and joined the Royal Guards; the guards were well trained and best in combat within hundreds of miles; the party that was supposed to open the castle gates contained a former pirate; and the party was accompanied by a wolf that could beat up any werewolf in Norene. Yet Ethan was getting more and more nervous. He was not sure if the plan was any good. There were just too many things entirely dependent on luck.

"Shh! Be quiet!" hissed Lord Adrian, giving Lord James a black look. Ethan turned around and looked at Lord James, who was climbing the steep rock behind him.

"Sorry," whispered Lord James. "I didn't see that twig. It's too dark."

Ethan moved forward, watching his feet. The walk was supposed to be short because there was a secret tunnel nearby, but it was harder in the darkness of the night. There was no moon in the sky. On one hand, that provided them with great cover, but on the other, they could hardly see anything.

Ethan hoped that their plan would work. Hardly anyone knew about the tunnel; it had always been kept a secret. It was supposed to be a path out of the castle if the castle ever fell. The point of any quick getaway was its secrecy. No king wanted to run out of the castle into the unwelcoming hands of his enemies.

This time, Ethan planned to use the secret tunnel as a way in. He wasn't sure if they could open it from the outside, but he knew it was worth a try. Besides, he had Lord James with him, and Lord James had supposedly once sneaked into Lord Eric's castle one night and stolen his coach without anyone noticing it until the next morning. If anyone could find a way in, it would be Lord James.

"It's over here," hissed Ethan from the darkness. Lord Adrian hurried after Ethan's voice with Lord James at his heals. Daniel sped up after the silhouettes, but as he stepped onto a rock, his foot slipped to the side. He hit the ground with a loud thud, and he slid down the hill a little. "Shh!" sounds echoed through the night. Several of the guards helped him to his feet, and he stepped after Ethan and the lords more carefully.

Ethan turned to the stone and ran his fingers on the stone's surface.

"Are we sure that this is the entrance?" Lord Adrian asked doubtfully, looking at the solid stone.

"Yes," answered Ethan absentmindedly. "This is it," he said suddenly and turned to face the soldiers. "Here's the gap."

Two men stepped forward with a very wide and very thick shovel. Ethan showed them the crack in the stone, and they pushed the blade of the shovel inside. Ethan stepped back, dusting off his hands. "Push to your right," he ordered quietly, and he watched the soldiers heave on the shovel. The stone didn't budge. The guards fought with the shovel for a minute or two without achieving anything. Ethan motioned to two more guards who came up to help, but the stone still didn't move.

The guards took the shovel out of the gap and stepped back. Ethan walked over to the wall and checked it once more. He was sure that this was the entrance. He walked to the side and looked at the castle towering high above them. It seemed that they would need to find another way in.

"Maybe we need to release the stone," Lord James said. He drew his dagger. "Maybe it's only stuck. When was it open the last time?"

"I honestly don't know," Ethan said, returning his attention to the secret passage. "I'm not even sure if the passage was ever used."

Suddenly, the stone opened, and torch light fell on the group in front of it. Daniel gasped and stepped back. Ethan turned around and exchanged a surprised look with Lord Adrian.

Two soldiers stepped out of the tunnel and froze, one holding the torch above his head, the other carrying some food in his arms. They scanned the group in front of them with their mouths gaped open, and their stares stopped on Ethan. At that moment, feeling completely astonished, Ethan couldn't think of anything better to do than smile at them.

Two daggers flew through the air and landed in the soldiers' chests. Both soldiers looked at their chests puzzled. Then they looked back up at Lord James, who watched them with his arm still extended after the throw. They watched Lord James for a while and then slid to the ground, dead. The torch fell to the ground and went out, leaving the group in front of the secret passage in the darkness.

"That ... was interesting," said Charles after they had stood for a little while in the darkness.

"The passage seems to be known," said Lord James nervously as he looked into the dark tunnel. Lord Adrian picked up the torch and turned to Lord James, who pulled two small stones from his belt bag. He smashed the stones against each other, and sparks flew in the air. A few of them landed on the hot torch, and it lit immediately.

Ethan hesitated and then stepped forward into the light. "Well, it's the way in, and it's open," he said. He motioned four guards to step inside. One of them took the torch, and they carefully entered the tunnel. Ethan followed them silently with the rest of the group at his heels.

A few minutes later, the tunnel made a sharp left turn. There was light ahead. The guards in front stopped and looked at Ethan, expecting orders. Ethan motioned to the torch and then to the ground. The guard understood immediately and put out the torch. The tunnel went dark. Only silhouettes were visible against the tunnel walls. Ethan turned around and motioned to the lords to get closer. "On the count of three we go out," he whispered. "And remember, we need to be quiet. No screaming, no shouting, no ..." His gaze fell upon Daniel, and he hesitated, "howling."

"Hey!" said Daniel angrily. There was a chorus of "Shh."

Ethan put up his hand, lifted three fingers, and one by one put them down. Inside his head, he counted: *Three ... two ... one ...*

The guards rushed out of the tunnel, followed by Ethan. He was ready for anything that could be there. However, there was one thing he definitely didn't expect.

"Well, well, well," said Captain Stuart cheerfully. "What a surprise!"

Bess spun around and looked at Captain Stuart, who was standing in the doorway. Bess was standing in the captain's room, going through papers on his desk. The only light in the room was from a candle on the table, which cast strange shadows over the place and gave Captain Stuart a dangerous look. Captain Stuart looked at a report in Bess's hands, and Bess followed his gaze. He looked up again and put the report onto the table. "I have a good reason to believe—"

"Ah! You think I'm that spy," said Captain Stuart with a manic grin. He closed the door of his room behind him.

"Well, it's definitely possible," Bess replied calmly. "You do have access to some important information, and on top of that, you can sniff out any secret within a mile. You would be a valuable ally to anyone."

Captain Stuart stepped closer and looked at his desk over Bess's shoulder. He smiled again and looked Bess in the eye. "What a coincidence," he said way too cheerfully for Bess's taste. "The enemy takes *my* prisoner, stops three of *my* resupply missions, kills a lot of *my* soldiers, and now I find you in *my* room with the list of routes in your hands. What will happen next? Will you send the information to Ethan so that he can hunt down my soldiers one by one?"

"I might ask you the same thing," said Bess calmly as he straightened up so that he was taller than Captain Stuart.

"Me?" Captain Stuart asked, and both his eyebrows flew up. "What would I gain if Ethan came back? I would only loose promotion to the captain of the Royal Guards and possibly to commander. Can you imagine that? *Lord* Stuart. Why should I want anything else?"

"Really? Blake is not even close to becoming king. He may have won the first battle, but he's not winning the war. Oh, by the way, did I mention that it was very interesting how you created that hole in the defence through which Lord James and his man ran away, taking the king with them?"

"True, I overestimated your soldiers and thought that they could ward off Ethan's Royal Guards. I won't make that mistake twice."

Bess's lips created a very thin line as he watched Captain Stuart. They stood still for a while fighting a silent battle. Who would look away first? Bess stared into Captain Stuart's eyes for a few more seconds and then looked away. Truth be told, he didn't have any proof of his hypothesis, though he didn't dismiss it entirely—at least not yet. He walked around Captain Stuart and opened the door.

"If I ever find you in here again," Captain Stuart said in a dangerous tone of voice, just as Bess stepped outside, "you will wake up in the middle of the night with a silver stick imbedded in your chest."

Bess looked over his shoulder and his eyes narrowed. "I'm keeping an eye on you," he hissed, and he closed the door behind him.

Before the door closed completely, he could hear Captain Stuart say, "I'm keeping two."

"What's this?" Charles asked as he lowered his sword.

Ethan walked around the guards who had preceded them into the castle and stopped in the centre of the room. There were torches on the walls illuminating the room and the things stocked there. He picked up a golden goblet and turned it around in his hand. "It looks like a museum," Lord Adrian said as he put his sword away.

Lord James walked along the wall and pulled one torch out of its stand. He walked to the centre of the room and lifted the torch high above his head. The light fell on the golden goblets, jewels, paintings, and pottery. All the things were stocked in the middle of the room with paths created around them.

Ethan put the goblet down and looked around. "It seems to be a storage space," Lord James said as he looked around. "It seems that all the paintings from the castle are here."

"It looks more like a hiding place," Ethan said quietly. He picked up a small painting that had been completely torn to pieces. He lifted the torn canvas only to stare at the portrait of his much younger self.

"Why did they bring it down here?" Lord James asked as he picked up a golden goblet nearby. It caught the light of the torches around them.

"We can try to find the answer to that later," said Ethan in a faraway voice. He put down his portrait and, with a beating heart, picked up a medallion embossed with an image of his father. It hadn't even been two weeks since his father died, yet it felt like ages. Only now he realized how much he missed him. He would give anything to see him once more, to hear his reassuring voice, his merry laughter. Even his frown would be very welcomed. A pressure tightened in his chest, and he felt his eyes burn. He took a deep breath and put the medallion into his belt bag. He knew it was ridiculous, but it made him feel better, as if his father was much closer, maybe even guiding his steps.

"I don't think the werewolves did this," Lord Adrian said quietly. Ethan put down his bow and picked up a book from the ground. When he looked at it much closer, he saw that it was his own diary. The diary was official, and he knew that it would be stored in the castle's library along with other diaries to possibly be read in the future. There were only a few days described there. He had written his first lines when his father died. He had described the news of the werewolf in Samforest and his coronation. There was also description of Lord Blake's preparation for the possible war. How naïve Ethan had been. Blake had never liked his father. Ethan just didn't believe that he would be willing to cooperate with the werewolves to gain the throne.

And then there was the description of the departure five days ago. The rest of the diary was empty. He hadn't taken it with him because he believed that he would come back and describe the battle afterwards. He closed the diary and looked around, but there were no other books in the room, at least none that were visible. Absentmindedly, he put the diary into the bag that was hanging from his belt.

"Put that back," Lord Adrian hissed. Ethan looked up, surprised, and noticed that Lord Adrian was not looking at him, but at Lord James who had the most innocent look his face. Dogs could have learned a valuable lesson from his expression.

"You're talking to me?" Lord James asked, pointing at his chest.

"That goblet—put it back."

Lord James stood still for a moment, watching Lord Adrian. Then he pulled a golden goblet out of his bag and put it on a box next to him. "It seemed so lonely there," he said conversationally. Lord Adrian gave him a black look, but didn't say anything else.

"Who's this?" asked Daniel and pointed at the old portrait of an old man. The man looked out at them with a serious look, holding a sword in his hands. The crown on his head was simple, yet it sent a very clear message. Lord Adrian walked around the soldiers and stopped next to Daniel. Lord James joined them and smiled when he saw the painting. "That's King John," Lord Adrian said. "He was actually the first king of Norene after we regained our freedom from Wolfast. Once he freed Norene from Wolfast's sovereignty, he divided the country to ten provinces, appointed nine lords, and kept the tenth part to himself. Then Flying Jimmy came along and became Lord James." He smiled and patted Lord James on the shoulder. "That's why we now have ten lords—"

"No!" Ethan shook his head. "We *had* ten lords. If we get back the castle and Norene, there will be some changes."

Lord James and Lord Adrian exchanged surprised looks.

"We should go," said Ethan suddenly and motioned to the guards. Two guards carefully opened the door to the room and peered outside. They both nodded to the rest and hurried out of the room. Lord Adrian and Lord James, with ten guards, went right; Ethan, Daniel, and Charles, with the rest of the guards, went left.

Ethan and his men moved forward as silently as they could. They walked through multiple secret passages, which Ethan knew by heart, and with each empty corridor, Ethan wondered where everyone was. They didn't meet a living soul in the castle, which was a little unnerving. Though it was way past midnight, a fortress like this should have been guarded by at least some soldiers.

Just as he thought this, a group of soldiers crossed their path. They marched through the corridors obviously bored and stopped on the spot when they saw the Royal Guards. The Royal Guards immediately charged, with Charles in the lead.

The soldiers drew their swords and charged as well, but two of them sprinted the other way. The soldiers and the Royal Guards clashed, and

Charles ran around the fighting group and hurried after the two men who had left. Daniel stepped forward and hesitated. Ethan realized that Daniel was thinking of following Charles, but he needed him elsewhere. He grabbed Daniel's shoulder and pulled him into another corridor. He broke into run and, half leading, half dragging Daniel behind him, reached the end of the corridor. They turned into a small hall. Several doors led off the hall.

"This is it," said Ethan calmly as he looked over his shoulder to make sure that no one was following them. "If anything happens, you know the way out?" He turned to face Daniel.

Daniel watched Ethan wide eyed for a while and then nodded.

Ethan had the impression that Daniel had no idea where they were, but he had no time to explain the way out. Besides, it wasn't probable that they would split up. Ethan opened the closest door and gestured to Daniel to follow him. They both entered a great hall, and Ethan closed the door behind him. Daniel stopped in the middle of the room, and his mouth dropped open.

"This is the throne hall," Ethan said from behind him. He put the bow on his back and his arrow back into his quiver. Daniel looked at the tall windows above his head and then looked further up at the ceiling. He turned around, and his gaze fell on the marble throne. During the daytime, the sun would be shining down upon it, illuminating the white stone, but even in the light of the torches on the walls, it looked magnificent.

Ethan grabbed Daniel's arm and tugged him towards the far end.

"I've never been in a throne hall before," Daniel breathed out still looking around.

"If we win," whispered Ethan as he led Daniel to another secret door, "I'll show you around myself."

Daniel didn't respond. He looked up at the ceiling while Ethan grabbed one of the torches from the wall and opened a secret passage. He pulled Daniel into the tunnel and closed the door behind them.

Ethan sniffed the air and retched. He put his hand against his mouth and nose and tried to breathe through his mouth. The stench was unbearable. Ethan raised the torch high above his head to have a better look at the corridor. It was dark and empty. And then he realized that something was very wrong. He could clearly hear that Daniel was breathing deeply. He lowered the torch and turned around. His gaze fell upon Daniel, but somehow it wasn't Daniel anymore. His eyes were closed, and his features were wild, unhuman even. "Are you all right?" Ethan asked with his hand still pressed against his nose. He could feel the skin on his neck crawl.

"There are corpses in the tunnel," Daniel said in a hoarse whisper that echoed in the tunnel. Ethan stepped back, watching Daniel nervously and moved his hand from his mouth to the hilt of the sword. He turned around and raised the torch high above his head, but all he could see was a dark and cold tunnel.

A low rasp of Daniel's breath reached Ethan's ears. He slowly turned around and watched Daniel with raising terror. The rasp changed to a growl, and Daniel opened his eyes. They were glassy and out of focus. They slowly changed colour from the dark brown to orange.

"Are you all right?" Ethan asked again with a trembling voice. Daniel smiled maniacally and revealed his teeth. Ethan stepped back, hit the wall, and cursed. Daniel growled and stepped closer. Ethan stepped back and drew his sword. Daniel's face started to change, and his arms were getting hairier beneath the shirt.

"Rrrrun!" Daniel growled, and he fell on all fours. Ethan didn't have to be told twice. He spun around and broke into a sprint, holding the torch above his head in one hand and carrying the sword in his other hand. His heart was beating painfully in his chest as he hurried along the corridor. He didn't know what Daniel would do, but his imagination supplied a lot of varieties of the same outcome. He sprinted around the corner and entered a wider corridor. Two more corridors led out in different directions. And his heart missed a beat.

He stopped abruptly and cursed under his breath. Two werewolves in wolf form looked up from a fresh corpse. It was the maid who had made the sofa for Ethan when he'd decided to remain by his father's side. He noticed that it was not the first corpse in the corridor, but he didn't take a better look because their bloodied jaws and teeth caught his attention. The surprise was mutual, which gave Ethan enough time to slide along the wall and run up the tunnel closest to him.

He sprinted through the tunnel as he had never sprinted in his life. He was thinking about what to do once he got out of the tunnel, but all the thoughts were driven out of his mind by the pounding of the soft feet behind him. He sped up. The sound was very rhythmical and getting closer and closer with each step and with each second. He didn't need to look behind him to realize that the werewolves were gaining on him. He didn't have a very big head start, and the tunnel was way too long.

He sped up even more in his futile attempt to overrun the werewolves. As he sprinted forward, something hit him hard in his back and threw him to the ground knocking the breath out of his lungs. The sword and the torch flew out of his hands, and he felt the coldness of the stone beneath his sweating body. Something soft slid down his calf. While he fought for breath, expecting teeth in his calf or neck any minute, he desperately crawled forward to the exit. He was partially aware of fighting nearby, but he didn't dare to stop. Several painful seconds later, he took a deep breath and cursed. The sounds behind him were terrifying. He risked a peek over his shoulder and saw three wolves fighting in the tunnel. He had trouble distinguishing them from one another. The torch had fallen ahead of him, and the flame was throwing a lot of shadows.

Ethan jumped to his feet, picked up his sword, and stepped back. His heart was beating painfully in his chest, and his lungs hurt. He put the sword away and quickly pulled his bow from his back. Before he could pull a silver-tipped arrow out of the quiver, one werewolf fell to the ground heavily, blood gushing from his throat.

Ethan stepped further back, lost his balance, and fell to the ground. The other werewolf and Daniel didn't pay him any attention. Ethan quickly pulled an arrow from the quiver and stood up. He aimed at the werewolf, but the fight was so vigorous that he wasn't able to aim properly. His hands were shaking too much to stay still for even a few seconds, and he didn't dare to shoot for fear of hitting Daniel. Then, suddenly, the werewolf lay still on the ground, Daniel above him with his jaws in the werewolf's throat. Ethan put the bow down and stepped further back, watching Daniel in horror. It seemed that the werewolves were dead. The only other living being that remained in the tunnel was Ethan.

Daniel let go off the werewolf and looked up at Ethan, the white fur around his jaws dripping with blood. He stood still and watched Ethan with glassy eyes. Ethan took a step back, but Daniel didn't do anything. Ethan took a few more steps back, but Daniel still didn't move an inch.

Ethan spun around and sprinted forward, leaving the torch and Daniel behind. He was expecting Daniel to catch up with him any second, but nothing pursued him.

Ethan didn't doubt that Daniel was still on his side, but he wasn't sure how lucid Daniel was at the moment. It had to be really hard for him to control himself when there was blood all around the place.

The light from the torch faded with each step until Ethan ran in complete darkness. He stretched his right hand to the side and used the side of the tunnel for guidance as he ran forward. And then he hit the wall. He staggered back and massaged his forehead. He hadn't expected the tunnel to end so soon.

Much more carefully, he pushed against the end of the tunnel. The wall slid aside. He rushed out of the tunnel, slammed the door behind him, and leaned against it, fighting for his breath. He stood still for a while listening to the silence of the castle. A few moments later, his breath deepened and his heartbeat slowed down. He wiped his forehead. With his entire body shaking, he walked to the window. He looked down and frowned.

Lord James opened a side door a fraction and peered through the little gap. He could see the front gate and quite a lot of soldiers walking around the castle walls and the yard. There were four fires lit in the middle, creating a lot of shadows. Two soldiers sat by one of the fires talking together. "Damn," he said calmly and quietly closed the door.

"Are there a lot of soldiers?" Lord Adrian asked.

"The trouble is they are scattered all around. We cannot take them one by one because they would notice us, and it would take too long. We cannot sneak to the gate because they lit so many fires the yard is sort of illuminated. On top of that, we are running out of time, since the moon is supposed to rise soon. There is another way in, isn't there?"

Lord Adrian leaned against the wall and looked at the corridor. The guards were standing on both sides of the corridor checking the situation.

"As I recall, there is a sewer underneath the northern tower leading to the walls," he said at last.

"That doesn't sound very inviting," Lord James said, deep in thought. "I don't like that version. We need another plan."

They stood silently for a while, but nothing crossed Lord James's mind. He knew that the castle was empty, but they needed to get out. Lord Adrian opened the door a fraction and peered outside. Lord James stepped forward and peaked over Lord Adrian's shoulder. "I have an idea," he said. "And I think it could work."

"What do you need from us?" Lord Adrian asked calmly as he closed the door.

Lord James stroked his chin deep in thought. "I need a uniform," he said. "The uniform of Blake's soldiers ... or better yet, two of them."

"We didn't meet anyone in the castle, and we have no idea where the spare uniforms are," Lord Adrian pointed out. "I'm not sure—"

One guard to their left hissed, and Lord Adrian stopped midsentence. The guard hurried to Lord Adrian and whispered something to his ear.

"It seems you are in luck, my lord," Lord Adrian said. He turned to Lord James with a happy smile. "Two uniforms are approaching as you ordered."

They stood in silence for a while, the Royal Guards ready for the new arrivals. Then two guards sprinted to the corridor and were knocked out immediately. Charles turned the corner and stopped. "What are you doing here?" he asked, surprised. He lowered his sword.

Lord Adrian looked at him in astonishment. "What are *you* doing *here*? You were supposed to be with the king? What happened?"

"We met some soldiers," Charles explained. He stepped closer. Lord James walked pass Lord Andrew and started to strip the first soldier. "These two hurried away, and I didn't want them to raise the alarm," Charles continued. "It seemed that they were trying to get out of the castle."

"So it would seem," Lord James said slowly as he threw Charles the first soldier's clothes. Charles caught them reflexively and looked at Lord James.

"Put these on," Lord James said without looking up. "You will help me to get to the gate."

Charles looked at the tunic and chain mail in his hands, surprised.

"Why Charles and not one of our guards?" Lord Adrian asked while Lord James stripped the second soldier.

"The soldiers on the walls are from the same army as the Royal Guards. There is a possibility that they would recognize our man. Charles is a new face to everyone."

"But your face is even more recognizable than anyone else's," Charles pointed out still holding the tunic and mail in his hand. "If you don't want other guards to accompany you, because the soldiers could recognize them, what makes you think the soldiers won't recognize you?"

"Because they won't *see* me," Lord James replied, pulling the mail over his head. "You are a decoy. I will use the shadows and chaos that you will create for me."

"What chaos?" Charles asked suspiciously. Lord James looked up with a devious smile.

Lord Thomas motioned to the Royal Guards to stop. They stood in the forest, two minutes away from the castle. Lord Eric stopped his horse next to Lord Thomas and looked at the castle through the branches of the nearest trees. "I hope they will manage to lower the bridge," Lord Eric said quietly. "It would be very boring to stand out there all night, watching the walls."

"I'm sure they will manage," Lord Thomas replied, scratching his beard. "Don't forget that Lord James is in there. He got into three of your castles, didn't he? This one's only bigger."

Lord Eric shot a side glance at Lord Thomas but didn't say anything. Lord Thomas found the fact that Flying Jimmy could get anywhere very reassuring. He only hoped that Lord James didn't lose touch and, hopefully, this place would be like any other.

Lord Thomas looked over his shoulder and motioned to the guards to follow him. Slowly, he and Lord Eric set out for the castle, followed by one portion of the army. The rest of the soldiers were to stay in the forest in case the bridge wasn't lowered and a siege of the castle was necessary. Lord Thomas certainly hoped it would not come to that.

They left the security of the forest and moved towards the castle. The moon was hidden below the horizon, which gave them cover, though it made the approach a little more difficult.

Lord Thomas had to agree that the plan was simple. The group that was inside had to open the gates before anyone noticed the army outside. He spotted a dim orange light arising from the yard and assumed that it came from fires. That would help them. The light in the castle would make it more difficult for the soldiers on the walls to notice anything outside the castle walls. With the bridge up, the troops inside would believe that they were protected and might neglect the night watch.

As they approached the castle, they heard screams from the other side of the walls. These were not battle cries, but screams of panic. Lord Eric looked at Lord Thomas with a wide happy smile. "You were right, My Lord," he said, "Lord James has made sure we can get inside. I think that's our signal that the bridge will go down soon."

Lord Adrian peered through the window at the castle yard. He watched a blooded soldier with only one hand running away from the castle. The soldier stopped after fifty feet and fell to the ground. He hit the tiles hard and lay still. Soldiers not far away looked at each other in surprise and then hurried to the soldier. The rest looked on in alarm. Lord Adrian noticed that all eyes in the yard were turned to the soldier or the castle.

Three soldiers leaned above the blooded soldier and turned him over. There was some talk, and then they all jumped back and turned to look at the castle. Lord Adrian was happy to see that they were terrified. Their plan was working.

"What happened?" a familiar voice shouted from the walls. Lord Adrian leaned to the side and saw Lord James's figure running alongside the wall, partially hidden in the shadow. No one was paying him any attention. Some soldiers were running through the yard, mostly to the castle or to the blooded soldier.

"One of the werewolves attacked him!" one of the soldiers by the blooded soldier shouted back. "He said that they are all on a hunt!"

A complete silence fell after this statement, and everyone stopped. Lord Adrian noticed that even Lord James stopped and hid near the stables. Everyone stood still for a few seconds, and then all hell broke loose. Complete chaos overtook the yard. Most of the soldiers hurried to the gate. They opened it, lowered the bridge, and ran away from the castle as if there was a fire.

Lord Adrian could see the bridge through the gate. He really hadn't expected the soldiers to open the gates so willingly. Soldiers suddenly crowded the gate, and Lord Adrian came to the conclusion that the running soldiers had spotted the Royal Guards positioned just outside the gates. The soldiers behind them didn't know about the army and were pushing their way through, determined to get as far away from the castle as possible.

Lord Adrian could pinpoint the moment when they all noticed the Royal Guards. It took a few seconds, but then mayhem continued. Some soldiers jumped to the water of the moat, but most hurried back to the castle. Lord Adrian could see through the gate that some just continued running from the castle, ignoring the Royal Guards in front of them. Ethan's army let the running guards get through. Then they quickly crossed the bridge and entered the castle.

Lord Adrian nodded to the guards behind him, and they all hurried to the yard to join the fight. Lord Adrian hurried towards Lord James, who still stood by the stables. Charles jumped up, pulled his arm completely out of the blooded shirt, and hurried after Lord Adrian. Lord Adrian reached Lord James by the stables, hiding in the shadow and watching the fights in front of him with a genuine shock on his face. "That was interesting," Lord Adrian said.

"Yeah." Lord James nodded slowly as Charles joined them. "It seems that the fear of the werewolves was much stronger than I anticipated. I thought that Charles would be a distraction and I would get to the gate, but it seems that he caused quite a bit of havoc. Well done!" he added with a big smile as he slapped Charles on the back.

"Well, I always wanted to be an actor—"

"We shouldn't waste time," Lord James said suddenly, and he turned to face Charles. "Follow me, we need to get ready."

"Ready for what?!" Lord Adrian asked, surprised, and he grabbed Lord James's arm before he could run away.

"There are some werewolves in the castle," Lord James said quietly. "And they may not go easily. Luckily, there is one sure way to kill a werewolf."

"Silver?"

"Fire."

Mors was in the office, reading a report when he heard some shouts. He stood up and walked over to the window, frowning. He hadn't expected any disturbance during the night. The castle was a fortress with a drawbridge, and there was no chance of getting inside easily.

There was a blooded soldier on the ground, and there was a lot of shouting and running going on. No one paid the blooded soldier any attention. It seemed to Mors that panic must have started because of the soldier.

He watched in amazement as the soldiers started to run back and forth, and then some of them lowered the bridge and hurried out of the castle. One minute later, an army reached the yard. And this army was not Blake's. Mors was sure that the army was the one that he hadn't managed to destroy five days ago.

Mors wanted Ethan dead, and instead, Ethan was in the castle. Captain Stuart had warned him against sending the troops away, and then suddenly, on the very first night, the king, whom he was trying to find outside the castle walls, was *in* the castle.

Mors screamed, grabbed the closest book, and threw it at the bookshelves. The book bounced off and fell to the floor. He grabbed another book and threw it after the first one. He looked at the table, but there were no other books, and he still didn't feel any better. He threw off the papers and kicked away the chair. Then he screamed some more, grabbed the table, and threw it into the air. The table flipped upside down and heavily fell to the floor.

The door flew open, and something hit him in the chest. He staggered back, hit the wall, and looked down astonished. There was an arrow sticking out of his chest, and the blood was pouring out of the wound, colouring his shirt. He could even taste blood in his mouth. He looked up and saw Ethan with another silver-tipped arrow in his bow, aiming at him. "How ..." he breathed as he slid along the wall to the ground with his arms spread. He remained quietly on the ground, his empty eyes looking at the ceiling.

Ethan lowered the bow and heaved a huge sigh. He was still shaking from his last meeting with the werewolves. He swallowed and hurried to the window. There in the yard was his army. At least something had gone swimmingly.

CHAPTER 13

Daniel changed back to human form and stood swaying. He felt dizzy, sick, and confused. The smell of blood was awful, and he couldn't focus. The necklace shone for a brief moment and illuminated the place. He looked at the bodies by his feet and stepped back. He remembered the fight, but he preferred not to think about it too much. The scared look on Ethan's face afterwards had been even worse.

He tore his eyes off the dead werewolves and noticed some clothes nearby. He walked over to the clothes and picked up a shirt and a pair of trousers. They were stained with blood, which was still fresh. He assumed that, though the clothes had belonged to one of the werewolves, the blood had belonged to the dead maid. He hesitated, but he was getting cold and he didn't want to walk back to his own clothes through the tunnel and around all those corpses of innocent people.

He put the clothes on gingerly and found that they were too big for him. The trousers were falling down, and the shirt was slipping off his shoulders, but he couldn't be picky. He tightened the belt as much as he could and tucked the shirt inside.

He tried on the shoes, but they were too big, so he threw them aside. He picked up the torch Ethan had left behind and hurried out of the tunnel. The pictures of all the corpses and of the dead maid kept on returning to him, and he had to shake his head to get rid of the memories.

After travelling a few yards, he came to a dead end. His heart started to pound hard, and he became scared. He wanted to get out. Nothing else mattered at that moment. He hit the wall, but nothing happened. He looked around, surprised, but didn't see anywhere to turn. He could still smell Ethan in the place, so he assumed that this was a way out. He leaned against the wall and pushed as hard as he could. The wall slid to the side so fast that he fell through and hit the cold stone floor. The torch flew out of his hand and landed far behind him. Daniel looked at the dark tunnel, his heart beating fast. He kicked the door closed and pushed himself away from it.

A strange noise from the yard caught his attention. Cautiously, he stood up and walked to the window. He peered at the castle yard and saw a battle below. The army was inside the castle. That meant that the plan had worked, even though Daniel had screwed up.

He looked up and down the corridor, but had no idea where he was or which way to go. He turned on the spot three times, trying to figure out which way to go. He stopped and looked once more at the yard below. Then he hurried down the corridor, hoping that it was a way out.

Captain Stuart sprinted down the corridor. The battle cries from the yard were audible throughout the castle. His soldiers were fighting an uneven fight with the Royal Guards. He had to get to them as fast as he could. He turned the corner and crashed into a tall figure. He bounced off and fell to the ground. He looked up at the towering figure of Hans, who was standing in the corridor looking at Captain Stuart curiously.

"What's going on?" Hans asked calmly. "What's the rush?"

"Didn't you see?" Captain Stuart asked and stood up. "The Royal Guards are in the castle. One soldier caused panic, and the soldiers lowered the drawbridge to get out of the castle. Now the yard is full of Ethan's army."

"And where are *you* going?" Hans asked quietly while Captain Stuart massaged his elbow. "Shouldn't you go and look for the soon-to-be-dead king?"

Captain Stuart hesitated and looked at the end of the corridor. He then walked to the window and looked at the yard. He couldn't see Ethan anywhere, though he saw Lord Eric carrying what appeared to be two battle axes. "Ethan's not down there," he said quietly. "Maybe you're right and he's in the castle."

"We should go and look for him," Hans said calmly. He stepped closer to the captain.

Icy chills race down Captain Stuart's spine. He wasn't thrilled of being this close to Hans. "I will look for him," he said as calmly as he could, "you go and warn Mors."

"Warn Mors?" Hans laughed heartily, yet there was no merriness in the laughter. "Why? He already knows … Hmm …" he added and sniffed the air. "I like the smell of nervous pray."

Another chill ran down Captain Stuart's spine. He turned around and looked at Hans, but didn't step back. Hans watched Captain Stuart intently. He smiled at him, revealing all his teeth.

The hair on the Captain Stuart's back stood up. He straightened up and put his hand on the hilt of his sword. He had an important job ahead of him, and no werewolf was to stop him.

Lord James ran into the warehouse and stopped so abruptly that dust flew into the air. The torch in his hands illuminated vast space around him. He looked around the spacious wooden building, which was filled with food and clothes. Weapons were kept in the armoury in the lower levels of the castle under lock and key, so he didn't expect to find any in there, but then again, he wasn't after weapons.

Charles ran inside and crashed into Lord James. They both staggered, and Lord James turned around with his eyebrow raised. Charles stepped back and looked around. There were hundreds of boxes, barrels, and bags neatly placed, creating aisles.

"What the hell was all that about?" Charles asked, little annoyed. He folded his arms. "You ran to the castle, but before I could follow, you ran outside and then in here. Where are we, anyway?"

"This is the castle warehouse," Lord James said as he turned around. "I needed a torch for my plan. And here are other necessary things. We're going to make a fire that can be thrown, my friend," he added quietly, and he walked to the wall. He put the torch into the holder on the wall and marched to the boxes nearby. He threw the lid off the first box, leaned over the box, and picked up an apple. He bit off a piece and threw it back inside. He stepped towards the next box and threw its lid aside. Charles watched him with interest. Lord James sighed and walked away from the box, which contained potatoes. He walked through the aisle and opened another box. Silently, he pulled out a few shirts and threw them to Charles. "Tear these to small pieces for me, please."

Charles caught most of the shirts and looked at them surprised. Lord James didn't pay him any attention, but continued looking through the boxes. Charles threw all the shirts to the ground and then, one by one, tore them to smaller pieces.

Lord James walked to another aisle and opened another box. He rubbed his hands together happily and picked up a bottle of wine. He put it back and dragged the whole box to Charles. Charles froze in the middle of the tearing of the shirts and watched Lord James with his mouth hanging open. Lord James walked away and continued his search. In the next aisle, he located a corkscrew. He continued to the big barrels at the centre of the warehouse, grabbed the crowbar that was leant against one barrel, and smashed the top of one of the barrels. Charles watched Lord James, fascinated. Lord James smiled widely and grabbed a tin cup that was sitting nearby. He dipped it inside and took a long sip. He then threw the cup to the ground and smashed open the barrel that was standing next to the first. "This is quite a lot of rum," he said with a wide smile.

"I hope you are not planning on drinking it all," Charles said with a frown and a little concern in his voice. Lord James looked at Charles with a manic grin and continued to the next barrel. He smashed it open and peered inside. "Perfect!" he said happily, and he hurried back to Charles. He took one wine bottle from the box and opened it with the corkscrew. He handed the corkscrew to Charles, who threw down the shirt he'd been holding and took it. Lord James poured the wine out of the bottle onto the ground while Charles opened another bottle.

Lord James grabbed the pieces of cloth and returned to the barrels. Using the tin cup, he poured rum and then oil to the bottle, splashing much of the liquid onto the ground. It wasn't easy to hit the slim neck of the bottle. He pushed a piece of cloth inside the bottle, leaving part of the cloth hanging from the neck. Then he hurried to Charles for other bottles. He took three bottles and poured out their contents as he hurried back to the barrels. He poured rum and oil into these bottles as well, and pushed pieces of cloth into the bottle necks. He repeated the process with another ten bottles, breaking one bottle in the process, and stacked them into the emptied wine box. He had been in such a hurry that he'd spilled the mixture almost everywhere, but luckily there had been enough rum and oil in the barrels.

"Okay," Lord James said happily once they were done. He wiped his hands on the shirts that remained on the ground. "Let's go." He grabbed the box of bottles and carried it in his hands as if it were empty.

Charles followed him, still not completely sure what the plan was. "Why are we creating these mixtures?" he asked as he followed Lord James outside.

"If the werewolves get out, we light these and throw them at them. The oil and alcohol are easily ignited, but not so easily extinguished. The werewolves will light up immediately, and since the fire can kill them for sure, they will actually … Damn!" he said suddenly and looked down at the box. He stopped, looked at the yard where the fighting was still going on, and turned to Charles. "That reminds me—I forgot the torch. And we'll need it for this."

Charles turned on his heel and hurried back to the warehouse. He ran inside and stopped by the door. Then he noticed the torch on the wall and jumped to it. He pulled it out of the holder so fast that it flew out of his hands and fell to the ground. He cursed, grabbed it, and hurried after Lord James.

Ethan sprinted down the corridor. He wanted to get to the yard or at least to find some of the Royal Guards. He had no idea where the werewolves were and definitely didn't want to meet them. He turned around the corner and came face to face with Hans and Captain Stuart. Hans was very close to Captain Stuart, obviously saying something Captain Stuart didn't like.

Ethan stopped abruptly, trying to change the direction, but his feet continued forward, and he fell to the ground heavily. His bow flew out of his hands and hit the wall with a soft thud.

Captain Stuart looked away from the werewolf's face, and his stare fell on the king on the floor. Shock appeared on his face. The werewolf looked over his shoulder, and when he noticed Ethan, he smiled happily.

"What do we have here?" he said as he stepped towards Ethan. "I think Mors will be more than happy when he finds out that I killed the king. I told you, Captain, that there was no need to go running to the yard."

Captain Stuart blinked and looked from Ethan to Hans, who was slowly walking forward, enjoying the moment. Ethan pushed himself away. He peeked quickly at his bow and tried to calculate how fast he could get to it.

Captain Stuart suddenly jumped forward and threw Hans to the wall. Hans hit the stone and fell to the ground. Captain Stuart drew his sword and turned to Ethan whose jaw dropped open.

"Run, Your Majesty!" he shouted, and he jumped towards Hans. Hans screamed and jumped up so fast that he threw Captain Stuart to the ground. He threw off his coat and changed in front of Ethan to wolf. Captain Stuart staggered to his feet and pointed his sword at the approaching werewolf. Ethan noticed that his hand was shaking a little.

"Run!" Captain Stuart screamed at Ethan without taking his eyes off Hans. Ethan just lay on the floor unable to comprehend what was going on. Hans stepped closer and jumped at Captain Stuart, who jumped aside and slashed his back. Hans yelped and landed on the cold stone. He stood up, growled, and stepped towards Captain Stuart. Captain Stuart stood with his sword ready, shock visible on his face, and watched Hans approaching.

Ethan finally gathered his wits, jumped to his feet, and hurried to his bow. He pulled a silver-tipped arrow out of his quiver on his way, but before he could reach the bow, Hans turned around and stepped towards him. He revealed his teeth and snarled at Ethan. Ethan stopped and looked at the bow between him and Hans. Captain Stuart lifted his sword and attacked, but Hans was ready this time. He spun quickly and knocked the sword out of Captain Stuart's hands, throwing the captain to the floor. The sword flew through the air and landed on the other end of the corridor. Captain Stuart hit the floor hard and groaned.

Hans turned towards Ethan, ignoring Captain Stuart. Growling, he stepped forward. Ethan stepped back and drew his sword. It wasn't silver, but it was still better than nothing.

Captain Stuart jumped up and grabbed Hans from behind. The werewolf tried to shake him off, but Captain Stuart was too strong and too heavy. Hans started to change back to human, and Captain Stuart staggered aside, still grabbing the growing beast. He screamed at the top of his lungs and pulled the werewolf after him to the window. Hans completely changed to human and managed to grab Captain Stuart's head, but Captain Stuart reached the window and threw himself at it, pushing Hans through.

A look of utter shock spread across Hans's face as they both flew through the closed window, shattering it to pieces. Ethan hurried to the window and looked out of it. He watched the two men struggle in the air, each trying to get on top of the other.

Several soldiers and members of the Royal Guards stopped fighting and looked at the falling men. And then the captain and the werewolf both hit the stone tiles of the yard and remained lying still, broken and covered in blood.

Ethan watched them. His entire body was shaking. He still wasn't sure what had happened. He looked at the bodies below in disbelief. He stepped away from the window and leaned against the wall. He stood still for a while, trying to gather his thoughts. Then he remembered the plan and the fight in the yard. He picked up his bow and restlessly walked down the corridor.

Daniel hurried through the corridors. As he turned around the corner, he smelled a familiar scent behind him. He spun around just in time to see Lord Eric jump from behind a statue with a battle axe in each hand. Daniel jumped back, startled, but Lord Eric simply lowered the axes and looked at Daniel, stupefied. Then his gaze fell on the blood-stained clothes that were different from the ones Daniel had been wearing earlier. His gaze continued down to the bare feet. "What happened to you?" he asked.

Daniel looked at his shirt and shrugged. "We got separated," he explained. "First Ethan and I had to run away from the soldiers after we got attacked in the corridors, and then we met two werewolves, and we split. I have no idea where I am ... or where he is."

"So that ..." Lord Eric motioned one of his battle axes towards blood stains on Daniel's shirt.

"That's not mine," Daniel said. "Neither the shirt, nor the blood. As I said, we met the werewolves. The clothes belonged to one of them."

"Why are you wearing them?"

Daniel hesitated. He remembered the strange feeling, the urge to kill, and then Ethan's scared look. Then he remembered the dead girl in the tunnels. He was glad he wasn't the one who had killed her, but he could have just done the same to Ethan. He probably would have.

"That's a long story," he said at last. "The less you know, the happier you will be."

Lord Eric looked down at the stained shirt and nodded.

"Do you know where the exit is?" Daniel asked to draw the conversation away from the blooded clothes. Lord Eric nodded and motioned for Daniel to follow. They walked through the corridors, and Lord Eric told Daniel how the soldiers had opened the gate and lowered the bridge because they believed that the werewolves were on a hunt. Daniel once more saw the dead bodies in his mind but decided to keep this as a secret. It seemed that the werewolves were hunting that night after all.

Daniel stopped and turned around. A strange scent reached his nose, but he couldn't place it. There was something in the air there. A feeling that someone was watching him grew inside him. He looked at the corridor, but except a few shadows, didn't see anything. Yet, he could smell a woman's scent.

Lord Eric was halfway along the corridor when he noticed that Daniel wasn't with him anymore. He stopped and looked around. "What's going on?" he asked, and he walked back to Daniel. Daniel didn't answer; he just watched the shadow nearby. Then footsteps reached their ears. They both turned towards the further end of the corridor, but before they could even blink, a group of men appeared.

Bess stopped, and the rest of the werewolves, who had been following him, stopped as well. Daniel's heart started to beat hard as if it was trying to escape. He understood immediately that these were the werewolves.

There was something unmistakeable about them. And they all immediately understood that they were facing the famous wolf that had killed Axel and caused so much trouble to Hans.

Five werewolves out of the fifteen started to change. Bess looked around, surprised, and frowned.

Daniel could feel the hair on his neck standing up. He stepped back and grabbed Lord Eric's shoulder. Lord Eric looked at him with a question in his eyes. Then the werewolves sprinted after Daniel, and Daniel spun around, pulling Lord Eric after him. The forward motion was so strong that Lord Eric's battle axes fell to the ground and his feet left the ground for whole five seconds. Daniel sprinted so fast that even the transformed werewolves were unable to catch him. Lord Eric tried to keep off the floor most of the time, looking like a piece of cloth in the air. They reached a crossroad, and Daniel stopped on the spot. Lord Eric landed on the ground heavily and stopped at Daniel's feet. Daniel was still holding his arm, not paying him any attention.

"To your right!" Lord Eric shouted as he staggered to his feet. Before he could stand up properly, Daniel sprinted to his right, dragging Lord Eric after him. They reached the staircase, and Daniel looked down three stories. He looked at the corridor and saw five strange wolves running around the corner. He heaved Lord Eric up and put him over his shoulder.

"No!" Lord Eric shouted, but it was too late. In one quick move, Daniel jumped over the staircase railings and into the empty space. They flew in the air for a while and then landed heavily three floors below. Daniel lost his balance and fell to the ground. Lord Eric rolled down from his shoulder. Daniel stood up immediately and looked up. The werewolves stopped at the railings, pushed their snouts through the iron bars, and looked down. None of them dared to follow Daniel the same way.

Daniel grabbed Lord Eric and lifted him up. Lord Eric watched Daniel wide eyed, with his mouth agape. Daniel looked at him and quickly checked his clothes for blood stains. None appeared. "We should go," Daniel said quietly, and he turned to watch the stairs. The werewolves were sprinting down.

"What the hell just happened?" Lord Eric asked shocked. "How come I'm still alive? How come you're not even hurt?"

"I don't know." Daniel shook his head. "But we don't have time to discuss this. A bunch of werewolves is after us, remember? I cannot kill them all."

Lord Eric blinked and looked up at the stairs. The werewolves were in the middle of the stairs. Daniel looked up as well and gulped. He had to come up with some solution, and quickly.

"Get them to the yard!" Lord Eric said. "There are plenty of our men there. Just don't turn into a wolf or they might think that you are a werewolf too."

Daniel nodded, glanced at the stairs, and sprinted towards the main door. Out of the corner of his eye, he saw that Lord Eric had run the other way. Daniel sprinted through the main gate, and the werewolves followed. He peeked over his shoulder and saw that the werewolves were completely ignoring the guards and the soldiers and were following only him. And Daniel kept on running. He was faster than the werewolves, and while he was running he could come up with a solution to his little problem. He sprinted around the castle and emerged in another part of the yard. He immediately noticed the burning warehouse. And there, in the doorway, stood Lord Eric, waving at him.

The hot flames from the burning building were eating away the wood inside, and Daniel understood immediately Lord Eric's plan. They had to close the werewolves inside the burning building. Daniel sprinted towards the burning warehouse, trying to figure out how to get the werewolves inside. Lord Eric sprinted into the warehouse and vanished in the flames and smoke.

Daniel saw that Ethan had run into the yard and stopped on the spot. They exchanged a quick look, and Daniel hoped that the werewolves would be more interested in him and would not notice Ethan at all. He looked over his shoulder to see that the werewolves were still following him. He slowed down a little to make sure that he would still be the most desired target, and then rushed through the open door into the warehouse. He noticed that the smaller door on the other side of the building was open as well. He continued through the warehouse with the werewolves at his heels, trying to solve the question of how to keep the werewolves inside the burning building.

He sprinted between the aisles created by barrels and boxes and saw Lord Eric out of the corner of his eye. As in slow motion, he saw that

Lord Eric, his mouth covered with a piece of cloth, rolled one barrel after another into the path as soon as Daniel ran past him. Daniel sprinted forward, trying to keep the werewolves on his tail.

When the werewolves reached the centre of the building, a barrel crashed into the first werewolf and knocked him aside. The second barrel followed right after and hit another werewolf. The third barrel reached the second, and they both crashed, spilling wine all over the place.

The fire gushed into the air, and the building blew up.

Ethan was thrown to the ground. He could feel the stone tiles below his body. His head spun, and his left arm hurt. He rolled to his back and remained on the ground for a while, trying to catch his breath. Finally, he sat up and looked at the burning building. The flames were reaching high into the sky, and a lot of castle windows had shattered from the explosion. Lord Adrian and the Royal Guards were getting back to their feet, and Lord Thomas watched the warehouse with his mouth agape. Someone dragged Ethan to his feet, and he looked up into Lord James's face.

"Daniel and Lord Eric are inside!" Lord James shouted, but Ethan could hardly hear him. His ears were ringing, and Lord James's voice came as from far away. Ethan looked at the burning building, trying to process the last information he'd heard.

Someone bumped into Ethan and ran on. Ethan turned around, feeling confused. Lord James sprinted after the running man immediately, and it took Ethan a while to recognize Charles. Hesitantly, he stepped after them and watched Lord James catch up with Charles and pull him away from the burning building.

"Let me go!" Charles shouted, trying to shake Lord James off.

"You will be killed!" Lord James shouted back, pulling him away. "There's nothing you can do now."

"No! He's in there! We have to get him out!"

"He's dead," Lord James said quietly, and Charles fell to the ground, dragging Lord James with him.

"No." Charles shook his head, watching the warehouse. "No, he can't be."

"Even a werewolf wouldn't survive an explosion like that."

Ethan reached them and stopped. Holding onto his left arm, which hurt like hell, he watched the flames. His heart was beating painfully in his chest. Lord Eric and Daniel were both gone, taking five werewolves with them. He had lost another lord. He had lost another friend.

Charles shook his head and put his head into his hands. Lord James let go of him and stood up. Ethan collapsed to the ground, watching the burning warehouse. He felt tired, weak, dizzy, and useless.

All of the soldiers and the guards were running through the yard, putting out the fire. Buckets of water were thrown at the burning building, and the empty buckets were sent from hand to hand all the way to the moat. Ethan looked around. The werewolves' deaths seemed to put an end to the fights. Captain Stuart was dead; Hans and Mors had been killed. There was no one to listen to.

"There's someone here!" a soldier shouted. He was looking towards the back door of the warehouse. Charles lifted his head. Lord James stepped closer and then looked at Charles. Charles lifted himself off the ground and stepped towards the soldier. With each step, he walked faster and faster, until he was running all the way with Lord James at his heels.

Ethan stood up and hurried after them. When he reached the other side of the warehouse, he immediately recognized Daniel's lifeless body. Charles pushed his way through the standing soldiers and knelt by Daniel. Lord James stopped nearby. "Go help the others put out the fire," Lord James ordered the soldiers. The soldiers hesitated for a second, and then one by one, saluted to Lord James. Lord James nodded, and the soldiers hurried back to work in the bucket brigade.

"We have to get him inside," Charles said to Lord James. "He probably needs a doctor."

"Does that mean he's alive?" Lord James asked as he leaned over Daniel. Blood was dripping down Daniel's face and neck, and his clothes were completely blooded and burnt.

Charles grabbed Daniel's arms, lifted him off the ground, and put him over his shoulder. He stumbled and then hurried away from the burning building. Ethan watched him walk into the castle. He was still grabbing his left arm, which was now bleeding heavily. Then his gaze fell upon the soldiers who were dragging Hans's body into the warehouse fire. As soon as they reached the warehouse, they threw the body into the flames.

Ethan looked at his left arm. He wasn't sure if it was the wound from the first battle or a new one, but it sure hurt like hell. He wiped his blooded hand against his trousers and walked to Captain Stuart's body. He knelt by him and turned his face up. The captain's body was still warm, and the blood was still dripping down his face. Ethan pressed his fingers against Captain Stuart's neck and tried to find the pulse. He found it.

"Quickly, get him to a doctor!" he shouted at the closest soldier. The man jumped up and turned around nervously. It took him a second or two to notice Ethan, but then he went pale. His jaw dropped as he watched the king wide eyed. Ethan raised his eyebrow and was about to repeat the order when the soldier nodded nervously. He stepped towards the castle, not taking his eyes off Ethan, and staggered on the stone tiles. He spun around and sprinted into the castle.

Ethan watched the entrance to the castle uncertainly and then scanned the yard, looking for another soldier or guard he could send for a doctor. Suddenly, the man came out with three other soldiers. They all seemed very nervous and were avoiding Ethan's stare. They knelt by their captain, picked him up, and clumsily carried him inside the castle.

Ethan still wasn't sure what the captain's angle was, but he was thankful to him for saving his life in that corridor. Maybe once the captain woke up, he would be able to explain the situation to Ethan.

CHAPTER 14

B ess stood up and dusted broken glass off his shirt. He was cut in many places, but that didn't bother him. He didn't need to see the yard to know that the werewolves were dead. It was only their fault. They had hurried after the wolf on their own accord. "We should leave," he said quietly. "Now, before we all get killed."

"We have to get Mors," another werewolf said.

Bess shook his head. "I bet that Mors is dead," he said, and he began to walk down the corridor. "I bet that was the part of the plan. Find and kill Mors while no one knows they're here and then open the gates and lower the bridge."

"How do we get out?" another werewolf asked behind Bess. There was panic in his voice.

"There is a secret tunnel out of the castle," Bess said over his shoulder. "It's only a one-way tunnel because it cannot be opened from the outside. It leads to the forest. We can get out of the castle, and then we'll need to hurry south. Once we are in Wolfast, we will send the treaty to Ethan. We'll pay for the damages we caused and promise not to return to Norene. In return, we will demand that Norene doesn't enter one foot into our domain."

"Why?" the werewolf to Bess's right asked.

Bess stopped and looked at him. "Look outside," he said quietly, motioning towards the broken windows. "We are not a match for Norene's army. I don't want it in our country. Do you?"

There was a long silence. Three of the werewolves looked at their toes. Bess did a quick calculation in his head. Hans and Axel were dead. They had been the most aggressive. Mors was most likely dead, and if he wasn't, he at least was doomed. Two werewolves were nowhere to be found, but those two were the most savage and stupid, and Bess didn't miss them at all. Five of the most stupid werewolves had just run after the wolf and Lord Eric and had been blown up. All that meant that Bess was left with the most timid werewolves. They accepted him as alpha as soon as they found out that they were the last ones. This should been easy.

Bess turned around and hurried to the staircase. The werewolves followed him like little ducklings. He could smell their fear and panic. None of them noticed that the shadow moved and was following them. "How do you know where to go?" one of the werewolves asked.

Bess didn't look around to find out who had spoken; he knew that they all had that same question on their minds. "I read about this tunnel in a journal. If the tunnel is not real, we are as good as dead."

In total silence, they walked down the stairs and through the corridors. Luckily, everyone was in the yard or in the entrance hall, and the rest of the castle was empty. Bess led the werewolves to the underground corridors. He stopped in front of an open door and looked inside. The place was supposed to be unknown, yet it was open and well lit. "Well," he said as he stepped inside. "We know now where the spy was hiding."

He looked around the room and picked up a small painting. It was Ethan's childhood portrait. He looked at it and threw it back on top of the boxes. He noticed another open corridor leading out of the room and motioned to the werewolves to follow him. He pulled a torch out of a holder and hurried inside the secret tunnel.

His heart was beating like crazy. He was really hoping that no one knew about this tunnel, but it was clear that the tunnel wasn't totally secret. There was a strong possibility that Ethan had known about it all along. In fact, he could have left his guards outside. Even if he hadn't, he could send someone to check the tunnel. Bess needed to get out—out of the castle, and out of Norene.

They reached the end of the tunnel and stopped. It was a dead end. Bess lifted the torch and looked at the wall. He scanned the tunnel's end, looking for a switch, but couldn't find anything. He pressed his hand against the stone, but nothing happened. He leaned against the wall and tried to push it. At first, it moved very slowly, but then the hinges squeaked, and the door opened.

It opened all the way and the torchlight fell on two dead bodies by the entrance. Bess stepped outside and stopped next to the dead soldiers. He had been right. Ethan had known about this secret tunnel and had probably used it to get inside. The rest of the werewolves walked around Bess outside, ignoring the dead soldiers. Bess looked at the castle above them and stepped to the side. It felt like ages since they had arrived at the castle for the first time.

He was standing still, watching the castle, when a soft bark made him turn around. All the werewolves stood there in wolf form and watched him. He realized that they were waiting for him to lead the way. He threw the torch to the entrance, changed, and ran towards the forest with the rest of the pack at his heels.

The secret door stood opened for a while and then slowly, by the force of gravity, started to close. Amy stepped out of the tunnel and looked after the werewolves. The shapes were sprinting in the darkness towards rising moon. They reached the forest and disappeared among the trees.

A loud thud made her turn around. The entrance was gone. The torch on the ground illuminated the impenetrable stone wall.

"Damn!" She cursed and hurried to the wall. She pressed against the stone, but nothing happened.

"You got locked out, didn't you?" Rex's voice said.

She spun around and folded her arms when she spotted the tall figure in front of her. She wasn't really keen on meeting Rex there. She felt as if he was checking up on her. "Yeah." She nodded and stepped closer. "But they will open the gates soon, and I will find that wolf once more. And this time, there won't be over a dozen werewolves nearby to stop me."

"Does it mean that they didn't manage to kill it?" Rex asked quietly as he stepped closer.

Amy shook her head. "He actually killed off five of them. Maybe he died in the process, but I don't think so. And I found two corpses earlier that had been attacked by some third werewolf or wolf, so I'm guessing he has seven notches in his belt at least. He definitely didn't look so tough when I saw him in the corridor."

"Did you get the necklace?"

"No. I saw it, but before I could try to get it, he was chased away by five werewolves. I didn't have a chance to get close to him."

Rex nodded slowly and looked into the forest where the werewolves had disappeared. The light from the castle was slowly dimming, which meant that the fire was under control. "Five days," Rex said with a sigh. He shook his head. "They kept Norene for five days and then they lost it again. And the wolf is still alive and carrying that necklace. I shouldn't have sent werewolves to do a man's job."

Amy looked at him. His eyes were glowing in the darkness, an unmistakeable sign that he was angry. He looked at her and then at the castle. "I count on you," he said at last. "I don't want to be too close to the necklace. It's too dangerous. I could attract the wrong kind of people, if you get my drift. Get me that necklace, but don't try to kill the wolf; he's too strong and too hard to kill. I underestimated the whole situation when I thought that the werewolves would be able to take care of it; and if the werewolves cannot kill it ... Well, you are a very good thief ..."

"I will get it," she said confidently. "Just leave that to me."

He nodded and walked into the darkness of the night. Amy stood by the rock wall and watched after him. She knew he trusted her, but the fact that he had come to check up on her was a little unnerving. Did it mean that he was reluctant to trust her as much as he used to, or that he distrusted the werewolves?

She sighed and looked at the castle above her. There was no point in trying to get inside. There were too many people and too much going on up there. Besides, the building was not Wolfast's palace. This was a fortress, and it was really difficult to sneak into.

She sighed and stepped towards the city. Whatever she needed to do could wait a day.

Ethan walked up the stairs. He wore a new tunic, and his shoulder had already been cleaned and bandaged. Soldiers and guards were still running all around, saluting him on the go. The castle was too small for the army, so

Ethan had ordered to empty as many rooms as possible and accommodate some guards inside. The first floor was turned into a field hospital, the other five into sleeping accommodations. He slowly walked by the rooms, watching the doctors running up and down with blooded bandages and buckets of boiling water. He tried to stay out of the way as he walked from one room to the next.

He entered a room where Captain Stuart lay and stopped at the threshold. A doctor was bandaging his left arm while his assistant was cleaning the captain's face with a wet cloth. "How is he doing?" Ethan asked quietly.

"Hard to tell," the doctor answered without even looking up. "The fall was too long. Even though he fell onto the werewolf's body, the impact caused major injuries. His left leg and left arm are broken, but they should heal. He also has broken ribs, but none of them penetrated his heart or his lungs. Now it's up to him."

"What about his head?" Ethan asked, watching the assistant wiping off the blood from the captain's face.

"That's even harder to tell," the doctor answered. He looked up. When he saw Ethan at the door, he hesitated. He watched the king for a while and then decided to treat him as before. "We will be sure once he wakes up."

"*If* he wakes up," the assistant specified. He wrung the cloth out in the warm water and continued wiping the captain's face.

"Take a good care of him," Ethan said, and he stepped out of the room.

"You want him fit for the gallows?"

Ethan stopped in the doorway and looked over his shoulder at the doctor. The doctor blushed and looked down. Ethan sighed and turned to leave. "No, I want to promote him," he said, and he left the room. Out of the corner of his eye he saw surprised looks on the doctor's and the assistant's faces.

The more he thought about it, the more confused he was. The possibility that Captain Stuart had just wanted to change sides quickly crossed his mind, but the situation hadn't been that favourable for Ethan in that corridor. He shook his head and decided to deal with the situation if Captain Stuart regained consciousness. He would have until then to decide what to do with the man.

He stopped at another door and watched another doctor removing

Daniel's bloodied clothes. Daniel was bleeding quite a lot, and his right arm was dark and burnt. Charles paced the room anxiously, occasionally stopping and checking the progress. Ethan watched Charles for a while and then coughed. Charles stopped pacing and looked towards the doorway. Ethan motioned to Charles. Charles looked at Daniel over his shoulder, left the room, and stepped into the corridor.

"He'll be all right," Ethan said quietly when Charles joined him outside. Charles nodded, looking at the ground in front of him. "He survived the fire, and that's the most important part," Ethan continued. "In a week or two, he'll be up and running."

"If I'm to judge," Charles whispered, "he'll be up and running much sooner. He heals really quickly. I've seen a bite heal in two days that should have left a scar."

"So, why the anxiety?"

Charles sighed and folded his arms. Ethan patiently waited for Charles to gather his thoughts. Charles opened his mouth, hesitated, and then shook his head. Ethan still waited. "He wanted to leave," Charles said at last. "He wanted to leave right before the fair. I made him stay. He didn't want to, but he stayed because of me. And then it all went wrong. He got attacked, arrested, attacked again, dragged into the castle, attacked again, and blown up. All because of me."

"He would be still running if it were not for you," Ethan argued back. "He chose to go to the castle because he realized that the werewolves wanted him dead, and the only way out of that was to attack them before they attacked him. He knew the situation he was getting into. And the most important part is that he survived it. True, it could have gone better, but he will be all right. And I'm sure that once he wakes up, he will tell you that you have no reason to feel guilty about anything."

Charles nodded, still looking at the floor. Lord Adrian approached them, but kept a discreet distance. Ethan looked up, and their eyes met. He patted Charles on the shoulder, leaving him to his thoughts, and walked over to Lord Adrian. "Report?" he asked with a sign when he reached him.

Lord Adrian looked at papers in his hands and flipped through them. "We have two hundred seventeen injured members of the Royal Guards and seventy-eight dead. The enemy soldiers suffered bigger losses, almost three hundred. Seven hundred and fourteen soldiers are injured. The rest were disarmed and are now being interrogated by Lord Thomas. We have also about seventy deserters who returned from the surrounding forest. Lord Thomas is doing some cross-checking on everyone and everything."

"What about Lords Michael, Martin, and Blake?"

"We don't have any information on them. They all left the castle this afternoon. The bigger trouble will be the soldiers who went out to look for you."

"What should we do with them?" Ethan asked, looking out of the window.

"There will be quite a lot of deserters. The moment the soldiers left the castle, they left the army. They should—"

"Sorry, I meant what should we do with the betraying lords?" Ethan specified his question.

Lord Adrian stood still for a while, thinking hard. "Well," he said slowly, "I wouldn't behead them. There would be consequences. They are still lords and heirs to the old families. But I would not let them go either. That would send the wrong message, as if saying that their behaviour was all right."

"That's what I thought too." Ethan nodded and stepped forward. "What is your view on exile and confiscation of their properties? Their families can stay, but they will lose everything."

Lord Adrian thought about this while walking silently by Ethan's side. They reached the staircase, and Ethan continued to the next floor. "That might work, but they could still unite some soldiers and try to counterattack," Lord Adrian answered while they climbed the stairs. "On the other hand, if you locked them up, they could try to manipulate the situation from within, having more direct access to the soldiers. The dungeons are breakable."

"Plus, there is the cost of feeding them," Ethan added and stopped on the stairs. "And then the cost for the guards who would look after them."

"I think that exile and confiscation of their properties is a good idea. I assume that they will lose their titles as well?"

Ethan nodded and continued climbing the stairs. Lord Adrian followed him. "However," Ethan continued, "If we lose three lords, I need to make some arrangements. Unfortunately, neither Lord Eric nor Lord Jonathan has a male heir. Their lines end with them."

"Didn't Lord Eric have children?" Lord Adrian asked.

"He had two daughters," Ethan nodded. "And neither has a son. Lord Jonathan was too young to have any children at all. His father died too young, and he had no brother. That means that I need a new lord, someone who shows a lot of courage and a good heart."

"Are you thinking of Charles?" Lord Adrian asked in an even voice. Ethan stopped at the top of the stairs on the fourth floor and turned to face Lord Adrian.

"You disagree?" he asked calmly.

"He doesn't really know anything about ruling," he pointed out, and they continued down the corridor. "He's a good man, true. He was willing to join us, and he was a great help to us, but he did it to protect Daniel."

"But when they got separated, he helped you and Lord James get the gates open," Ethan pointed out. "He didn't run after Daniel. He fought bravely and showed true courage. As for his ability to rule and make important decisions, even the first lords had to learn those skills the hard way. Besides, you can keep an eye on him while he learns his ways around."

"True." Lord Adrian nodded as they stopped in front of the library. "And I'm sure he would learn quickly. If you really wish it, My Liege, I will happily take Lord Charles under my wing."

Ethan looked at Lord Adrian, frowning, and Lord Adrian looked back at him. They stared at each other for a few seconds and then both burst out laughing. They laughed merrily for almost a minute. Soldiers passing by nervously looked at them and changed their direction. When Ethan's stomach started to hurt, he leaned forward and rested his hands against his knees. Lord Adrian wiped his eyes and took a deep breath.

"Sorry," Ethan said at last and straightened up. "I am really tired and hurting … but *my liege*? That one really made my day."

"Yeah." Lord Adrian smiled widely and nodded. "When I'm tired, I sometimes use very archaic words."

Ethan patted Lord Adrian on the shoulder and entered the library with smile on his lips. Lord Adrian followed him inside. "It's always good to see you laugh," Lord Adrian said. "I hope that from now on you can rule peacefully and officially."

Ethan nodded and pulled his diary from the leather pouch on his belt. He sat behind the table, opened to the last used page, and looked at the entry. "The weird part is that it feels like ages since I sat here and wrote these words, yet it happened only a few days ago. Who would have thought that my life would take this strange detour?"

Lord Adrian smiled and left the library, leaving Ethan alone with his thoughts. Ethan picked up the quill and dipped it into the inkbottle. He wrote the current date and hesitated. He watched the empty page for a while and then decided to write the last few days as truthfully as possible. He placed the tip of the quill on the paper and wrote:

> The battle didn't go as planned, and I was forced to leave the warmth and security of Royal Castle. To my best recollection, this is what happened …

Daniel opened his eyes and looked around. The sun was setting over the castle walls. He sat up and threw off the blanket. His right arm was scarred, but didn't hurt at all. It seemed he had been burnt. That meant that burns were not healable. He looked at his hand curiously from all sides. He touched the scarred skin with his other hand, but it didn't hurt, though it felt weird. He wondered if his paw would be hairless, but didn't wish to find out right away. He rolled up his sleeve, but the burnt area ended by his elbow. He looked beneath his shirt, but couldn't see any scars there. He relaxed a little, and then a thought occurred to him. He quickly looked inside his pants and smiled happily. The hand seemed to be the only part of his body that was marked. He put his feet down and stood up.

His legs easily supported him, which was very reassuring. He wasn't hurting anywhere. He jumped up and down, but still nothing hurt. He couldn't remember what really had happened, but he remembered some parts of the previous night. He remembered the two werewolves in the tunnel and quickly suppressed that memory. Then he remembered meeting Lord Eric in the corridor and then the werewolves. He vividly remembered the chase and how he had run into the burning warehouse.

He walked to the window and looked out onto the yard, but his window wasn't facing the warehouse. Since the castle was still standing, he assumed that the guards had managed to get the fire under control.

He was really glad that he had managed to get the werewolves into the burning warehouse. And then he remembered Lord Eric's face covered with a piece of cloth. Daniel's smile froze as he recalled the events of that night. He wanted to find someone quickly and find out if Lord Eric had made it out of the building, but at the same time was scared to ask the question because he already knew the answer.

Then he remembered Charles running after the soldiers in that corridor. He hadn't seen Charles anywhere after that. What if he never saw Charles again? His chest tightened, and he felt a big lump in his throat. The idea was unbearable, and the possibility that it may be true was scary. He had never felt so lonely in his life. He leaned against the cold glass of the window, closed his eyes, and tried to calm down a little.

"Daniel," Charles's voice came from the door.

Daniel spun around and blinked away tears. Charles stood by the door. A wide smile appeared on Daniel's face. "I'm so glad you're all right," he said happily as he stepped forward. "I was worried that you got hurt during that fight—or worse."

"No, I'm fine. You actually got *me* really scared," Charles said with a smile. He came into the room. "I thought you didn't make it out of that building before it blew up."

"Why did it blow up in the first place?" Daniel asked as he sat down on the bed. His legs were suddenly very shaky, and he felt dizzy.

"I don't know exactly." Charles shrugged and sat next to Daniel. "There was nothing in there that should have exploded."

"Lord Eric threw wine barrels at the werewolves," Daniel said remembering the small figure between the flames. "Is he all right?"

Charles pressed his lips together and shook his head. Daniel gulped and nodded. He had expected this answer, but it still hurt. "Well," Charles said quietly, "I think that the oil caught fire and was really hot when the barrels of much colder wine landed on top of it, and the oil exploded. It sure got rid of those werewolves and actually ended the fight. You should be proud of Lord Eric. He died a hero."

Daniel nodded, looking to the floor. His vision got a little blurry. He rubbed his eyes, but they still burnt.

"The king wants to see you," Charles said. Daniel looked up scared. "Don't worry," Charles added with a wide smile. "He's just concerned about you and wants to make sure you are all right,"

Daniel nodded and looked at the door. The last time he had seen Ethan, they were in a dark tunnel with dead werewolves, and Ethan was looking really scared. Well, Daniel couldn't blame him. He hadn't really been himself, and the worst part was that he wasn't really sure whether he would have hurt Ethan if the werewolves had not been in the tunnel. Who knows what would have happened?

Charles stood up, and Daniel absentmindedly followed him out of the room, through the corridors, and up the stairs. A few silent minutes later they stopped in front of the office, and Charles knocked on the door. They heard a muffled "Come in!" from inside, and Charles opened the door.

Daniel nervously entered the office. Ethan was sitting behind the table with a quill in his hand, watching the door curiously. When he saw Daniel, a wide smile spread across his face. He put the quill down, stood up, and walked over to Daniel, who looked really scared and nervous, like a dog that had done something wrong and was awaiting some form of punishment. "Daniel!" Ethan said happily. "I'm so glad to see you finally awake."

Charles smiled and closed the door. Daniel peeked over his shoulder at the door and nervously turned to face Ethan. "I ..." he said hesitantly, trying to find words that would express how sorry he was for what had happened.

Ethan returned to his chair at the table and gestured for Daniel to sit in the chair opposite him. "I wanted to thank you," Ethan said.

Daniel's mouth gaped open. "*Thank* me?" he asked incredulously as he sat down. "For what?"

"For saving my life in that tunnel and for risking your life in a successful attempt to kill the werewolves," Ethan answered. He sat behind the table. "It definitely ended the fight."

"But ... I nearly attacked you in that tunnel."

"I don't think you would have done. Maybe I am delusional, but you did attack the werewolves, and afterwards you let me leave. You just had a difficult moment in there. That was all. Though I have to admit that I nearly shit my pants after we entered that tunnel. And again the second time, when I saw two werewolves in that tunnel. I will have nightmares for a while now, but still, you saved my life. Thanks."

Daniel nodded slowly, his mouth still hanging open. He watched Ethan, unable to find any words to say. He wasn't sure if he was dreaming, but it seemed real enough. He thought about the situation in the tunnel and then shook his head, trying to suppress the memory of the dead maid.

"There's something else I wanted to talk to you about," Ethan continued. Daniel straightened up in the chair and looked at him. "I discussed this with Charles, and he came up with the idea. He feels responsible for the whole situation, since you wanted to leave on the day of the fair ... whatever that means. And he would like you to accompany him to his new home. You will be safe with him. Of course, if you wish to stay here, you are more than welcome."

Daniel's mouth dropped opened once more. He watched the king wide eyed. "Thank you! Thank you so much!" he said happily, and he jumped in excitement. "I didn't dare hope ... I wasn't sure ... I mean ... Thank you!" He ran around the table and hugged surprised Ethan.

Ethan patted Daniel's back, laughing merrily. "Don't mention it," Ethan said when Daniel let go. He stood up to be at the same level and patted his shoulder. "You were a great help. You promised to help me get rid of the werewolves, and you did just that, saving my life in the process. I consider you my friend, and I hope you will take me for yours."

"I will, I will!" Daniel nodded. He looked Ethan in the eye, and then put his hands around his neck and pulled off the necklace. "This is for you," he said, and handed the necklace to Ethan.

Ethan took it and looked at the small light blue stone. "I cannot accept this," he shook his head and looked up at Daniel.

"I want you to have it," Daniel insisted with a wide smile. "It brought me luck. Maybe it will bring you some luck, too."

Ethan smiled at Daniel and pulled the necklace over his head. He looked at the small stone and then looked back at Daniel, who watched Ethan with a wide happy smile. "Thank you," Ethan said. "If you ever want it back, you know where it is."

CHAPTER 15

E than was glad to see that the place was returning to the old routine.
He found the next day rather uneventful until the armies returned.
They didn't seem to be surprised to see the king in the castle; quite the
contrary. The army was getting too big to stay in the castle, so Ethan
ordered that a camp be set up not far away.

In the evening, Ethan returned to his office and stood by the window
watching the life in the yard. A few soldiers were walking around the
castle with bandages on their heads or arms. Captain Stuart was still
unconscious, and Ethan still hadn't made up his mind about the whole
situation. The werewolves had escaped, as had the lords, including Blake,
who had left his castle the morning after the battle. Ethan wished from
the bottom of his heart to get his hands on Blake.

The leaflet *The Freedom Speaker* had quickly spread the word of the
battle and Ethan's victory. Ethan didn't know the people behind it but
was very keen to meet them one day. He wanted to thank them. He
thought that people who were issuing *The Royal Messenger* and printing
books for the royal family were behind this leaflet too. There were two
other places with printing machines in Norene. Ethan found out that all
the premises had been searched while Lord Blake was trying to find the
people responsible. There had to be a printing machine somewhere that
they didn't know about.

A soft knock sounded on the door. Ethan turned around and sat
behind the table. He looked at the papers he'd been reading, and when
he was sure that he hadn't left anything important visible, he called,
"Come in."

The door opened, and a very skinny man peeked inside. Ethan watched
him with his eyebrow raised. The man gulped and entered. He seemed

extremely nervous as he closed the door behind him and stepped forward. Ethan grabbed a sword hidden beneath the table, but remained seated, awaiting further development.

"Your Majesty," the man said and bowed a little.

"Who are you? How did you get here?" Ethan asked sharply.

"The guards let me get through, Sire," the man replied in a surprised tone of voice. "I came to talk to you about Captain Stuart. You see, he asked me for help before the first battle, so I came to speak on his behalf."

Ethan tightened his grip on the sword, but didn't charge. He was getting more and more curious. With his free hand, he motioned to the chair in front of the table, and the man sat down. He hunched in the chair and nervously looked at Ethan. "Before the battle," he continued in a shaky voice, "Captain Stuart got some background information on the betrayal, but he didn't have time to warn you or your lords, so he sent me home. I was in charge of the communication and had my carrier pigeons with me. I left them with the captain. I believe that he hid them somewhere in the castle. Some pigeons arrived at my home during the following days, bringing messages with them. I was to bring them to you. When the battle started, Captain Stuart was leading part of the army. He deliberately made a mistake that led to Lord James's successful retreat and—"

"You mean that the gap in the line was his *deliberate* doing?" Ethan asked. He let go of the sword. The man nodded vigorously. Ethan leaned back and motioned to the man to continue his story.

"Afterwards, he was collecting information from the castle and sending it to me. He knew of the cave system in the Simels Mountains, though he didn't know where exactly the entrances were and expected Lord James to use it as a camp. He instructed me to leave the message nearby, but never to bring it too close."

"That message about the human wolf was from you?"

"Oh, yes." The man nodded. "A friend of mine tipped me off, and then I saw them on the other side of the hill. I knew they had decided to take the longer but safer road. You know … the road with fewer villages and fewer curious villagers. I didn't have time or means to notify Captain Stuart, so I quickly wrote you a note. At first, I thought you didn't get it on time, but luckily, you did manage to get that boy."

Ethan leaned his head against his hand and watched the man in front of him. He wasn't sure if the man was telling the truth, but there was one thing that didn't fit the description. "Captain Stuart always wanted to be the captain of the Royal Guards," Ethan said slowly. "Everyone knew that. If Blake had become king, he would get the post for sure. Why did he help *me*?"

"Well, if you knew Captain Stuart, you would have noticed that he was very loyal to your father. He risked his life in Flying Jimmy's crew for his king and country. He really wants to be the captain of the Royal Guards, but not like this. He actually never liked Lord Blake, and this betrayal was way too much for his taste. That's why he wanted to help you. At first, he was thinking of deserting and hurrying to warn you, but he was risking that he would not get to you in time. Instead, he decided to remain with Lord Blake and to find a way to help you on the battlefield. Afterwards, he wanted to leave and find you in the forest, but he realized that he could be much more useful to you in the castle, next to the source of all the troubles."

Ethan nodded absentmindedly. Captain Stuart's actions had helped them a lot. And Captain Stuart was high enough in rank to have a lot of information. And, apparently, he was devious enough to get the rest. And the fact that he had risked his life to save Ethan from Hans supported this theory, however crazy it seemed.

The man suddenly stood up and stepped to the table. Ethan grabbed the sword and readied himself, but the man only put a golden medallion on the table. Ethan picked it up with his free hand. It was very small and was attached to a long slim gold chain. The medallion was embossed with a little bird. "Blackbird?" he asked, and he looked at the man. The man nodded with a smile. Ethan let go of the sword and rubbed the bridge of his nose. "So," he said, "Captain Stuart found out about the treason, but instead of trying to inform me and risking that he would not manage to do so in time, he let Lord Blake attack my troops, and then he created a gap for us to escape through and then remained in the castle next to Blake and sent the secret information to you, and you brought them to our hiding place?"

"I ...," the man opened his mouth, but paused for a long time, obviously trying to process the question. "Please, could you repeat the question?" he asked at last.

Someone knocked and opened the door before Ethan could react. Lord Adrian entered and stopped in the doorway. He looked from the man to Ethan and placed his hand on the hilt of his swords. "I'm sorry, Your Majesty," he said hesitantly as he looked at the man standing in front of the king's table. "There is a messenger from Wolfast. He brought you a message."

Ethan's eyebrows raised in surprise. He watched Lord Adrian for a while and then turned to the man. "Thank you for the information," he said. "I will definitely consider it."

The man bowed and left the office, leaving the medallion on Ethan's table. Lord Adrian looked after the man curiously. He watched him close the door and then handed Ethan a thick parchment. Ethan took it and opened it. He read the message for a while and the further down he went, the wider was the smile that appeared on his face. Lord Adrian waited patiently for Ethan to break the silence. "Truce!" Ethan said, and he looked up. "They want a truce. They will pay us four boxes of iron, seven boxes of copper, and one box of gold to help us repair the damaged castle. And we have to promise not to enter Wolfast with the army for at least one hundred years. Of course, Wolfast promises the same."

"Why would they be willing to do this?"

"Well, they have almost no army. Thanks to our brave Royal Guards they suffered huge losses. If we attacked now, we would crush them. Their new leader—." He looked at the parchment. "Bess ... wants to ensure that that doesn't happen."

"But why pay us? They wanted Norene for our resources, and now they give us theirs?"

"No, they wanted to open trade with Norene. I suspect that Mors was more interested in our weapons than our minerals. They have a lot of minerals of their own; they just lack our knowledge in working with them. And Bess wants the treaty to be irresistible."

Ethan put the parchment down and leaned back in his chair. Lord Adrian watched him in silence. "Are you going to sign it?" he asked.

Ethan sighed and shrugged. "I see no reason why I shouldn't," he said at last. "But first I want to read this thoroughly, to make sure there is no catch. If I see none, I will sign this." Then he noticed another piece of parchment, much smaller, attached to the larger one. He picked it up and read the personal letter from Bess. As he came to the end of the letter, he burst out laughing and handed the letter to Lord Adrian. Lord Adrian took it while Ethan leaned against the table.

"Your Majesty," Lord Adrian read out loud. "I understand that you have no reason to trust us, and I understand completely if you want a few days to study the treaty I sent you. Please, take as much time as you need. I am wishing only for peace between our two countries. I hope you will find the treaty acceptable. If you have any objections or improvements, please, send the word via the messenger ... I don't see what's so funny," he said, furrowing his brow, and looked at Ethan.

"Read the post scriptum," Ethan said, still smiling.

Lord Adrian looked at the letter and continued reading: "P.S. Lords Michael and Martin of Norene were caught in Wolfast hiding in a small village near the borders. Since we are still officially at war with you, they are now in our custody charged with spying. If you decide to sign the treaty, let me also know if you wish your former lords to return. If you don't request otherwise or don't sign the treaty, we will execute them ... Consider this my coronation gift to you."

Lord Adrian looked up and put the letter down on the table.

"Will you request their return?" he asked curiously.

"No," Ethan shook his head, "but I will let Bess know that they are exiled from Norene and therefore he can do with them whatever he pleases."

Two days later, Bess was sitting in the palace's library, checking letters that had been placed on a table in front of him. The letters were rather old and faded. Most were still in good condition, but some were illegible.

An old man entered the library, his hands filled with parchments and old and faded scrolls, which he added to the documents already on the desk. He straightened up, and his back cracked in protest.

Bess looked up with a smile. "You need some exercise, Steven," he said to the man.

Steven waved his hand dismissively and picked up a much newer piece of paper. "I need a lesson on your handwriting," he said and walked around the table with the paper in his hand. "This letter you sent me from Norene is indecipherable. What's this word?"

Bess looked at the letter and frowned. He picked up the letter and scratched his jaw. Steven stood by him awaiting an answer patiently.

"You have no idea, do you?" Steven asked two minutes later.

"No, no. I will remember. I needed all records on the mines in north of Wolfast."

"I could read that part," Steven nodded. "Records for the first and second year after the battle for Norene and letters sent during that period in Wolfast."

"No." Bess shook his head. "Not first and second, but the year after and the year before."

The man blinked and looked at the letter. He picked it up and walked to the window. He read the letter in the sunlight for a minute and then shook his head. "Sorry, but this really doesn't look like *before*. It looks like *second*."

"Why would I write 'year first and second'? It would make much more sense to write 'first and second year'."

"That's what I thought, but that was the only thing that would have made sense. Okay, so one year prior as well," he said with a sigh as he returned to Bess. He walked around the table and leaned against it. "But still, I cannot decipher this part: 'if I can find *resorts of a pan in green byes*?'"

"No, it's not *resorts*." Bess shook his head. "But you're right. It looks a lot like *resorts*. Maybe, it's reports … or records. Yes, it would be records." Bess nodded and stood up. "I really have to write more legibly. It's definitely records of a … of a …"

"Of a pan," Steven said in a matter-of-fact tone of voice.

"No!" Bess shook his head and bit his lip. "Records of a man!" he said finally. Steven looked up at him with his eyebrow raised. "Yes, I remember. Records of a man with glowing green eyes."

"Don't you have a more difficult request?" Steven asked sarcastically. Bess looked at him with a frown. Steven sighed, took the letter, and walked out of the library, mumbling something under his breath. Bess shook his head and sat down. He went through the letters on the table until the door opened once more and a guard entered. He saluted and nervously waited for Bess to notice him. Bess looked up from an old letter, and when he noticed the guard, he stood up, excitement rising inside him.

"The messenger is here," the guard said. "The one from Norene."

Bess nodded and hurried out of the library, leaving the guard behind. He quickened his pace as he made his way to the entrance hall. The messenger stood by the main door with a thick parchment in his hands. Bess descended the stairs two at the time and wrenched the parchment out of the messenger's hands. He broke the seal on the personal letter and opened it. He read it quickly and smiled. "Did Ethan Philipson say anything?" he asked the messenger, checking the truce.

"No." The messenger shook his head. "Actually, I never met him. I met Adrian Johnson, who took the papers to the king. He also brought the letter and the treaty back to me."

Bess didn't even look up from the treaty. He looked at the letter again and then slowly walked back to the library. He climbed the stairs, still reading the letter. So, the lords were no longer lords; neither did they belong to Norene anymore. He was tempted to behead them, but decided to follow Ethan's example. They could travel further south and try their luck somewhere else in Lanland. If they ever came back to Wolfast, he would behead them then.

Bess returned to the library and put the treaty and the letter down. He tossed the letters and parchments to the side, and the pile fell off the table onto the floor. He jumped after the letters, but was too slow to catch them. He cursed and walked around the table. As he was picking up the parchments, he noticed a strange piece of information on one of the parchments. He picked it up and sat on the cold stone floor. The information, dated almost a hundred years back said:

Order for search for a precious gem stone located in the Minerst Mine.

He scanned the order but didn't find any specific information on the stone or the reason for the search. He picked up all the letters, stood up, and put the letters and the parchments on the table. He sat behind the table and scanned the piles for a similar date or anything about the Minerst Mines. Ten minutes later, he found another paper:

The tunnels in the Minerst Mines were dug almost one quarter of the way when the funding stopped. The work on the passage through the hill will continue when the funding is renewed. The miners were all sent home.

He checked the dates and found out the difference was three weeks—three weeks from the search for the stone and then the change to the tunnelling projects. Three weeks until the funds supposedly had stopped. This was very suspicious. The weirdest part was that the signature at the end of the notice was the same. This meant that the same person had to forget within three weeks what the reason of mining in their mine was. If they didn't want anyone to know about the stone, why write order to search for it and then claim that the tunnelling couldn't be finished?

He grabbed the quill and quickly wrote a simple note on a clean parchment: "Steven, please, bring me all information you have on Minerst Mines from thirty-fourth Moonday of Year 735 till today." He looked at the note and then at all papers on his table. He was more than determined to find out as much about the strange necklace as possible. However, there was something else connected to the necklace. He didn't think he could find any information on the subject, but he dipped the quill and wrote an addition to the note: "Check to see if some stranger was working in the mines or funding it—anyone out of place." He looked at the sentence, and as an afterthought added: "Thanks for your patience with me."

A man hid behind a bush in the forest near Royal City and looked at the road. A dark hat was throwing a shadow over his eyes, and the rest of his face was covered with a piece of dark cloth. The dark coat and dark clothes made the man blend in with the shadow of the bush. In his right hand, he held a small crossbow.

The road was empty and quiet. Occasionally a bird flew down, picked up a twig from the road, and flew away. The masked man watched a rabbit hop to the centre of the road and stop in the middle. It raised its long ears and turned to watch the road.

The masked man looked in the same direction. Charles and Daniel, followed by a group of fifty soldiers, appeared on the road. Daniel was on a horse, but didn't look too happy about it. He held the saddle tight, trying not to fall off.

The rabbit sniffed the air, sprinted to the other side of the road, and vanished between the bushes not far away from the masked man. The man was watching the group, waiting. The soldiers were either half sleeping or watching the trees, and Charles was having a discussion with Daniel. No one was paying attention to the forest.

Silently and carefully, the masked man nocked a silver-tipped bolt onto the string of his crossbow. He looked at the approaching group, adjusting his posture. The horses were slowly walking towards him. The man lifted the crossbow and aimed at Daniel's heart. He watched the group for a while and then lowered the crossbow. He crawled to his left and lifted the crossbow once more. He aimed at Daniel and put his finger on the trigger.

Leaves rustled nearby. The masked man lowered the crossbow and looked over his shoulder into the forest. He waited for a while, but nothing happened. Then he remembered the rabbit and suppressed an urge to curse loudly.

He turned to the group in front of him and quickly crouched down. His window of opportunity had passed. They were way too close. He watched Daniel through the gap between the branches, trying not to move a muscle. At close range, the boy seemed much younger than he had from a distance. His shirt was unbuttoned all the way to his belly, yet he was sweating, though not as much as Charles was.

The masked man leaned close to the ground as he watched the group walk by. He was sure that he was hidden completely and the wind was blowing against him, but he wanted to make sure that they would not see him.

When the soldiers disappeared behind the trees, the masked man stood up and leaned the crossbow against his shoulder. He looked at the empty forest and sighed. He looked up the forest road and then after the soldiers. Shaking his head, he stepped after Charles and Daniel.

TO BE CONTINUED...

Printed in the United States
By Bookmasters